"YOU MUST GO THROUGH ME."

"I don't know what you mean," said Diamond.

"I mean just what I say," said the North Wind. "To reach the country at my back, you must walk *through* me as if I were an open door."

"But that will hurt you!"

"Not in the least. It will hurt you, though."

"I don't mind that, if you tell me to do it," said Diamond.

"Do it."

Diamond walked toward her. When he reached her knees, he felt an intense cold. All grew white about him, and the cold stung like fire. But he kept going. . . .

AT THE BACK OF THE NORTH WIND

George MacDonald

TOR ®

A TOM DOHERTY ASSOCIATES BOOK
NEW YORK

This is a work of fiction. All the characters and events portrayed in this book are either products of the author's imagination or are used fictitiously.

AT THE BACK OF THE NORTH WIND

All new material in this edition is copyright © 1998 by Tom Doherty Associates, Inc.

A Tor Book
Published by Tom Doherty Associates, Inc.
175 Fifth Avenue
New York, NY 10010

Tor® is a registered trademark of Tom Doherty Associates, Inc.

ISBN: 0-812-56712-9

First Tor edition: May 1998

Printed in the United States of America

0 9 8 7 6 5 4 3 2 1

CONTENTS

Contents

Contents

Foreword

Hyperborea.

Hyper = beyond. Boreas = the north wind, the wind from the mountains. According to the ancient Greeks, Boreas was a god, son of Astraeus and Aurora, a cold, blustery fellow. But beyond those mountains from which the north wind blew, said the Greeks, lay a paradise of sunshine and everlasting spring. Hyperboreans lived there, crowned with bay-leaves of gold and dancing to the music of flute and lyre.

Obviously, the Greeks had never experienced the Arctic. But before we laugh at them, let us call to mind our own speculations about distant planets. To the ancients, earth was a place of wonders unexplored, as vast and resonant as the universe is to us. Anything could be out there. Eternal sunshine. People who lived a thousand years. Anything.

We do not know whether the Greeks in general, and Herodotus in particular, really believed what they heard of this place called Hyperborea. Perhaps they did. But certainly by the nineteenth century, educated people had stopped believing in such places, hadn't they?

Enter the fantastic imagination of George MacDonald.

As a fantasy writer myself, I find myself dithering in awe at MacDonald's vision in *At the Back of the North Wind.* I know how easy it is to make imaginative leaps but how difficult to land on sure footing; I know how hard it is to do what MacDonald has done.

His purest, truest creation, of course, is the character of North Wind herself, no longer just another Greek god, but now a mighty, beautiful woman whose black tresses fill the night, whose dark eyes flash like lightning or sparkle like starlight, whose smile plays breezily around her lovely mouth. North Wind whispers, commands, teases; she can be tiny or as big as the sky; she can be human or a serpent or a tiger; she sings, nurses the flowers, topples chimneys, and sinks ships.

Some truths can be told only in story; MacDonald's North Wind is the characterization of such a profound truth. When I was a child, in the My Book House books I read an excerpt of her story, and I studied the pen-and-ink illustration of the North Wind with her masses and waves and curls and tendrils of black hair flying, with Diamond riding in a braided nest at the back of her neck. Again and again I dreamed over that picture, I imagined riding so high in that wild mane of windy hair, at the back of the North Wind.

Diamond. A little English boy. Again, I stand in awe of MacDonald's achievement; I know how difficult it is to write fantasy set in one's own time. Go long ago and far away, and readers will be more willing to be believe you, but write of how the impossible impinges upon the here and now, and they will sniff. Oh, *certainly,* they will scoff. But Diamond has the strength of character to make the scoffers believe. Diamond is an adorable little boy, a charmer, tough and vulnerable and shy and articulate and innocent and wise. Diamond stopped on his way to ride the North Wind to give the old horse's ears a pull. Diamond is perfect.

Quite literally perfect. First of all, he has the perfect name; he is named after his father's favorite horse. (As one besotted by horses, immediately I adore Diamond's family.) The name sets him apart, makes him special, as befits one who is also perfect in goodness: Diamond speaks truth, loves his horse and his mother, soothes babies, takes over the family business when his father is sick, impresses important people, inspires improved behavior in those around him—he is just too cute to shoot. Psychologically speaking, Diamond is implausible—but it doesn't matter, for you see, Diamond has been to the back of the North Wind. And somehow MacDonald makes this work. I ought to detest Diamond for being so inhumanly good, yet I find myself loving him. Somehow MacDonald makes me love him.

Diamond is, I think, a peculiarly Victorian superhero, Little Child As Godlike Being. Look at a collection of books of that era and you will see a proliferation of "little" titles: little angels, little women, little men, little lame princes. Usually, in these stories, the perfect little child humbles and enlightens those around him/her, then dies. (The Victorians loved a good, weepy, nose-honking death scene.) MacDonald plays on this familiar theme—but with important variations. You might say that, consciously or not, he uses the expectations of his readership to pull them in, and then he has them where he wants them—facing the North Wind.

His readership consisted, quite simply, of the general public of the time. Like Dickens, MacDonald wrote his novels for the newspapers, where they appeared in serialized form. He had deadlines when he had to come up with something. *At the Back of the North Wind* is not a children's book, or not originally; it is popular entertainment, like a weekly TV show. This fact goes a long way to explain its ragged structure and the odd turns it sometimes takes.

Structure is, I'd say, MacDonald's chief weakness as a writer, aside from his penchant for including his own poetry. Okay, I plead guilty, I've done it myself, this thing of getting the poetry published by slipping it into the novel—but just the same, you have my permission to skip the poetry. It does not pertain to the plot, and most of it is, well, it's not that great.

Don't skip anything else, though. Sometimes this book veers like a sailboat tacking against the wind, and there are stretches where characters disappear altogether and others pop up; it is episodic—but every episode is worth reading.

This is not a lightweight book, although MacDonald likes to let you think it is. Just family entertainment, he seems to assure you; he lulls you with his chatty, comfortable voice and he diverts you with his reassuring, down-to-earth knowledge of kitchens and stableyards; he pulls you in—and then he has you out there in the night, and North Wind and Diamond are having conversations that will take your breath away.

Our hero, Diamond, a sort of Victorian Forrest Gump, at the back of the North Wind—who wouldn't want to go along for the ride? It can be a chilly one, but it will also thrill you and grab you by the heart, and never mind that it's good for you. Have you ever been to Hyperborea? No? Well, then, venture there along with Diamond. Remember to breathe. Enjoy.

Nancy Springer

Chapter I
THE HAY-LOFT

I HAVE been asked to tell you about the back of the North Wind. An old Greek writer mentions a people who lived there, and were so comfortable that they could not bear it any longer, and drowned themselves. My story is not the same as his. I do not think Herodotus had got the right account of the place. I am going to tell you how it fared with a boy who went there.

He lived in a low room over a coach-house; and that was not by any means at the back of the North Wind, as his mother very well knew. For one side of the room was built only of boards, and the boards were so old that you might run a penknife through into the north wind. And then let them settle between them which was the sharper! I know that when you pulled it out again the wind would be after it like a cat after a mouse, and you would know soon enough you were *not* at the back of the North Wind. Still, this room was not very cold, except when the North Wind blew stronger than usual: the room I have to do with now was always cold, except in summer, when the sun took the matter into his own hands. Indeed, I am not sure whether I ought to call it a room at all; for it was just a loft where they kept hay and straw and oats for the horses. And when little Diamond—but stop: I must tell you that his father, who was a coachman, had named him after a favorite horse, and his mother had had no objection:—when little Diamond then lay there in bed, he could hear the horses under him munching away in the dark, or moving sleepily in their dreams. For Diamond's father had built him a bed in the loft with boards all round it, because they had so little room in their own end over the coach-house; and Diamond's father put old Diamond in the stall under the bed, because he was a quiet horse, and did not go to sleep standing, but lay down like a reasonable creature. But, although he was a surprisingly reasonable creature, yet, when young Diamond woke in the middle of the night, and felt the bed shaking in the blasts of the north wind, he could not help wondering whether, if the wind should blow the house down, and he were to fall through into the manger, old Diamond mightn't eat him up before he knew him in his nightgown. And although old Diamond was very quiet all night long, yet when he woke he got up like an earthquake, and then young Diamond knew what o'clock it was, or at least what was to be done next, which was—to go to sleep again as fast as he could.

There was hay at his feet and hay at his head, piled up in great trusses to the very roof. Indeed it was sometimes only through a little lane with several turnings, which looked as if it had been sawn out for him, that he could reach his bed at all. For the stock of hay was, of course, always in a state either of slow ebb or of sudden flow. Sometimes the whole space of the loft, with the little panes in the roof for the stars to look in, would lie open before his open eyes as he lay in bed; sometimes a yellow wall of sweet-smelling fibres closed up his view at the distance of half a yard. Sometimes, when his mother had undressed him in her room, and told him to trot away to bed by himself, he would creep into the heart of the hay, and lie there thinking how cold it was outside in the wind, and how warm it was inside there in his bed, and how he could go to it when he pleased, only he wouldn't just yet; he would get a little colder first. And ever as he grew colder, his bed would grow warmer, till at last he would scramble out of the hay, shoot like an arrow into his bed, cover himself up, and snuggle down, thinking what a happy boy he was. He had not the least idea that the wind got in at a chink in the wall, and blew about him all night. For the back of his bed was only of boards an inch thick, and on the other side of them was the north wind.

Now, as I have already said, these boards were soft and crumbly. To be sure, they were tarred on the outside, yet in many places they were more like tinder than timber. Hence it happened that the soft part having worn away from about it, little Diamond found one night, after he lay down, that a knot had come out of one of them, and that the wind was blowing in upon him in a cold and rather imperious fashion. Now he had no fancy for leaving things wrong that might be set right; so he jumped out of bed again, got a little strike of hay, twisted it up, folded it in the middle, and, having thus made it into a cork, stuck it into the hole in the wall. But the wind began to blow loud and angrily, and, as Diamond was falling asleep, out blew his cork and hit him on the nose, just hard enough to wake him up quite, and let him hear the wind whistling shrill in the hole. He searched for his hay-cork, found it, stuck it in harder, and was just dropping off once more, when, pop! with an angry whistle behind it, the cork struck him again, this time on the cheek. Up he rose once more, made a fresh stopple of hay, and corked the hole severely. But he was hardly down again before—pop! it came on his forehead. He gave it up, drew the clothes above his head, and was soon fast asleep.

Although the next day was very stormy, Diamond forgot all about the hole, for he was busy making a cave by the side of his mother's fire, with a broken chair, a three-legged stool, and a blanket, and then sitting in it. His mother, however, discovered it, and pasted a bit of brown paper over it, so that, when Diamond had snuggled down the next night, he had no occasion to think of it.

Presently, however, he lifted his head and listened. Who could that be talking to him? The wind was rising again, and getting very loud, and full of rushes and whistles. He was sure some one was talking—and very near him too it was. But he was not frightened, for he had not yet learned how to be; so he sat up and hearkened. At last the voice, which, though quite gentle, sounded a little angry, appeared to come from the back of the bed. He crept nearer to it, and laid his ear against the wall. Then he heard nothing but the wind, which sounded very loud indeed. The moment, however, that he moved his head from the wall, he heard the voice again, close to his ear. He felt about with his hand, and came upon the piece of paper his mother had pasted over the hole. Against this he laid his ear, and then he heard the voice quite distinctly. There was, in fact, a little corner of the paper loose, and through that, as from a mouth in the wall, the voice came.

"What do you mean, little boy—closing up my window?"

"What window?" asked Diamond.

"You stuffed hay into it three times last night. I had to blow it out again three times."

"You can't mean this little hole! It isn't a window; it's a hole in my bed."

"I did not say it was *a* window: I said it was *my* window."

"But it can't be a window, because windows are holes to see out of."

"Well, that's just what I made this window for."

"But you are outside: you can't want a window."

"You are quite mistaken. Windows are to see out of, you say. Well, I'm in my house, and I want windows to see out of it."

"But you've made a window into my bed."

"Well, your mother has got three windows into my dancing-room, and you have three into my garret."

"But I heard father say, when my mother wanted him to make a window through the wall, that it was against the law for it would look into Mr. Dyves's garden."

The voice laughed.

"The law would have some trouble to catch me!" it said.

"But if it's not right, you know," said Diamond, "that's no matter. You shouldn't do it."

"I am so tall I am above *that* law," said the voice.

"You must have a tall house, then," said Diamond.

"Yes; a tall house: the clouds are inside it."

"Dear me!" said Diamond, and thought a minute. "I think, then, you can hardly expect me to keep a window in my bed for you. Why don't you make a window into Mr. Dyves's bed?"

"Nobody makes a window into an ash-pit," said the voice rather sadly. "I like to see nice things out of my windows."

"But he must have a nicer bed than I have, though mine is *very* nice—so nice that I couldn't wish a better."

"It's not the bed I care about: it's what is in it. But you just open that window."

"Well, mother says I shouldn't be disobliging; but it's rather hard. You see the north wind will blow right in my face if I do."

"I am the North Wind."

"O-o-oh!" said Diamond, thoughtfully. "Then will you promise not to blow on my face if I open your window?"

"I can't promise that."

"But you'll give me the toothache. Mother's got it already."

"But what's to become of me without a window?"

"I'm sure I don't know. All I say is, it will be worse for me than for you."

"No; it will not. You shall not be the worse for it—I

promise you that. You will be much the better for it. Just you believe what I say, and do as I tell you."

"Well, I *can* pull the clothes over my head," said Diamond, and feeling with his little sharp nails, he got hold of the open edge of the paper and tore it off at once.

In came a long whistling spear of cold, and struck his little naked chest. He scrambled and tumbled in under the bed-clothes, and covered himself up: there was no paper now between him and the voice, and he felt a little—not frightened exactly—I told you he had not learned that yet—but rather queer; for what a strange person this North Wind must be that lived in the great house—"called Out-of-Doors, I suppose," thought Diamond—and made windows into people's beds! But the voice began again; and he could hear it quite plainly, even with his head under the bed-clothes. It was a still more gentle voice now, although six times as large and loud as it had been, and he thought it sounded a little like his mother's.

"What is your name, little boy?" it asked.

"Diamond," answered Diamond, under the bed-clothes.

"What a funny name!"

"It's a very nice name," returned its owner.

"I don't know that," said the voice.

"Well, I do," retorted Diamond, a little rudely.

"Do you know to whom you are speaking?"

"No," said Diamond.

And indeed he did not. For to know a person's name is not always to know the person's self.

"Then I must not be angry with you. You had better look and see, though."

"Diamond is a very pretty name," persisted the boy, vexed that it should not give satisfaction.

"Diamond is a useless thing rather," said the voice.

"That's not true. Diamond is very nice—as big as two—and so quiet all night! And doesn't he make a jolly row in the morning, getting up on his four great legs! It's like thunder."

"You don't seem to know what a diamond is."

"Oh, don't I just! Diamond is a great and good horse; and he sleeps right under me. He is Old Diamond, and I am Young Diamond; or, if you like it better, for you're very particular, Mr. North Wind, he's Big Diamond, and I'm Little Diamond; and I don't know which of us my father likes best."

A beautiful laugh, large but very soft and musical, sounded somewhere beside him, but Diamond kept his head under the clothes.

"I'm not Mr. North Wind," said the voice.

"You told me that you were the North Wind," insisted Diamond.

"I did not say *Mister* North Wind," said the voice.

"Well, then, I do; for mother tells me I ought to be polite."

"Then let me tell you I don't think it at all polite of you to say *Mister* to me."

"Well, I didn't know better. I'm very sorry."

"But you ought to know better."

"I don't know that."

"I do. You can't say it's polite to lie there talking—with your head under the bed-clothes, and never look up to see what kind of person you are talking to.—I want you to come out with me."

"I want to go to sleep," said Diamond, very nearly crying, for he did not like to be scolded, even when he deserved it.

"You shall sleep all the better to-morrow night."

"Besides," said Diamond, "you are out in Mr. Dyves's garden, and I can't get there. I can only get into our own yard."

"Will you take your head out of the bed-clothes?" said the voice, just a little angrily.

"No!" answered Diamond, half peevish, half frightened.

The instant he said the word, a tremendous blast of wind crashed in a board of the wall, and swept the clothes off Diamond. He started up in terror. Leaning over him was the large beautiful pale face of a woman. Her dark eyes looked a little angry, for they had just begun to flash; but a quivering in her sweet upper lip made her look as if she were going to cry. What was most strange was that away from her head streamed out her black hair in every direction, so that the darkness in the hayloft looked as if it were made of her hair; but as Diamond gazed at her in speechless amazement, mingled with confidence—for the boy was entranced with her mighty beauty—her hair began to gather itself out of the darkness, and fell down all about her again, till her face looked out of the midst of it like a moon out of a cloud. From her eyes came all the light by which Diamond saw her face and her hair; and that was all he did see of her yet. The wind was over and gone.

"Will you go with me now, you little Diamond? I am sorry I was forced to be so rough with you," said the lady.

"I will; yes, I will," answered Diamond, holding out both his arms. "But," he added, dropping them, "how shall I get my clothes? They are in mother's room, and the door is locked."

"Oh, never mind your clothes. You will not be cold. I shall take care of that. Nobody is cold with the North Wind."

"I thought everybody was," said Diamond.

"That is a great mistake. Most people make it, however. They are cold because they are not with the North Wind, but without it."

If Diamond had been a little older, and had supposed himself a good deal wiser, he would have thought the lady was joking. But he was not older, and did not fancy himself wiser, and therefore understood her well enough. Again he stretched out his arms. The lady's face drew back a little.

"Follow me, Diamond," she said.

"Yes," said Diamond, only a little ruefully.

"You're not afraid?" said the North Wind.

"No, ma'am; but mother never would let me go without

shoes: she never said anything about clothes, so I dare say she wouldn't mind that."

"I know your mother very well," said the lady. "She is a good woman. I have visited her often. I was with her when you were born. I saw her laugh and cry both at once, I love your mother, Diamond."

"How was it you did not know my name, then, ma'am? Please am I to say *ma'am* to you, ma'am?"

"One question at a time, dear boy. I knew your name quite well, but I wanted to hear what you would say for it. Don't you remember that day when the man was finding fault with your name—how I blew the window in?"

"Yes, yes," answered Diamond, eagerly. "Our window opens like a door, right over the coach-house door. And the wind—you, ma'am—came in, and blew the bible out of the man's hands, and the leaves went all flutter flutter on the floor, and my mother picked it up and gave it back to him open, and there—"

"Was your name in the bible,—the sixth stone in the highpriest's breast-plate."

"Oh!—a stone, was it?" said Diamond. "I thought it had been a horse—I did."

"Never mind. A horse is better than a stone any day. Well, you see, I know all about you and your mother."

"Yes. I will go with you."

"Now for the next question: you're not to call me *ma'am*. You must call me just my own name—respectfully, you know—just North Wind."

"Well, please, North Wind, you are so beautiful, I am quite ready to go with you."

"You must not be ready to go with everything beautiful all at once, Diamond."

"But what's beautiful can't be bad. You're not bad, North Wind?"

"No; I'm not bad. But sometimes beautiful things grow bad by doing bad, and it takes some time for their badness to spoil their beauty. So little boys may be mistaken if they go after things because they are beautiful."

"Well, I will go with you because you are beautiful and good too."

"Ah, but there's another thing, Diamond:—What if I should look ugly without being bad—look ugly myself because I am making ugly things beautiful?—What then?"

"I don't quite understand you, North Wind. You tell me what then."

"Well, I will tell you. If you see me with my face all black, don't be frightened. If you see me flapping wings like a bat's, as big as the whole sky, don't be frightened. If you hear me raging ten times worse than Mrs. Bill, the blacksmith's wife—even if you see me looking in at people's windows like Mrs. Eve Dropper, the gardener's wife—you must believe that I am doing my work. Nay, Diamond, if I change into a serpent or a tiger, you must not let go your hold of me, for my hand will never change in yours if you keep a good hold. If you keep a hold, you will know who I am all the time, even when you look at me and can't see me the least like the North Wind. I may look something very awful. Do you understand?"

"Quite well," said little Diamond.

"Come along, then," said North Wind, and disappeared behind the mountain of hay.

Diamond crept out of bed and followed her.

Chapter II
THE LAWN

WHEN Diamond got round the corner of the hay, for a moment he hesitated. The stair by which he would naturally have gone down to the door was at the other side of the loft, and looked very black indeed; for it was full of North Wind's hair, as she descended before him. And just beside him was the ladder going straight down into the stable, up which his father always came to fetch the hay for Diamond's dinner. Through the opening in the floor the faint gleam of the stable-lantern was enticing, and Diamond thought he would run down that way.

The stair went close past the loose-box in which Diamond the horse lived. When Diamond the boy was half-way down, he remembered that it was of no use to go this way, for the stable-door was locked. But at the same moment there was horse Diamond's great head poked out of his box on to the ladder, for he knew boy Diamond although he was in his night-gown, and wanted him to pull his ears for him. This Diamond did very gently for a minute or so, and patted and stroked his neck too, and kissed the big horse, and had begun to take the bits of straw and hay out of his mane, when all at once he recollected that the Lady North Wind was waiting for him in the yard.

"Good night, Diamond," he said, and darted up the ladder, across the loft, and down the stair to the door. But when he got out into the yard, there was no lady.

Now it is always a dreadful thing to think there is somebody and find nobody. Children in particular have not made up their minds to it; they generally cry at nobody, especially when they wake up at night. But it was an especial disappointment to Diamond, for his little heart had been beating with joy: the face of the North Wind was so grand! To have a lady like that for a friend—with such long hair, too! Why, it was longer than twenty Diamonds' tails! She was gone. And there he stood, with his bare feet on the stones of the paved yard.

It was a clear night overhead, and the stars were shining. Orion in particular was making the most of his bright belt and golden sword. But the moon was only a poor thin crescent. There was just one great, jagged, black and grey cloud in the sky, with a steep side to it like a precipice; and the moon was against this side, and looked as if she had tumbled off the top of the cloud-hill, and broken herself in rolling down the precipice. She did not seem comfortable, for she was looking down into the deep pit waiting for her. At least that was what Diamond thought as he stood for a moment staring at her. But he was quite wrong, for the moon was not afraid, and there was no pit she was going down into, for there were no sides to it, and a pit without sides to it is not a pit at all. Diamond, however, had not been out so late before in all his life, and things looked so strange about him!—just as if he had got into Fairyland, of which he knew quite as much as anybody; for his mother had no money to buy books to set him wrong on the subject. I have seen this world—only sometimes, just now and then, you know—look as strange as ever I saw Fairyland. But I confess that I have not yet seen Fairyland at its best. I am always *going* to see it so some time. But if you had been out in the face and not at the back of the North Wind, on a cold *rather* frosty night, and in your night-gown, you would have felt it all quite as strange as Diamond did. He cried a little, just a little, he was so disappointed to lose the lady: of course, you, little man, wouldn't have done that! But for my part, I don't mind people crying, so much as I mind what they cry about, and how they cry—whether they cry quietly like ladies and gentlemen, or go shrieking like vulgar emperors, or ill-natured cooks; for all emperors are not gentlemen, and all cooks are not ladies—nor all queens and princesses for that matter, either.

But it can't be denied that a little gentle crying does one good. It did Diamond good; for as soon as it was over he was a brave boy again.

"She shan't say it was my fault anyhow!" said Diamond. "I daresay she is hiding somewhere to see what I will do. I will look for her."

So he went round the end of the stable towards the kitchen-garden. But the moment he was clear of the shelter of the stable, sharp as a knife came the wind against his little chest and his bare legs. Still he would look in the kitchen-garden, and went on. But when he got round the weeping-ash that stood in the corner, the wind blew much stronger, and it grew stronger and stronger till he could hardly fight against it. And it was so cold! All the flashy spikes of the stars seemed to have got somehow into the wind. Then he thought of what the lady had said about people being cold because they were not *with* the North Wind. How it was that he should have guessed what she meant at that very moment I cannot tell, but I have observed that the most wonderful thing in the world is how people come to understand anything. He turned his back to the wind, and trotted again towards the yard; whereupon, strange to say, it blew so much more gently against his calves than it had blown against his shins, that he began to feel almost warm by contrast.

You must not think it was cowardly of Diamond to turn

his back to the wind: he did so only because he thought Lady North Wind had said something like telling him to do so. If she had said to him that he must hold his face to it, Diamond would have held his face to it. But the most foolish thing is to fight for no good, and to please nobody.

Well, it was just as if the wind was pushing Diamond along. If he turned round, it grew very sharp on his legs especially, and so he thought the wind might really be Lady North Wind, though he could not see her, and he had better let her blow him wherever she pleased. So she blew and blew, and he went and went, until he found himself standing at a door in a wall which door led from the yard into a little belt of shrubbery, flanking Mr. Coleman's house. Mr. Coleman was his father's master, and the owner of Diamond. He opened the door, and went through the shrubbery, and out into the middle of the lawn, still hoping to find North Wind. The soft grass was very pleasant to his bare feet, and felt warm after the stones of the yard; but the lady was nowhere to be seen. Then he began to think that after all he must have done wrong, and she was offended with him for not following close after her, but staying to talk to the horse, which certainly was neither wise nor polite.

There he stood in the middle of the lawn, the wind blowing his night-gown till it flapped like a loose sail. The stars were very shiny over his head; but they did not give light enough to show that the grass was green; and Diamond stood alone in the strange night, which looked half solid all about him. He began to wonder whether he was in a dream or not. It was important to determine this; "for," thought Diamond, "if I am in a dream, I am safe in my bed, and I needn't cry. But if I'm not in a dream, I'm out here, and perhaps I had better cry, or, at least, I'm not sure whether I can help it." He came to the conclusion, however, that, whether he was in a dream or not, there could be no harm in not crying for a little while longer: he could begin whenever he liked.

The back of Mr. Coleman's house was to the lawn, and

one of the drawing-room windows looked out upon it. The ladies had not gone to bed; for the light was still shining in that window. But they had no idea that a little boy was standing on the lawn in his night-gown, or they would have run out in a moment. And as long as he saw that light, Diamond could not feel quite lonely. He stood staring, not at the great warrior Orion in the sky, nor yet at the disconsolate, neglected moon going down in the west, but at the drawing-room window with the light shining through its green curtains. He had been in that room once or twice that he could remember at Christmas times; for the Colemans were kind people, though they did not care much about children.

All at once the light went nearly out: he could only see a glimmer of the shape of the window. Then, indeed, he felt that he was left alone. It was so dreadful to be out in the night after *everybody* was gone to bed! That was more than he *could* bear. He burst out crying in good earnest, beginning with a wail like that of the wind when it is waking up.

Perhaps you think this was very foolish; for could he not go home to his own bed again when he liked? Yes; but it looked dreadful to him to creep up that stair again and lie down in his bed again, and know that North Wind's window was open beside him, and she gone, and he might never see her again. He would be just as lonely there as here. Nay, it would be much worse if he had to think that the window was nothing but a hole in the wall.

At the very moment when he burst out crying, the old nurse, who had grown to be one of the family, for she had not gone away when Miss Coleman did not want any more nursing, came to the back-door, which was of glass, to close the shutters. She thought she heard a cry, and, peering out with a hand on each side of her eyes like Diamond's blinkers, she saw something white on the lawn. Too old and too wise to be frightened, she opened the door, and went straight towards the white thing to see what it was. And when Diamond saw her coming he was not frightened either, though Mrs. Crump was a little cross sometimes; for there is a good kind of crossness that is only disagreeable, and there is a bad kind of crossness that is very nasty indeed. So she came up with her neck stretched out, and her head at the end of it, and her eyes foremost of all, like a snail's, peering into the night to see what it could be that went on glimmering white before her. When she did see, she made a great exclamation, and threw up her hands. Then without a word, for she thought Diamond was walking in his sleep, she caught hold of him and led him towards the house. He made no objection, for he was just in the mood to be grateful for notice of any sort, and Mrs. Crump led him straight into the drawing-room.

Now, from the neglect of the new housemaid, the fire in Miss Coleman's bed-room had gone out, and her mother had told her to brush her hair by the drawing-room fire—a disorderly proceeding which a mother's wish could justify. The young lady was very lovely, thought not nearly so beautiful as North Wind; and her hair was extremely long, for it came down to her knees—though that was nothing at all to North Wind's hair. Yet when she looked round, with her hair all about her, as Diamond entered, he thought for one moment that it was North Wind, and, pulling his hand from Mrs. Crump's, he stretched out his arms and ran towards Miss Coleman. She was so pleased that she threw down her brush, and almost knelt on the floor to receive him in her arms. He saw the next moment that she was not Lady North Wind, but she looked so like her he could not help running into her arms and bursting into tears afresh. Mrs. Crump said the poor child had walked out in his sleep, and Diamond thought she ought to know, and did not contradict her: for anything he knew, it might be so indeed. He let them talk on about him, and said nothing; and when, after their astonishment was over, and Miss Coleman had given him a sponge-cake, it was decreed that Mrs. Crump should take him to his mother, he was quite satisfied.

His mother had to get out of bed to open the door when Mrs. Crump knocked. She was indeed surprised to see her boy; and having taken him in her arms and carried him to his bed, returned and had a long confabulation with Mrs. Crump, for they were still talking when Diamond fell fast asleep, and could hear them no longer.

Chapter III
OLD DIAMOND

DIAMOND woke very early in the morning, and thought what a curious dream he had had. But the memory grew brighter and brighter in his head, until it did not look altogether like a dream, and he began to doubt whether he had not really been abroad in the wind last night. He came to the conclusion that, if he had really been brought home to his mother by Mrs. Crump, she would say something to him about it, and that would settle the matter. Then he got up and dressed himself, but, finding that his father and mother were not yet stirring, he went down the ladder to the stable. There he found that even old Diamond was not awake yet, for he, as well as young Diamond, always got up the moment he woke, and now he was lying as flat as a horse could lie upon his nice trim bed of straw.

"I'll give old Diamond a surprise," thought the boy; and creeping up very softly, before the horse knew, he was astride of his back. Then it was young Diamond's turn to have more of a surprise than he had expected; for as with an earthquake, with a rumbling and a rocking hither and thither, a sprawling of legs and heaving as of many backs, young Diamond found himself hoisted up in the air, with both hands twisted in the horse's mane. The next instant old Diamond lashed out with both his hind legs, and giving one cry of terror young Diamond found himself lying on his neck, with his arms as far round it as they would go. But then the horse stood as still as a stone, except that he lifted his head gently up, to let the boy slip down to his back. For when he heard young Diamond's cry he knew that there was nothing to kick about; for young Diamond was a good boy, and old Diamond was a good horse, and the one was all right on the back of the other.

As soon as Diamond had got himself comfortable on the saddle place, the horse began pulling at the hay, and the boy began thinking. He had never mounted Diamond himself before, and he had never got off him without being lifted down. So he sat, while the horse ate, wondering how he was to reach the ground.

But while he meditated, his mother woke, and her first thought was to see her boy. She had visited him twice during the night, and found him sleeping quietly. Now his bed was empty, and she was frightened.

"Diamond! Diamond! Where are you, Diamond?" she called out.

Diamond turned his head where he sat like a knight on his steed in enchanted stall, and cried aloud,—

"Here, mother!"

"Where, Diamond?" she returned.

"Here, mother, on Diamond's back."

She came running to the ladder, and peeping down, saw him aloft on the great horse.

"Come down, Diamond," she said.

"I can't," answered Diamond.

"How did you get up?" asked his mother.

"Quite easily," answered he; "but when I got up, Diamond would get up too, and so here I am."

His mother thought he had been walking in his sleep

again, and hurried down the ladder. She did not much like going up to the horse, for she had not been used to horses; but she would have gone into a lion's den, not to say a horse's stall, to help her boy. So she went and lifted him off Diamond's back, and felt braver all her life after. She carried him in her arms up to her room; but, afraid of frightening him at his own sleep-walking, as she supposed it, said nothing about last night. Before the next day was over, Diamond had almost concluded the whole adventure a dream.

For a week his mother watched him very carefully— going into the loft several times a night,—as often, in fact, as she woke. Every time she found him fast asleep.

All that week it was hard weather. The grass showed white in the morning with the hoar-frost which clung like tiny comfits to every blade. And as Diamond's shoes were not good, and his mother had not quite saved up enough money to get him the new pair she so much wanted for him, she would not let him run out. He played all his games over and over indoors, especially that of driving two chairs harnessed to the baby's cradle; and if they did not go very fast, they went as fast as could be expected of the best chairs in the world, although one of them had only three legs, and the other half a back.

At length his mother brought home his new shoes, and no sooner did she find they fitted him than she told him he might run out in the yard and amuse himself for an hour.

The sun was going down when he flew from the door like a bird from its cage. All the world was new to him. A great fire of sunset burned on the top of the gate that led from the stables to the house; above the fire in the sky lay a large lake of green light, above that a golden cloud, and over that the blue of the wintry heavens. And Diamond thought that, next to his own home, he had never seen any place he would like so much to live in as that sky. For it is not fine things that make home a nice place, but your mother and your father.

As he was yet looking at the lovely colors, the gates

were thrown open, and there was old Diamond and his friend in the carriage, dancing with impatience to get at their stalls and their oats. And in they came. Diamond was not in the least afraid of his father driving over him, but, careful not to spoil the grand show he made with his fine horses and his multitudinous cape, with a red edge to every fold, he slipped out of the way and let him dash right on to the stables. To be quite safe he had to step into the recess of the door that led from the yard to the shrubbery.

As he stood there he remembered how the wind had driven him to this same spot on the night of his dream. And once more he was almost sure that it was no dream. At all events, he would go in and see whether things looked at all now as they did then. He opened the door, and passed through the little belt of shrubbery. Not a flower was to be seen in the beds on the lawn. Even the brave old chrysanthemums and Christmas roses had passed away before the frost. What? Yes! There was one! He ran and knelt down to look at it.

It was a primrose—a dwarfish thing, but perfect in shape—a baby-wonder. As he stooped his face to see it close, a little wind began to blow, and two or three long leaves that stood up behind the flower shook and waved and quivered, but the primrose lay still in the green hollow, looking up at the sky, and not seeming to know that the wind was blowing at all. It was just a one eye that the dull black wintry earth had opened to look at the sky with. All at once Diamond thought it was saying its prayers, and he ought not to be staring at it so. He ran to the stable to see his father make Diamond's bed. Then his father took him in his arms, carried him up the ladder, and set him down at the table where they were going to have their tea.

"Miss is very poorly," said Diamond's father; "Mis'ess has been to the doctor with her to-day, and she looked very glum when she came out again. I was a-watching of them to see what doctor had said."

"And didn't Miss look glum too?" asked his mother.

"Not half as glum as Mis'ess," returned the coachman. "You see—"

But he lowered his voice, and Diamond could not make out more than a word here and there. For Diamond's father was not only one of the finest of coachmen to look at, and one of the best of drivers, but one of the most discreet of servants as well. Therefore he did not talk about family affairs to anyone but his wife, whom he had proved better than himself long ago, and was careful that even Diamond should hear nothing he could repeat again concerning master and his family.

It was bed-time soon, and Diamond went to bed and fell fast asleep.

He awoke all at once, in the dark.

"Open the window, Diamond," said a voice.

Now Diamond's mother had once more pasted up North Wind's window.

"Are you North Wind?" said Diamond: "I don't hear you blowing."

"No; but you hear me talking. Open the window, for I haven't overmuch time."

"Yes," returned Diamond. "But, please, North Wind, where's the use? You left me all alone last time."

He had got up on his knees, and was busy with his nails once more at the paper over the hole in the wall. For now that North Wind spoke again, he remembered all that had taken place before as distinctly as if it had happened only last night.

"Yes, but that was your fault," returned North Wind. "I had work to do; and, besides, a gentleman should never keep a lady waiting."

"But I'm not a gentleman," said Diamond, scratching away at the paper.

"I hope you won't say so ten years after this."

"I'm going to be a coachman, and a coachman is not a gentleman," persisted Diamond.

"We call your father a gentleman in our house," said North Wind.

"He doesn't call himself one," said Diamond.

"That's of no consequence: every man ought to be a gentleman, and your father is one."

Diamond was so pleased to hear this that he scratched at the paper like ten mice, and getting hold of the edge of it, tore if off. The next instant a young girl glided across the bed, and stood upon the floor.

"Oh dear!" said Diamond, quite dismayed; "I didn't know—who are you, please?"

"I'm North Wind."

"Are you really?"

"Yes. Make haste."

"But you're no bigger than me."

"Do you think I care about how big or how little I am? Didn't you see me this evening? I was less then."

"No. Where was you?"

"Behind the leaves of the primrose. Didn't you see them blowing?"

"Yes."

"Make haste, then, if you want to go with me."

"But you are not big enough to take care of me. I think you are only Miss North Wind."

"I am big enough to show you the way, anyhow. But if you won't come, why, you must stay."

"I must dress myself. I didn't mind with a grown lady, but I couldn't go with a little girl in my night-gown."

"Very well. I'm not in such a hurry as I was the other night. Dress as fast as you can, and I'll go and shake the primrose leaves till you come."

"Don't hurt it," said Diamond.

North Wind broke out in a little laugh like the breaking of silver bubbles, and was gone in a moment. Diamond saw—for it was a starlit night, and the mass of hay was at a low ebb now—the gleam of something vanishing down the stair, and, springing out of bed, dressed himself as fast as ever he could. Then he crept out into the yard, through the door in the wall, and away to the primrose. Behind it stood North Wind, leaning over it, and looking at the flower as if she had been its mother.

"Come along," she said, jumping up and holding out her hand.

Diamond took her hand. It was cold, but so pleasant and full of life, it was better than warm. She led him across the garden. With one bound she was on the top of the wall. Diamond was left at the foot.

"Stop, stop!" he cried. "Please, I can't jump like that."

"You don't try," said North Wind, who from the top looked down a foot taller than before.

"Give me your hand again, and I will try," said Diamond.

She reached down, Diamond laid hold of her hand, gave a great spring, and stood beside her.

"This *is* nice!" he said.

Another bound, and they stood in the road by the river. It was full tide, and the stars were shining clear in its depths, for it lay still, waiting for the turn to run down again to the sea. They walked along its side. But they had not walked far before its surface was covered with ripples, and the stars had vanished from its bosom.

And North Wind was now tall as a full-grown girl. Her hair was flying about her head, and the wind was blowing a breeze down the river. But she turned aside and went up a narrow lane, and as she went her hair fell down around her.

"I have some rather disagreeable work to do to-night," she said, "before I get out to sea, and I must set about it at once. The disagreeable work must be looked after first."

So saying, she laid hold of Diamond and began to run, gliding along faster and faster. Diamond kept up with her as well as he could. She made many turnings and windings, apparently because it was not quite easy to get him over walls and houses. Once they ran through a hall where they found back and front doors open. At the foot of the stair North Wind stood still, and Diamond, hearing a great growl, started in terror, and there, instead of North Wind, was a huge wolf by his side. He let go his hold in dismay, and the wolf bounded up the stair. The windows of the house rattled and shook as if guns were firing, and the sound of a great fall came from above. Diamond stood with white face staring up at the landing.

"Surely," he thought, "North Wind can't be eating one of the children!" Coming to himself all at once, he rushed after her with his little fist clenched. There were ladies in long trains going up and down the stairs, and gentlemen in white neckties attending on them, who stared at him, but none of them were of the people of the house, and they said nothing. Before he reached the head of the stair, however, North Wind met him, took him by the hand, and hurried down and out of the house.

"I hope you haven't eaten a baby, North Wind!" said Diamond, very solemnly.

North Wind laughed merrily, and went tripping on faster. Her grassy robe swept and swirled about her steps, and wherever it passed over withered leaves, they went fleeing and whirling in spirals, and running on their edges like wheels, all about her feet.

"No," she said at last, "I did not eat a baby. You would not have had to ask that foolish question if you had not let go your hold of me. You would have seen how I served a nurse that was calling a child bad names, and telling her she was wicked. She had been drinking. I saw an ugly gin bottle in a cupboard."

"And you frightened her?" said Diamond.

"I believe so!" answered North Wind, laughing merrily. "I flew at her throat, and she tumbled over on the floor with such a crash that they ran in. She'll be turned away tomorrow—and quite time, if they knew as much as I do."

"But didn't you frighten the little one?"

"She never saw me. The woman would not have seen me either if she had not been wicked."

"Oh!" said Diamond, dubiously.

"Why should you see things," returned North Wind,

"that you wouldn't understand or know what to do with? Good people see good things; bad people, bad things."

"Then are you a bad thing?"

"No. For *you* see me, Diamond, dear," said the girl, and she looked down at him, and Diamond saw the loving eyes of the great lady beaming from the depths of her falling hair.

"I had to make myself look like a bad thing before she could see me. If I had put on any other shape than a wolf's she would not have seen me, for that is what is growing to be her own shape inside of her."

"I don't know what you mean," said Diamond, "but I suppose it's all right."

They were now climbing the slope of a grassy ascent. It was Primrose Hill, in fact, although Diamond had never heard of it. The moment they reached the top, North Wind stood and turned her face towards London. The stars were still shining clear and cold overhead. There was not a cloud to be seen. The air was sharp, but Diamond did not find it cold.

"Now," said the lady, "whatever you do, do not let my hand go. I might have lost you the last time, only I was not in a hurry then: now I am in a hurry."

Yet she stood still for a moment.

Chapter IV
NORTH WIND

A ND as she stood looking towards London, Diamond saw that she was trembling.

"Are you cold, North Wind?" he asked.

"No, Diamond," she answered, looking down upon him with a smile; "I am only getting ready to sweep one of my rooms. Those careless, greedy, untidy children make it in such a mess."

As she spoke he could have told by her voice, if he had not seen with his eyes, that she was growing larger and larger. Her head went up and up towards the stars; and as she grew, still trembling through all her body, her hair also grew—longer and longer, and lifted itself from her head, and went out in black waves. The next moment, however, it fell back around her, and she grew less and less till she was only a tall woman. Then she put her hands behind her head, and gathered some of her hair, and began weaving and knotting it together. When she had done, she bent down her beautiful face close to his, and said—

"Diamond, I am afraid you would not keep hold of me,

and if I were to drop you, I don't know what might happen; so I have been making a place for you in my hair. Come."

Diamond held out his arms, for with that grand face looking at him, he believed like a baby. She took him in her hands, threw him over her shoulder, and said, "Get in, Diamond."

And Diamond parted her hair with his hands, crept between, and feeling about soon found the woven nest. It was just like a pocket, or like the shawl in which gipsy women carry their children. North Wind put her hands to her back, felt all about the nest, and finding it safe, said,—

"Are you comfortable, Diamond?"

"Yes, indeed," answered Diamond.

The next moment he was rising in the air. North Wind grew towering up to the place of the clouds. Her hair went streaming out from her, till it spread like a mist over the stars. She flung herself abroad in space.

Diamond held on by two of the twisted ropes which, parted and interwoven, formed his shelter, for he could not help being a little afraid. As soon as he had come to himself, he peeped through the woven meshes, for he did not dare to look over the top of the nest. The earth was rushing past like a river or a sea below him. Trees, and water, and green grass hurried away beneath. A great roar of wild animals rose as they rushed over the Zoological Gardens, mixed with a chattering of monkeys and a screaming of birds; but it died away in a moment behind them. And now there was nothing but the roofs of houses, sweeping along like a great torrent of stones and rocks. Chimney-pots fell, and tiles flew from the roofs; but it looked to him as if they were left behind by the roofs and the chimneys as they scudded away. There was a great roaring, for the wind was dashing against London like a sea; but at North Wind's back Diamond, of course, felt nothing of it all. He was in a perfect calm. He could hear the sound of it, that was all.

By and by he raised himself and looked over the edge

of his nest. There were the houses rushing up and shooting away below him, like a fierce torrent of rocks instead of water. Then he looked up to the sky, but could see no stars; they were hidden by the blinding masses of the lady's hair which swept between. He began to wonder whether she would hear him if he spoke. He would try.

"Please, North Wind," he said, "what is that noise?"

From high over his head came the voice of North Wind, answering him gently,—

"The noise of my besom. I am the old woman that sweeps the cobwebs from the sky; only I'm busy with the floor now."

"What makes the houses look as if they were running away?"

"I am sweeping so fast over them."

"But, please, North Wind, I knew London was very big, but I didn't know it was so big as this. It seems as if we should never get away from it."

"We are going round and round, else we should have left it long ago."

"Is this the way you sweep, North Wind?"

"Yes; I go round and round with my great besom."

"Please, would you mind going a little slower, for I want to see the streets?"

"You won't see much now."

"Why?"

"Because I have nearly swept all the people home."

"Oh! I forgot," said Diamond, and was quiet after that, for he did not want to be troublesome.

But she dropped a little towards the roofs of the houses, and Diamond could see down into the streets. There were very few people about, though. The lamps flickered and flared again, but nobody seemed to want them.

Suddenly Diamond espied a little girl coming along a street. She was dreadfully blown by the wind, and a broom she was trailing behind her was very troublesome. It seemed as if the wind had a spite at her—it kept worrying her like a wild beast, and tearing at her rags. She was so lonely there!

"Oh! please, North Wind," he cried, "won't you help that little girl?"

"No, Diamond; I mustn't leave my work."

"But why shouldn't you be kind to her?"

"I am kind to her: I am sweeping the wicked smells away."

"But you're kinder to me, dear North Wind. Why shouldn't you be as kind to her as you are to me?"

"There are reasons, Diamond. Everybody can't be done to all the same. Everybody is not ready for the same thing."

"But I don't see why I should be kinder used than she."

"Do you think nothing's to be done but what you can see, Diamond, you silly! It's all right. Of course you can help her if you like. You've got nothing particular to do at this moment; I have."

"Oh! do let me help her, then. But you won't be able to wait, perhaps?"

"No, I can't wait; you must do it yourself. And, mind, the wind will get a hold of you too,"

"Don't you want me to help her, North Wind?"

"Not without having some idea what will happen. If you break down and cry, that won't be much of a help to her, and it will make a goose of little Diamond."

"I want to go," said Diamond. "Only there's just one thing—how am I to get home?"

"If you're anxious about that, perhaps you had better go with me. I am bound to take you home again, if you do."

"There!" cried Diamond, who was still looking after the little girl; "I'm sure the wind will blow her over, and perhaps kill her. Do let me go."

They had been sweeping more slowly along the line of the street. There was a lull in the roaring.

"Well, though I cannot promise to take you home," said North Wind, as she sank nearer and nearer to the tops of the houses, "I can promise you it will be all right in the end. You will get home somehow. Have you made up your mind what to do?"

"Yes; to help the little girl," said Diamond firmly.

The same moment North Wind dropt into the street and stood, only a tall lady, but with her hair flying up over the housetops. She put her hands to her back, took Diamond, and set him down in the street. The same moment he was caught in the fierce coils of the blast, and all but blown away. North Wind stepped back a pace, and at once towered in stature to the height of the houses. A chimney-pot clashed at Diamond's feet. He turned in terror, but it was to look for the little girl, and when he turned again the lady had vanished, and the wind was roaring along the street as if it had been the bed of an invisible torrent. The little girl was scudding before the blast, her hair flying too, and behind her she dragged her broom. Her little legs were going as fast as ever they could to keep her from falling. Diamond crept into the shelter of a doorway, thinking to stop her; but she passed him like a bird, crying gently and pitifully.

"Stop! stop! little girl," shouted Diamond, starting in pursuit.

"I can't," wailed the girl; "the wind won't leave go of me."

Diamond could run faster than she, and he had no broom. In a few moments he had caught her by the frock. But it tore in his hand, and away went the little girl. So he had to run again, and this time he ran so fast that he got before her, and turning round caught her in his arms, when down they went both together, which made the little girl laugh in the midst of her crying.

"Where are you going?" asked Diamond, rubbing the elbow that had stuck farthest out. The arm it belonged to was twined around a lamp-post as he stood between the little girl and the wind.

"Home," she said, gasping for breath.

"Then I will go with you," said Diamond.

And then they were silent for a while, for the wind blew

worse than ever, and they had both to hold on to the lamp-post.

"Where is your crossing?" asked the girl at length.

"I don't sweep," answered Diamond.

"What *do* you do, then?" asked she. "You ain't big enough for most things."

"I don't know what I do do," answered he, feeling rather ashamed. "Nothing, I suppose. My father's Mr. Coleman's coachman."

"Have you à father?" she said, staring at him as if a boy with a father was a natural curiosity.

"Yes. Haven't *you?*" returned Diamond.

"No; nor mother neither. Old Sal's all I've got."

And she began to cry again.

"I wouldn't go to her if she wasn't good to me," said Diamond.

"But you must go somewheres."

"Move on," said the voice of a policeman behind them.

"I told you so," said the girl. "You must go somewheres. They're always at it."

"But old Sal doesn't beat you, does she?"

"I wish she would."

"What do you mean?" asked Diamond, quite bewildered.

"She would if she was my mother. But she wouldn't lie abed a-cuddlin' of her ugly old bones, and laugh to hear me crying at the door."

"You don't mean she won't let you in to-night?"

"It'll be a good chance if she does."

"Why are you out so late, then?" asked Diamond.

"My crossing's a long way off at the West End, and I had been indulgin' in door-steps and mewses."

"We'd better have a try anyhow," said Diamond. "Come along."

As he spoke Diamond thought he caught a glimpse of North Wind turning a corner in front of them; and when they turned the corner too, they found it quite quiet there, but he saw nothing of the lady.

"Now you lead me," he said, taking her hand, "and I'll take care of you."

The girl withdrew her hand, but only to dry her eyes with her frock, for the other had enough to do with her broom. She put it in his again, and led him, turning after turning, until they stopped at a cellar-door in a very dirty lane. There she knocked.

"I shouldn't like to live here," said Diamond.

"Oh yes, you would, if you had nowheres else to go to," answered the girl. "I only wish we may get in."

"I don't want to go in," said Diamond.

"Where do you mean to go, then?"

"Home to my home."

"Where's that?"

"I don't exactly know."

"Then you're worse off than I am."

"Oh no, for North Wind—" began Diamond, and stopped, he hardly knew why.

"*What?*" said the girl, as she held her ear to the door listening.

But Diamond did not reply. Neither did old Sal.

"I told you so," said the girl. "She is wide awake hearkening. But we don't get in."

"What will you do, then?" asked Diamond.

"Move on," she answered.

"Where?"

"Oh, anywheres. Bless you, I'm used to it."

"Hadn't you better come home with me, then?"

"That's a good joke, when you don't know where it is. Come on."

"But where?"

"Oh, nowheres in particular. Come on."

Diamond obeyed. The wind had now fallen considerably. They wandered on and on, turning in this direction and that, without any reason for one way more than another, until they had got out of the thick of the houses into a waste kind of place. By this time they were both very tired. Diamond felt a good deal inclined to cry, and thought he had been very silly to get down from the back of the North Wind; not that he would have minded it if he had done the girl any good; but he thought he had been of no use to her. He was mistaken there, for she was far happier for having Diamond with her than if she had been wandering about alone. She did not seem so tired as he was.

"Do let us rest a bit," said Diamond.

"Let's see," she answered. "There's something like a railway there. Perhaps there's an open arch."

They went towards it and found one, and, better still, there was an empty barrel lying under the arch.

"Hillo! here we are!" said the girl. "A barrel's the jolliest bed going—on the tramp, I mean. We'll have forty winks, and then go on again."

She crept in, and Diamond crept in beside her. They put their arms round each other, and when he began to grow warm, Diamond's courage began to come back.

"This *is* jolly!" he said. "I'm *so* glad!"

"I don't think so much of it," said the girl. "I'm used to it, I suppose. But I can't think how a kid like you comes to be out all alone this time o' the night."

She called him a *kid*, but she was not really a month older than he was; only she had had to work for her bread, and that so soon makes people older.

"But I shouldn't have been out so late if I hadn't got down to help you," said Diamond. "North Wind is gone home long ago."

"I think you must ha' got out o' one o' them Hidget Asylms," said the girl. "You said something about the north wind afore that I couldn't get the rights of."

So now, for the sake of his character, Diamond had to tell her the whole story.

She did not believe a word of it. She said she wasn't such a flat as to believe all that bosh. But as she spoke there came a great blast of wind through the arch, and set the barrel rolling. So they made haste to get out of it, for they had no notion of being rolled over and over as if they had been packed tight and wouldn't hurt, like a barrel of herrings.

"I thought we should have had a sleep," said Diamond; "but I can't say I'm very sleepy after all. Come, let's go on again."

They wandered on and on, sometimes sitting on a doorstep, but always turning into lanes or fields when they had a chance.

They found themselves at last on a rising ground that sloped rather steeply on the other side. It was a waste kind of spot below, bounded by an irregular wall, with a few doors in it. Outside lay broken things in general, from garden rollers to flower-pots and wine-bottles. But the moment they reached the brow of the rising ground, a gust of wind seized them and blew them down hill as fast as they could run. Nor could Diamond stop before he went bang against one of the doors in the wall. To his dismay it burst open. When they came to themselves they peeped in. It was the back door of a garden.

"Ah, ah!" cried Diamond, after staring for a few moments, "I thought so! North Wind takes nobody in! Here I am in master's garden! I tell you what, little girl, you just bore a hole in old Sal's wall, and put your mouth to it, and say, 'Please, North Wind, mayn't I go out with you?' and then you'll see what'll come."

"I daresay I shall. But I'm out in the wind too often already to want more of it."

"I said *with* the North Wind, not *in* it."

"It's all one."

"It's *not* all one."

"It *is* all one."

"But I know best."

"And I know better. I'll box your ears," said the girl.

Diamond got very angry. But he remembered that even if she did box his ears, he mustn't box hers again, for she was a girl, and all that boys must do, if girls are rude, is to go away and leave them. So he went in at the door.

"Good-bye, mister," said the girl.

This brought Diamond to his senses.

"I'm sorry I was cross," he said. "Come in, and my mother will give you some breakfast."

"No, thank you. I must be off to my crossing. It's morning now."

"I'm very sorry for you," said Diamond.

"Well, it *is* a life to be tired of—what with old Sal, and so many holes in my shoes."

"I wonder you're so good. I should kill myself."

"Oh no, you wouldn't! When I think of it, I always want to see what's coming next, and so I always wait till next is over. Well! I suppose there's somebody happy somewheres. But it ain't in them carriages. Oh my! *how* they *do* look sometimes—fit to bite your head off! Good-bye!"

She ran up the hill and disappeared behind it. Then Diamond shut the door as he best could, and ran through the kitchen-garden to the stable. And wasn't he glad to get into his own blessed bed again!

Chapter V
THE SUMMER-HOUSE

DIAMOND said nothing to his mother about his adventures. He had half a notion that North Wind was a friend of his mother, and that, if she did not know *all* about it, at least she did not mind his going anywhere with the lady of the wind. At the same time he doubted whether he might not appear to be telling stories if he told all, especially as he could hardly believe it himself when he thought about it in the middle of the day, although when the twilight was once half-way on to night he had no doubt about it, at least for the first few days after he had been with her. The girl that swept the crossing had certainly refused to believe him. Besides, he felt sure that North Wind would tell him if he ought to speak.

It was some time before he saw the lady of the wind again. Indeed nothing remarkable took place in Diamond's history until the following week. This was what happened then. Diamond the horse wanted new shoes, and Diamond's father took him out of the stable, and was just getting on his back to ride him to the forge, when he saw his little boy standing by the pump, and looking at him wistfully. Then the coachman took his foot out of the stirrup, left his hold of the mane and bridle, came across to his boy, lifted him up, and setting him on the horse's back, told him to sit up like a man. He then led away both Diamonds together.

The boy atop felt not a little tremulous as the great muscles that lifted the legs of the horse knotted and relaxed against his legs, and he cowered towards the withers, grasping with his hands the bit of mane worn short by the collar; but when his father looked back at him, saying once more, "Sit up, Diamond," he let the mane go and sat up, notwithstanding that the horse, thinking, I suppose, that his master had said to him, "*Come* up, Diamond," stepped out faster. For both the Diamonds were just grandly obedient. And Diamond soon found that, as he was obedient to his father, so the horse was obedient to him. For he had not ridden far before he found courage to reach forward and catch hold of the bridle, and when his father, whose hand was upon it, felt the boy pull it towards him, he looked up and smiled, and, well pleased, let go his hold, and left Diamond to guide Diamond; and the boy soon found that he could do so perfectly. It was a grand thing to be able to guide a great beast like that. And another discovery he made was that, in order to guide the horse, he had in a measure to obey the horse first. If he did not yield his body to the motions of the horse's body, he could not guide him; he must fall off.

The blacksmith lived at some distance, deeper into London. As they crossed the angle of a square, Diamond, who was now quite comfortable on his living throne, was glancing this way and that in a gentle pride, when he saw a girl sweeping a crossing scuddingly before a lady. The lady was his father's mistress, Mrs. Coleman, and the little girl was she for whose sake he had got off North Wind's back. He drew Diamond's bridle in eager anxiety to see whether her outstretched hand would gather a penny from Mrs. Coleman. But she had given one at the last crossing, and the hand returned only to grasp its broom. Diamond could not bear it. He had a penny in his pocket, the gift of the same lady the day before, and he tumbled off his horse to give it to the girl. He tumbled off, I say, for he did tumble when he reached the ground. But he got up in an instant, and ran, searching his pocket as he ran. She made him a pretty courtesy when he offered his treasure, but with a bewildered stare. She thought first: "Then he *was* on the back of the North Wind after all!" but, looking up at the sound of the horse's feet on the paved crossing, she changed her idea, saying to herself, "North Wind is his father's horse! That's the secret of it! Why couldn't he say so?" And she had a mind to refuse the penny. But his smile put it all right, and she not only took his penny but put it in her mouth with a "Thank you, mister. Did they wollop you then?"

"Oh no!" answered Diamond. "They never wollops me."

"Lor!" said the little girl, and was speechless.

Meantime his father, looking up, and seeing the horse's back bare, suffered a pang of awful dread, but the next moment catching sight of him, took him up and put him on, saying—

"Don't get off again, Diamond. The horse might have put his foot on you."

"No, father," answered the boy, and rode on in majestic safety.

The summer drew near, warm and splendid. Miss Coleman was a little better in health, and sat a good deal in the garden. One day she saw Diamond peeping through the shrubbery, and called him. He talked to her so frankly that she often sent for him after that, and by degrees it came about that he had leave to run in the garden as he pleased. He never touched any of the flowers or blossoms, for he was not like some boys who cannot enjoy a thing without pulling it to pieces, and so preventing every one from enjoying it after them.

A week even makes such a long time in a child's life,

that Diamond had begun once more to feel as if North Wind were a dream of some far-off year.

One hot evening, he had been sitting with the young mistress, as they called her, in a little summer-house at the bottom of the lawn—a wonderful thing for beauty, the boy thought, for a little window in the side of it was made of colored glass. It grew dusky, and the lady began to feel chill, and went in, leaving the boy in the summer-house. He sat there gazing out at a bed of tulips, which, although they had closed for the night, could not go quite asleep for the wind that kept waving them about. All at once he saw a great bumble-bee fly out of one of the tulips.

"There! that is something done," said a voice—a gentle, merry, childish voice, but *so* tiny. "At last it was. I thought he would have had to stay there all night, poor fellow! I did."

Diamond could not tell whether the voice was near or far away, it was so small and yet so clear. He had never seen a fairy, but he had heard of such, and he began to look all about for one. And there was the tiniest creature sliding down the stem of the tulip!

"Are you the fairy that herds the bees?" he asked, going out of the summer-house, and down on his knees on the green shore of the tulip-bed.

"I'm not a fairy," answered the little creature.

"How do you know that?"

"It would become you better to ask how *you* are to know it."

"You've just told me."

"Yes. But what's the use of knowing a thing only because you're told it?"

"Well, how *am* I to know you are not a fairy? You do look very like one."

"In the first place, fairies are much bigger than you see me."

"Oh!" said Diamond reflectively; "I thought they were very little."

"But they might be tremendously bigger than I am, and

yet not *very* big. Why, *I* could be six times the size I am, and not be very huge. Besides, a fairy can't grow big and little at will, though the nursery-tales do say so: they don't know better. You stupid Diamond! have you never seen me before?"

And, as she spoke, a moan of wind bent the tulips almost to the ground, and the creature laid her hand on Diamond's shoulder. In a moment he knew that it was North Wind.

"I *am* very stupid," he said; "but I never saw you so small before, not even when you were nursing the primrose."

"Must you see me every size that can be measured before you know me, Diamond?"

"But how could I think it was you taking care of a great stupid bumble-bee?"

"The more stupid he was the more need he had to be taken care of. What with sucking honey and trying to open the door, he was nearly dazed; and when it opened in the morning to let the sun see the tulip's heart, what would the sun have thought to find such a stupid thing lying there—with wings too?"

"But how do you have time to look after bees?"

"I don't look after bees. I had this one to look after. It was hard work, though."

"Hard work! Why, you could blow a chimney down, or—or—a boy's cap off," said Diamond.

"Both are easier than blow a tulip open. But I scarcely know the difference between hard and easy. I am always able for what I have to do. When I see my work, I just rush at it—and it is done. But I mustn't chatter. I have got to sink a ship to-night."

"Sink a ship! What! with men in it?"

"Yes, and women too."

"How dreadful! I wish you wouldn't talk so."

"It is rather dreadful. But it is my work. I must do it."

"I hope you won't ask me to go with you."

"No, I won't ask you. But you must come for all that."

"I won't, then."

"Won't you?"

And North Wind grew a tall lady, and looked him in the eyes, and Diamond said—

"Please take me. You cannot be cruel."

"No; I could not be cruel if I would. I can do nothing cruel, although I often do what looks like cruel to those who do not know what I really am doing. The people they say I drown, I only carry away to—to—to—well, the back of the North Wind—that is what they used to call it long ago, only *I* never saw the place."

"How can you carry them there if you never saw it?"

"I know the way."

"But how is it you never saw it?"

"Because it is behind me."

"But you can look round."

"Not far enough to see my own back. No; I always look before me. In fact, I grow quite blind and deaf when I try to see my back. I only mind my work."

"But how does it be your work?"

"Ah, that I can't tell you. I only know it is, because when I do it I feel all right, and when I don't I feel all wrong. East Wind says—only one does not exactly know how much to believe of what she says, for she is very naughty sometimes—she says it is all managed by a baby; but whether she is good or naughty when she says that, I don't know. I just stick to my work. It is all one to me to let a bee out of a tulip, or to sweep the cobwebs from the sky. You would like to go with me tonight?"

"I don't want to see a ship sunk."

"But suppose I had to take you?"

"Why, then, of course I must go."

"There's a good Diamond.—I think I had better be growing a bit. Only you must go to bed first. I can't take you till you're in bed. That's the law about the children. So I had better go and do something else first."

"Very well, North Wind," said Diamond. "What are you going to do first, if you please?"

"I think I may tell you. Jump up on the top of the wall, there."

"I can't."

"Ah! and I can't help you—you haven't been to bed yet, you see. Come out to the road with me, just in front of the coach-house, and I will show you."

North Wind grew very small indeed, so small that she could not have blown the dust off a dusty miller, as the Scotch children call a yellow auricula. Diamond could not even see the blades of grass move as she flitted along by his foot. They left the lawn, went out by the wicket in the coach-house gates, and then crossed the road to the low wall that separated it from the river.

"You can get up on this wall, Diamond," said North Wind.

"Yes; but my mother has forbidden me."

"Then don't," said North Wind.

"But I can see over," said Diamond.

"Ah! to be sure. I can't."

So saying, North Wind gave a little bound, and stood on the top of the wall. She was just about the height a dragon-fly would be, if it stood on end.

"You darling!" said Diamond, seeing what a lovely little toy-woman she was.

"Don't be impertinent, Master Diamond," said North Wind. "If there's one thing makes me more angry than another, it is the way you humans judge things by their size. I am quite as respectable now as I shall be six hours after this, when I take an East Indiaman by the royals, twist her round, and push her under. You have no right to address me in such a fashion."

But as she spoke, the tiny face wore the smile of a great grand woman. She was only having her own beautiful fun out of Diamond, and true woman's fun never hurts.

"But look there!" she resumed. "Do you see a boat with one man in it—a green and white boat?"

"Yes; quite well."

"That's a poet."

"I thought you said it was a bo-at."

"Stupid pet! Don't you know what a poet is?"

"Why, a thing to sail on the water in."

"Well, perhaps you're not so far wrong. Some poets do carry people over the sea. But I have no business to talk so much. The man is a poet."

"The boat is a boat," said Diamond.

"Can't you spell?" asked North Wind.

"Not very well."

"So I see. A poet is not a bo-at, as you call it. A poet is a man who is glad of something, and tries to make other people glad of it too."

"Ah! now I know. Like the man in the sweety-shop."

"Not very. But I see it is no use. I wasn't sent to tell you, and so I can't tell you. I must be off. Only first just look at the man."

"He's not much of a rower," said Diamond—"paddling first with one fin and then with the other."

"Now look here!" said North Wind.

And she flashed like a dragon-fly across the water, whose surface rippled and puckered as she passed. The next moment the man in the boat glanced about him, and bent to his oars. The boat flew over the rippling water. Man and boat and river were awake. The same instant almost, North Wind perched again upon the river wall.

"How did you do that?" asked Diamond.

"I blew in his face," answered North Wind.

"I don't see how that could do it," said Diamond.

"I daresay not. And therefore you will say you don't believe it could."

"No, no, dear North Wind. I know you too well not to believe you."

"Well, I blew in his face, and that woke him up."

"But what was the good of it?"

"Why! don't you see? Look at him—how he is pulling. I blew the mist out of him."

"How was that?"

"That is just what I cannot tell you."

"But you did it."

"Yes. I have to do ten thousand things without being able to tell how."

"I don't like that," said Diamond.

He was staring after the boat. Hearing no answer, he looked down to the wall.

North Wind was gone. Away across the river went a long ripple—what sailors call a cat's paw. The man in the boat was putting up a sail. The moon was coming to herself on the edge of a great cloud, and the sail began to shine white. Diamond rubbed his eyes, and wondered what it was all about. Things seemed going on around him, and all to understand each other; but he could make nothing of it. So he put his hands in his pockets, and went in to have his tea. The night was very hot, for the wind had fallen again.

"You don't seem very well to-night, Diamond," said his mother.

"I am quite well, mother," returned Diamond, who was only puzzled.

"I think you had better go to bed," she added.

"Very well, mother," he answered.

He stopped for one moment to look out of the window. Above the moon the clouds were going different ways. Somehow or other this troubled him, but, notwithstanding, he was soon fast asleep.

He woke in the middle of the night and the darkness. A terrible noise was rumbling overhead, like the rolling beat of great drums echoing through a brazen vault. The roof of the loft in which he lay had no ceiling; only the tiles were between him and the sky. For a while he could not come quite awake, for the noise kept beating him down, so that his heart was troubled and fluttered painfully. A second peal of thunder burst over his head, and almost choked him with fear. Nor did he recover until the great blast that followed, having torn some tiles off the roof, sent a spout of wind down into his bed and over his face, which brought him wide awake, and gave him back his courage.

The same moment he heard a mighty yet musical voice calling him.

"Come up, Diamond," it said. "It's all ready. I'm waiting for you."

He looked out of the bed, and saw a gigantic, powerful, but most lovely arm—with a hand whose fingers were nothing the less ladylike that they could have strangled a boa-constrictor, or choked a tigress off its prey—stretched down through a big hole in the roof. Without a moment's hesitation he reached out his tiny one, and laid it in the grand palm before him.

Chapter VI
OUT IN THE STORM

THE hand felt its way up his arm, and, grasping it gently and strongly above the elbow, lifted Diamond from the bed. The moment he was through the hole in the roof, all the winds of heaven seemed to lay hold upon him, and buffet him hither and thither. His hair blew one way, his night-gown another, his legs threatened to float from under him, and his head to grow dizzy with the swiftness of the invisible assailant. Cowering, he clung with the other hand to the huge hand which held his arm, and fear invaded his heart.

"Oh, North Wind!" he murmured, but the words vanished from his lips as he had seen the soap-bubbles that burst too soon vanish from the mouth of his pipe. The wind caught them, and they were nowhere. They couldn't get out at all, but were torn away and strangled. And yet North Wind heard them, and in her answer it seemed to Diamond that just because she was so big and could not help it, and just because her ear and her mouth must seem to him so dreadfully far away, she spoke to him more tenderly and graciously than ever before. Her voice was like the bass of a deep organ, without the groan in it; like the most delicate of violin tones without the wail in it; like the most glorious of trumpet-ejaculations without the defiance in it; like the sound of falling water without the clatter and clash in it: it was like all of them and neither of them—all of them without their faults, each of them without its peculiarity; after all, it was more like his mother's voice than anything else in the world.

"Diamond, dear," she said, "be a man. What is fearful to you is not the least fearful to me."

"But it can't hurt you," murmured Diamond, "for you're *it*."

"Then, if I'm *it*, and have you in my arms, how can it hurt you?"

"Oh yes! I see," whispered Diamond. "But it looks so dreadful, and it pushes me about so."

"Yes, it does, my dear. That is what it was sent for."

At the same moment, a peal of thunder which shook Diamond's heart against the sides of his bosom hurtled out of the heavens: I cannot say out of the sky, for there was no sky. Diamond had not seen the lightning, for he had been intent on finding the face of North Wind. Every moment the folds of her garment would sweep across his eyes and blind him, but between, he could just persuade himself that he saw great glories of woman's eyes looking down through rifts in the mountainous clouds over his head.

He trembled so at the thunder, that his knees failed him, and he sunk down at North Wind's feet, and clasped her round the column of her ankle. She instantly stooped and lifted him from the roof—up—up into her bosom, and held him there, saying, as if to an inconsolable child—

"Diamond, dear, this will never do."

"Oh yes, it will," answered Diamond. "I am all right now—quite comfortable, I assure you, dear North Wind. If you will only let me stay here, I shall be all right indeed."

"But you will feel the wind here, Diamond."

"I don't mind that a bit, so long as I feel your arms

through it," answered Diamond, nestling closer to her grand bosom.

"Brave boy!" returned North Wind, pressing him closer.

"No," said Diamond, "I don't see that. It's not courage at all, so long as I feel you there."

"But hadn't you better get into my hair? Then you would not feel the wind; you will here."

"Ah, but, dear North Wind, you don't know how nice it is to feel your arms about me. It is a thousand times better to have them and the wind together, than to have only your hair and the back of your neck and no wind at all."

"But it is surely more comfortable there?"

"Well, perhaps; but I begin to think there are better things than being comfortable."

"Yes, indeed there are. Well, I will keep you in front of me. You will feel the wind, but not too much. I shall only want one arm to take care of you; the other will be quite enough to sink the ship."

"Oh, dear North Wind! how can you talk so?"

"My dear boy, I never talk; I always mean what I say."

"Then you do mean to sink the ship with the other hand?"

"Yes."

"It's not like you."

"How do you know that?"

"Quite easily. Here you are taking care of a poor little boy with one arm, and there you are sinking a ship with the other. It can't be like you."

"Ah! but which is me? I can't be two mes, you know."

"No. Nobody can be two mes."

"Well, which me is me?"

"Now I must think. There looks to be two."

"Yes. That's the very point.—You can't be knowing the thing you don't know, can you?"

"No."

"Which me do you know?"

"The kindest, goodest, best me in the world," answered Diamond, clinging to North Wind.

"Why am I good to you?"

"I don't know."

"Have you ever done anything for me?"

"No."

"Then I must be good to you because I choose to be good to you."

"Yes."

"Why should I choose?"

"Because—because—because you like."

"Why should I like to be good to you?"

"I don't know, except it be because it's good to be good to me."

"That's just it; I am good to you because I like to be good."

"Then why shouldn't you be good to other people as well as to me?"

"That's just what I don't know. Why shouldn't I?"

"I don't know either. Then why shouldn't you?"

"Because I am."

"There it is again," said Diamond. "I don't see that you are. It looks quite the other thing."

"Well, but listen to me, Diamond. You know the one *me*, you say, and that is good."

"Yes."

"Do you know the other *me* as well?"

"No. I can't. I shouldn't like to."

"There it is. You don't know the other me. You are sure of one of them?"

"Yes."

"And you are sure there can't be two mes?"

"Yes."

"Then the me you don't know must be the same as the me you do know—else there would be two mes?"

"Yes."

"Then the other me you don't know must be as kind as the me you do know?"

"Yes."

"Besides, *I* tell you that it is so, only it doesn't look like it. That I confess freely. Have you anything more to object?"

"No, no, dear North Wind; I am quite satisfied."

"Then I will tell you something you might object. You might say that the me you know is like the other me, and that I am cruel all through."

"I know that can't be, because you are so kind."

"But that kindness might be only a pretence for the sake of being more cruel afterwards."

Diamond clung to her tighter than ever, crying—

"No, no, dear North Wind; I can't believe that. I don't believe it. I won't believe it. That would kill me. I love you, and you must love me, else how did I come to love you? How could you know how to put on such a beautiful face if you did not love me and the rest? No. You may sink as many ships as you like, and I won't say another word. I can't say I shall like to see it, you know."

"That's quite another thing," said North Wind; and as she spoke she gave one spring from the roof of the hayloft, and rushed up into the clouds, with Diamond on her left arm close to her heart. And as if the clouds knew she had come, they burst into a fresh jubilation of thunderous light. For a few moments, Diamond seemed to be borne up through the depths of an ocean of dazzling flame; the next, the winds were writhing around him like a storm of serpents. For they were in the midst of the clouds and mists, and they of course took the shapes of the wind, eddying and wreathing and whirling and shooting and dashing about like gray and black water, so that it was as if the wind itself had taken shape, and he saw the gray and black wind tossing and raving most madly all about him. Now it blinded him by smiting him upon the eyes; now it deafened him by bellowing in his ears; for even when the thunder came he knew now that it was the billows of the great ocean of the air dashing against each other in their haste to fill the hollow scooped out by the lightning; now it took his breath quite away by sucking it from his body with the speed of its rush. But he did not mind it. He only gasped first and then laughed, for the arm of North Wind was about him, and he was leaning against her bosom. It is quite impossible for me to describe what he saw. Did you ever watch a great wave shoot into a winding passage amongst rocks? If you ever did, you would see that the water rushed every way at once, some of it even turning back and opposing the rest; greater confusion you might see nowhere except in a crowd of frightened people. Well, the wind was like that, except that it went much faster, and therefore was much wilder, and twisted and shot and curled and dodged and clashed and raved ten times more madly than anything else in creation except human passions. Diamond saw the threads of the lady's hair streaking it all. In parts indeed he could not tell which was hair and which was black storm and vapor. It seemed sometimes that all the great billows of mist-muddy wind were woven out of the crossing lines of North Wind's infinite hair, sweeping in endless intertwistings. And Diamond felt as the wind seized on his hair, which his mother kept rather long, as if he too was a part of the storm, and some of its life went out from him. But so sheltered was he by North Wind's arm and bosom that only at times, in the fiercer onslaught of some curl-billowed eddy, did he recognize for a moment how wild was the storm in which he was carried, nestling in its very core and formative centre.

It seemed to Diamond likewise that they were motionless in this centre, and that all the confusion and fighting went on around them. Flash after flash illuminated the fierce chaos, revealing in varied yellow and blue and gray and dusky red the vaporous contention; peal after peal of thunder tore the infinite waste; but it seemed to Diamond that North Wind and he were motionless, all but the hair. It was not so. They were sweeping with the speed of the wind itself towards the sea.

Chapter VII
THE CATHEDRAL

I MUST not go on describing what cannot be described, for nothing is more wearisome.

Before they reached the sea, Diamond felt North Wind's hair beginning to fall about him.

"Is the storm over, North Wind?" he called out.

"No, Diamond. I am only waiting a moment to set you down. You would not like to see the ship sunk, and I am going to give you a place to stop in till I come back for you."

"Oh! thank you," said Diamond. "I shall be sorry to leave you, North Wind, but I would rather not see the ship go down. And I'm afraid the poor people will cry, and I should hear them. Oh, dear!"

"There are a good many passengers on board; and to tell the truth, Diamond, I don't care about your hearing the cry you speak of. I am afraid you would not get it out of your little head again for a long time."

"But how can you bear it then, North Wind? For I am sure you are kind. I shall never doubt that again."

"I will tell you how I am able to bear it, Diamond: I am always hearing, through every noise, through all the noise I am making myself even, the sound of a far-off song. I do not exactly know where it is, or what it means; and I don't hear much of it, only the odor of its music, as it were, flitting across the great billows of the ocean outside this air in which I make such a storm; but what I do hear, is quite enough to make me able to bear the cry from the drowning ship. So it would you if you could hear it."

"No, it wouldn't," returned Diamond, stoutly. "For *they* wouldn't hear the music of the far-away song; and if they did, it wouldn't do them any good. You see, you and I are not going to be drowned, and so *we* might enjoy it."

"But you have never heard the psalm, and you don't know what it is like. Somehow, I can't say how, it tells me that all is right; that it is coming to swallow up all cries."

"But that won't do them any good—the people, I mean," persisted Diamond.

"It must. It must," said North Wind, hurriedly. "It wouldn't be the song it seems to be if it did not swallow up all their fear and pain too, and set them singing it themselves with the rest. I am sure it will. And do you know, ever since I knew I had hair, ever since it began to go out and away, that song has been coming nearer and nearer. Only I must say it was some thousand years before I heard it."

"But how can you say it was coming nearer when you did not hear it?" asked doubting little Diamond.

"Since I began to hear it, I know it is growing louder, therefore I judge it was coming nearer and nearer until I did hear it first. I'm not so very old, you know—a few thousand years only—and I was quite a baby when I heard the noise first, but I knew it must come from the voices of people ever so much older and wiser than I was. I can't sing at all, except now and then, and I can never tell what my song is going to be; I only know what it is after I have sung it.—But this will never do. Will you stop here?"

"I can't see anywhere to stop," said Diamond. "Your

hair is all down like a darkness, and I can't see through it if I knock my eyes into it ever so much."

"Look then," said North Wind; and, with one sweep of her great white arm, she swept yards deep of darkness like a great curtain from before the face of the boy.

And lo! it was a blue night, lit up with stars. Where it did not shine with stars it shimmered with the milk of the stars, except where, just opposite to Diamond's face, the gray towers of a cathedral blotted out each its own shape of sky and stars.

"Oh! what's that?" cried Diamond, struck with a kind of terror, for he had never seen a cathedral, and it rose before him with an awful reality in the midst of the wide spaces, conquering emptiness with grandeur.

"A very good place for you to wait in," said North Wind. "But we shall go in, and you shall judge for yourself."

There was an open door in the middle of one of the towers, leading out upon the roof, and through it they passed. Then North Wind set Diamond on his feet, and he found himself at the top of a stone stair, which went twisting away down into the darkness. For only a little light came in at the door. It was enough, however, to allow Diamond to see that North Wind stood beside him. He looked up to find her face, and saw that she was no longer a beautiful giantess, but the tall gracious lady he liked best to see. She took his hand, and, giving him the broad part of the spiral stair to walk on, led him down a good way; then, opening another little door, led him out upon a narrow gallery that ran all around the central part of the church, on the ledges of the windows of the clerestory, and through openings in the parts of the wall that divided the windows from each other. It was very narrow, and except when they were passing through the wall, Diamond saw nothing to keep him from falling into the church. It lay below him like a great silent gulf hollowed in stone, and he held his breath for fear as he looked down.

"What are you trembling for, little Diamond?" said the

lady, as she walked gently along, with her hand held out behind her leading him, for there was not breadth enough for them to walk side by side.

"I am afraid of falling down there," answered Diamond. "It is so deep down."

"Yes, rather," answered North Wind; "but you were a hundred times higher a few minutes ago."

"Ah, yes, but somebody's arm was about me then," said Diamond, putting his little mouth to the beautiful cold hand that had a hold of his.

"What a dear little warm mouth you've got!" said North Wind. "It is a pity you should talk nonsense with it. Don't you know I have a hold of you?"

"Yes; but I'm walking on my own legs, and they might slip. I can't trust myself so well as your arms."

"But I have a hold of you, I tell you, foolish child."

"Yes, but somehow I can't feel comfortable."

"If you were to fall, and my hold of you were to give way, I should be down after you in a less moment than a lady's watch can tick, and catch you long before you had reached the ground."

"I don't like it, though," said Diamond.

"*Oh! oh! oh!*" he screamed the next moment, bent double with terror, for North Wind had let go her hold of his hand, and had vanished, leaving him standing as if rooted to the gallery.

She left the words, "Come after me," sounding in his ears.

But move he dared not. In a moment more he would from very terror have fallen into the church, but suddenly there came a gentle breath of cool wind upon his face, and it kept blowing upon him in little puffs, and at every puff Diamond felt his faintness going away, and his fear with it. Courage was reviving in his little heart, and still the cool wafts of the soft wind breathed upon him, and the soft wind was so mighty and strong within its gentleness, that in a minute more Diamond was marching along the narrow ledge as fearless for the time as North Wind herself.

He walked on and on, with the windows all in a row on one side of him, and the great empty nave of the church echoing to every one of his brave strides on the other, until at last he came to a little open door, from which a broader stair led him down and down and down, till at last all at once he found himself in the arms of North Wind, who held him close to her, and kissed him on the forehead. Diamond nestled to her, and murmured into her bosom,—

"Why did you leave me, dear North Wind?"

"Because I wanted you to walk alone," she answered.

"But it is so much nicer here!" said Diamond.

"I daresay; but I couldn't hold a little coward to my heart. I would make me so cold!"

"But I wasn't brave of myself," said Diamond, whom my older readers will have already discovered to be a true child in this, that he was given to metaphysics. "It was the wind that blew in my face that made me brave. Wasn't it now, North Wind?"

"Yes: I know that. You had to be taught what courage was. And you couldn't know what it was without feeling it: therefore it was given you. But don't you feel as if you would try to be brave yourself next time?"

"Yes, I do. But trying is not much."

"Yes, it is—a very great deal, for it is a beginning. And a beginning is the greatest thing of all. To try to be brave is to be brave. The coward who tries to be brave is before the man who is brave because he is made so, and never had to try."

"How kind you are, North Wind!"

"I am only just. All kindness is but justice. We owe it."

"I don't quite understand that."

"Never mind; you will some day. There is no hurry about understanding it now."

"Who blew the wind on me that made me brave?"

"I did."

"I didn't see you."

"Therefore you can believe me."

"Yes, yes; of course. But how was it that such a little breath could be so strong?"

"That I don't know."

"But you made it strong?"

"No: I only blew it. I knew it would make you strong, just as it did the man in the boat, you remember. But how my breath has that power I cannot tell. It was put into it when I was made. That is all I know. But really I must be going about my work."

"Ah! the poor ship! I wish you would stop here, and let the poor ship go."

"That I dare not do. Will you stop here till I come back?"

"Yes. You won't be long?"

"Not longer than I can help. Trust me, you shall get home before the morning."

In a moment North Wind was gone, and the next Diamond heard a moaning about the church, which grew and grew to a roaring. The storm was up again, and he knew that North Wind's hair was flying.

The church was dark. Only a little light came through the windows, which were almost all of that precious old stained glass which is so much lovelier than the new. But Diamond could not see how beautiful they were, for there was not enough of light in the stars to show the colors of them. He could only just distinguish them from the walls. He looked up, but could not see the gallery along which he had passed. He could only tell where it was far up by the faint glimmer of the windows of the clerestory, whose sills made part of it. The church grew very lonely about him, and he began to feel like a child whose mother has forsaken it. Only he knew that to be left alone is not always to be forsaken.

He began to feel his way about the place, and for a while went wandering up and down. His little footsteps waked little answering echoes in the great house. It wasn't too big to mind him. It was as if the church knew he was there, and meant to make itself his house. So it went on giving back an answer to every step, until at length Diamond thought he should like to say something out loud, and see what the church would answer. But he found he was afraid to speak. He could not utter a word for fear of the loneliness. Perhaps it was as well that he did not, for the sound of a spoken word would have made him feel the place yet more deserted and empty. But he thought he could sing. He was fond of singing, and at home he used to sing, to tunes of his own, all the nursery rhymes he knew. So he began to try *Hey diddle diddle*, but it wouldn't do. Then he tried *Little Boy Blue*, but it was no better. Neither would *Sing a Song of Sixpence* sing itself at all. Then he tried *Poor old Cockytoo*, but he wouldn't do. They all sounded so silly! and he had never thought them silly before. So he was quiet, and listened to the echoes that came out of the dark corners in answer to his footsteps.

At last he gave a great sigh, and said, "I'm *so* tired." But he did not hear the gentle echo that answered from far away over his head, for at the same moment he came against the lowest of a few steps that stretched across the church, and fell down and hurt his arm. He cried a little first, and then crawled up the steps on his hands and knees. At the top he came to a little bit of carpet, on which he lay down; and there he lay staring at the dull window that rose nearly a hundred feet above his head.

Now this was the eastern window of the church, and the moon was at that moment just on the edge of the horizon. The next, she was peeping over it. And lo! with the moon, St. John and St. Paul, and the rest of them, began to dawn in the window in their lovely garments. Diamond did not know that the wonder-working moon was behind, and he thought all the light was coming out of the window itself, and that the good old men were appearing to help him, growing out of the night and the darkness, because he had hurt his arm, and was very tired and lonely, and North Wind was so long in coming. So he lay and looked at them backwards over his head, wondering when they would come down or what they would do next. They were very dim, for the moonlight was not strong enough for the colors, and he had enough to do with his eyes trying to make out their shapes. So his eyes grew tired, and more and more tired, and his eyelids grew so heavy that they would keep tumbling down over his eyes. He kept lifting them and lifting them, but every time they were heavier than the last. It was no use: they were too much for him. Sometimes before he had got them half up, down they were again; and at length he gave it up quite, and the moment he gave it up, he was fast asleep.

Chapter VIII
THE EAST WINDOW

THAT Diamond had fallen fast asleep is very evident from the strange things he now fancied as taking place. For he thought he heard a sound as of whispering up in the great window. He tried to open his eyes, but he could not. And the whispering went on and grew louder and louder, until he could hear every word that was said. He thought it was the Apostles talking about him. But he could not open his eyes.

"And how comes he to be lying there, St. Peter?" said one.

"I think I saw him a while ago up in the gallery, under the Nicodemus window. Perhaps he has fallen down. What do you think, St. Matthew?"

"I don't think he could have crept here after falling from such a height. He must have been killed."

"What are we to do with him? We can't leave him lying there. And we could not make him comfortable up here in the window: it's rather crowded already. What do you say, St. Thomas?"

"Let's go down and look at him."

There came a rustling, and a chinking, for some time, and then there was a silence, and Diamond felt somehow that all the Apostles were standing round him and looking down on him. And still he could not open his eyes.

"What is the matter with him, St. Luke?" asked one.

"There's nothing the matter with him," answered St. Luke, who must have joined the company of the Apostles from the next window, one would think. "He's in a sound sleep."

"I have it," cried another. "This is one of North Wind's tricks. She has caught him up and dropped him at our door, like a withered leaf or a foundling baby. I don't understand that woman's conduct, I must say. As if we hadn't enough to do with our money, without taking care of other people's children! That's not what our forefathers built cathedrals for."

Now Diamond could not bear to hear such things against North Wind, who, he knew, never played anybody a trick. She was far too busy with her own work for that. He struggled hard to open his eyes, but without success.

"She should consider that a church is not a place for pranks, not to mention that *we* live in it," said another.

"It certainly is disrespectful of her. But she always is disrespectful. What right has she to bang at our windows as she has been doing the whole of this night? I dare say there is glass broken somewhere. I know my blue robe is in a dreadful mess with the rain first and the dust after. It will cost me shillings to clean it."

Then Diamond knew that they could not be Apostles, talking like this. They could only be the sextons and vergers, and such-like, who got up at night, and put on the robes of deans and bishops, and called each other grand names, as the foolish servants he had heard his father tell of call themselves lords and ladies, after their masters and mistresses. And he was so angry at their daring to abuse North Wind, then he jumped up, crying—

"North Wind knows best what she is about. She has a

good right to blow the cobwebs from your windows, for she was sent to do it. She sweeps them away from grander places, I can tell you, for I've been with her at it."

This was what he began to say, but as he spoke his eyes came wide open, and behold, there were neither Apostles nor vergers there—not even a window with the effigies of holy men in it, but a dark heap of hay all about him, and the little panes in the roof of his loft glimmering blue in the light of the morning. Old Diamond was coming awake down below in the stable. In a moment more he was on his feet, and shaking himself so that young Diamond's bed trembled under him.

"He's grand at shaking himself," said Diamond. "I wish I could shake myself like that. But then I can wash myself, and he can't. What fun it would be to see Old Diamond washing his face with his hoofs and iron shoes! Wouldn't it be a picture?"

So saying, he got up and dressed himself. Then he went out into the garden. There must have been a tremendous wind in the night, for although all was quiet now, there lay the little summer-house crushed to the ground, and over it the great elm-tree, which the wind had broken across, being much decayed in the middle. Diamond almost cried to see the wilderness of green leaves, which used to be so far up in the blue air, tossing about in the breeze, and liking it best when the wind blew it most, now lying so near the ground, and without any hope of ever getting up into the deep air again.

"I wonder how old the tree is!" thought Diamond. "It must take a long time to get so near the sky as that poor tree was."

"Yes, indeed," said a voice beside him, for Diamond had spoken the last words aloud.

Diamond started, and looking round saw a clergyman, a brother of Mrs. Coleman, who happened to be visiting her. He was a great scholar, and was in the habit of rising early.

"Who are you, my man?" he added.

"Little Diamond," answered the boy.

"Oh! I have heard of you. How do you come to be up so early?"

"Because the sham Apostles talked such nonsense, they waked me up."

The clergyman stared. Diamond saw that he had better have held his tongue, for he could not explain things.

"You must have been dreaming, my little man," said he. "Dear! dear!" he went on, looking at the tree, "there has been terrible work here. This is the north wind's doing. What a pity! I wish we lived at the back of it, I'm sure."

"Where is that, sir?" asked Diamond.

"Away in the Hyperborean regions," answered the clergyman, smiling.

"I never heard of the place," returned Diamond.

"I daresay not," answered the clergyman; "but if this tree had been there now, it would not have been blown down, for there is no wind there."

"But, please, sir, if it had been there," said Diamond, "we should not have had to be sorry for it."

"Certainly not."

"Then we shouldn't have had to be glad for it, either."

"You're quite right, my boy," said the clergyman, looking at him very kindly, as he turned away to the house, with his eyes bent towards the earth. But Diamond thought within himself, "I will ask North Wind next time I see her to take me to that country. I think she did speak about it once before."

Chapter IX
HOW DIAMOND GOT TO THE BACK OF THE NORTH WIND

WHEN Diamond went home to breakfast, he found his father and mother already seated at the table. They were both busy with their bread and butter, and Diamond sat himself down in his usual place. His mother looked up at him, and, after watching him for a moment, said:

"I don't think the boy is looking well, husband."

"Don't you? Well, I don't know. I think he looks pretty bobbish. How do you feel yourself, Diamond, my boy?"

"Quite well, thank you, father; at least, I think I've got a little headache."

"There! I told you," said his father and mother both at once.

"The child's very poorly," added his mother.

"The child's quite well," added his father.

And then they both laughed.

"You see," said his mother, "I've had a letter from my sister at Sandwich."

"Sleepy old hole!" said his father.

"Don't abuse the place; there's good people in it," said his mother.

"Right, old lady," returned his father; "only I don't believe there are more than two pair of carriage-horses in the whole blessed place."

"Well, people can get to heaven without carriages—or coachmen either, husband. Not that I should like to go without *my* coachman, you know. But about the boy?"

"What boy?"

"That boy, there, staring at you with his goggle-eyes."

"Have I got goggle-eyes, mother?" asked Diamond, a little dismayed.

"Not too goggle," said his mother, who was quite proud of her boy's eyes, only did not want to make him vain. "Not too goggle; only you need not stare so."

"Well, what about him?" said his father.

"I told you I had got a letter."

"Yes, from your sister; not from Diamond."

"La, husband! you've got out of bed the wrong leg first this morning, I do believe."

"I always get out with both at once," said his father, laughing.

"Well, listen then. His aunt wants the boy to go down and see her."

"And that's why you want to make out that he ain't looking well."

"No more he is. I think he had better go."

"Well, I don't care, if you can find the money," said his father.

"I'll manage that," said his mother; and so it was agreed that Diamond should go to Sandwich.

I will not describe the preparations Diamond made. You would have thought he had been going on a three months' voyage. Nor will I describe the journey, for our business is now at the place. He was met at the station by his aunt, a cheerful middle-aged woman, and conveyed in safety to the sleepy old town, as his father had called it. And no wonder that it was sleepy, for it was nearly dead of old age.

Diamond went about staring, with his beautiful goggle-eyes, at the quaint old streets, and the shops, and the houses. Everything looked very strange, indeed; for here was a town abandoned by its nurse, the sea, like an old oyster left on the shore till it gaped for weariness. It used to be one of the five chief seaports in England, but it began to hold itself too high, and the consequence was the sea grew less and less intimate with it, gradually drew back, and kept more to itself, till at length it left it high and dry; Sandwich was a seaport no more; the sea went on with its own tide-business a long way off, and forgot it. Of course it went to sleep, and had no more to do with ships. That's what comes to cities and nations, and boys and girls, who say, "I can do without *your* help. I'm enough for myself."

Diamond soon made great friends with an old woman who kept a toyshop, for his mother had given him two-pence for pocket-money before he left, and he had gone into her shop to spend it, and she got talking to him. She looked very funny, because she had not got any teeth, but Diamond liked her, and went often to her shop, although he had nothing to spend there after the twopence was gone.

One afternoon he had been wandering rather wearily about the streets for some time. It was a hot day, and he felt tired. As he passed the toyshop, he stepped in.

"Please may I sit down for a minute on this box?" he said, thinking the old woman was somewhere in the shop. But he got no answer, and sat down without one. Around him were a great many toys of all prices, from a penny up to shillings. All at once he heard a gentle whirring somewhere amongst them. It made him start and look behind him. There were the sails of a windmill going round and round almost close to his ear. He thought at first it must be one of those toys which are wound up and go with clockwork; but no, it was a common penny toy, with the windmill at the end of a whistle, and when the whistle blows the windmill goes. But the wonder was that there was no one at the whistle end blowing, and yet the sails were turning round and round—now faster, now slower, now faster again.

"What can it mean?" said Diamond, aloud.

"It means me," said the tiniest voice he had ever heard.

"Who are you, please?" asked Diamond.

"Well, really, I begin to be ashamed of you," said the voice. "I wonder how long it will be before you know me; or how often I might take you in before you got sharp enough to suspect me. You are as bad as a baby that doesn't know his mother in a new bonnet."

"Not quite so bad as that, dear North Wind," said Diamond, "for I didn't see you at all, and indeed I don't see you yet, although I recognise your voice. Do grow a little, please."

"Not a hair's-breadth," said the voice, and it was the smallest voice that ever spoke. "What are you doing here?"

"I am come to see my aunt. But, please, North Wind, why didn't you come back for me in the church that night?"

"I did. I carried you safe home. All the time you were dreaming about the glass apostles, you were lying in my arms."

"I'm so glad," said Diamond. "I thought that must be it, only I wanted to hear you say so. Did you sink the ship, then?"

"Yes."

"And drown everybody?"

"Not quite. One boat got away with six or seven men in it."

"How could the boat swim when the ship couldn't?"

"Of course I had some trouble with it. I had to contrive a bit, and manage the waves a little. When they're once thoroughly waked up, I have a good deal of trouble with them sometimes. They're apt to get stupid with tumbling over each other's heads. That's when they're fairly at it. However, the boat got to a desert island before noon next day."

"And what good will come of that?"

"I don't know. I obeyed orders. Good bye."

"Oh! stay, North wind, *do* stay!" cried Diamond, dismayed to see the windmill get slower and slower.

"What it is, my dear child?" said North Wind, and the windmill began turning again so swiftly that Diamond could scarcely see it. "What a big voice you've got! and what a noise you do make with it! What is it you want? I have little to do, but that little must be done."

"I want you to take me to the country at the back of the north wind."

"That's not so easy," said North Wind, and was silent for so long that Diamond thought she was gone indeed. But after he had quite given her up, the voice began again.

"I almost wish old Herodotus had held his tongue about it. Much he knew of it!"

"Why do you wish that, North Wind?"

"Because then that clergyman would never have heard of it, and set you wanting to go. But we shall see. We shall see. You must go home, now, my dear, for you don't seem very well, and I'll see what can be done for you. Don't wait for me. I've got to break a few of old Goody's toys: she's thinking too much of her new stock. Two or three will do. There! go now."

Diamond rose, quite sorry, and without a word left the shop, and went home.

It soon appeared that his mother had been right about him, for that same afternoon his head began to ache very much, and he had to go to bed.

He awoke in the middle of the night. The lattice window of his room had blown open, and the curtains of his little bed were swinging about in the wind.

"If that should be North Wind now!" thought Diamond. But the next moment he heard some one closing the window, and his aunt came to the bedside. She put her hand on his face, and said—

"How's your head, dear?"

"Better, auntie, I think."

"Would you like something to drink?"

"Oh, yes! I should, please."

So his aunt gave him some lemonade, for she had been used to nursing sick people, and Diamond felt very much refreshed, and laid his head down again to go very fast asleep, as he thought. And so he did, but only to come awake again, as a fresh burst of wind blew the lattice open a second time. The same moment he found himself in a cloud of North Wind's hair, with her beautiful face, set in it like a moon, bending over him.

"Quick, Diamond!" she said. "I have found such a chance!"

"But I'm not well," said Diamond.

"I know that, but you will be better for a little fresh air. You shall have plenty of that."

"You want me to go, then?"

"Yes, I do. It won't hurt you."

"Very well," said Diamond; and getting out of the bed-clothes, he jumped into North Wind's arms.

"We must make haste before your aunt comes," said she, as she glided out of the open lattice and left it swinging.

The moment Diamond felt her arms fold around him he began to feel better. It was a moonless night, and very dark, with glimpses of stars when the clouds parted.

"I used to dash the waves about here," said North Wind, "where cows and sheep are feeding now; but we shall soon get to them. There they are."

And Diamond, looking down, saw the white glimmer of breaking water far below him.

"You see, Diamond," said North Wind, "it is very difficult for me to get you to the back of the north wind, for that country lies in the very north itself, and of course I can't blow northwards."

"Why not?" asked Diamond.

"You little silly!" said North Wind. "Don't you see that if I were to blow northwards I should be South Wind, and that is as much as to say that one person could be two persons?"

"But how can you ever get home at all, then?"

"You are quite right—that is my home, though I never get farther than the outer door. I sit on the doorstep, and hear the voices inside. I am nobody there, Diamond."

"I'm very sorry."

"Why?"

"That you should be nobody."

"Oh, I don't mind it. Dear little man! you will be very glad some day to be nobody yourself. But you can't understand that now, and you had better not try; for if you do, you will be certain to go fancying some egregious nonsense, and making yourself miserable about it."

"Then I won't," said Diamond.

"There's a good boy. It will all come in good time."

"But you haven't told me how you get to the doorstep, you know."

"It is easy enough for me. I have only to consent to be nobody, and there I am. I draw into myself, and there I am on the doorstep. But you can easily see, or you have less sense than I think, that to drag you, you heavy thing, along with me, would take centuries, and I could not give the time to it."

"Oh, I'm so sorry!" said Diamond.

"What for now, pet?"

"That I'm so heavy for you. I would be lighter if I could, but I don't know how."

"You silly darling! Why, I could toss you a hundred miles from me if I liked. It is only when I am going home that I shall find you heavy."

"Then you are going home with me?"

"Of course. Did I not come to fetch you just for that?"

"But all this time you must be going southwards."

"Yes. Of course I am."

"How can you be taking me northwards, then?"

"A very sensible question. But you shall see. I will get rid of a few of these clouds—only they do come up so fast! It's like trying to blow a brook dry. There! What do you see now?"

"I think I see a little boat, away there, down below."

"A little boat, indeed! Well! She's a yacht of two hundred tons; and the captain of it is a friend of mine; for he is a man of good sense, and can sail his craft well. I've helped him many a time when he little thought it. I've heard him grumbling at me, when I was doing the very best I could for him. Why, I've carried him eighty miles a day, again and again, right north."

"He must have dodged for that," said Diamond, who had been watching the vessels, and had seen that they went other ways than the wind blew.

"Of course he must. But don't you see, it was the best I could do? I couldn't be South Wind. And besides it gave him a share in the business. It is not good at all—mind that, Diamond—to do everything for those you love, and not give them a share in the doing. It's not kind. It's making too much of yourself, my child. If I had been South Wind, he would only have smoked his pipe all day, and made himself stupid."

"But how could he be a man of sense and grumble at you when you were doing your best for him?"

"Oh! you must make allowances," said North Wind, "or you will never do justice to anybody. You do understand, then, that a captain may sail north—"

"In spite of a north wind—yes," supplemented Diamond.

"Now, I do think you must be stupid, my dear," said North Wind. "Suppose the north wind did not blow, where would he be then?"

"Why then the south wind would carry him."

"So you think that when the north wind stops the south wind blows. Nonsense. If I didn't blow, the captain couldn't sail his eighty miles a day. No doubt South Wind would carry him faster, but South Wind is sitting on her doorstep then, and if I stopped there would be a dead calm. So you are all wrong to say he can sail north in spite of me; he sails north by my help, and my help alone. You see that, Diamond?"

"Yes, I do, North Wind. I am stupid, but I don't want to be stupid."

"Good boy! I am going to blow you north in that little craft, one of the finest that ever sailed the sea. Here we are, right over it. I shall be blowing against you; you will be sailing against me; and all will be just as we want it. The captain won't get on so fast as he would like, but he will get on, and so shall we. I'm just going to put you on board. Do you see in front of the tiller—that thing the man is working, now to one side, now to the other—a round thing like the top of a drum?"

"Yes," said Diamond.

"Below that is where they keep their spare sails, and some stores of that sort. I am going to blow that cover off. The same moment I will drop you on deck, and you must tumble in. Don't be afraid, it is of no depth, and you will fall on a roll of sail-cloth. You will find it nice and warm and dry—only dark; and you will know I am near you by every roll and pitch of the vessel. Coil yourself up and go to sleep. The yacht shall be my cradle, and you shall be my baby."

"Thank you, dear North Wind. I am not a bit afraid," said Diamond.

In a moment they were on a level with the bulwarks, and North Wind sent the hatch of the after-store rattling away over the deck to leeward. The next, Diamond found himself in the dark, for he had tumbled through the hole as North Wind had told him, and the cover was replaced over his head. Away he went rolling to leeward, for the wind began all at once to blow hard. He heard the call of the captain, and the loud trampling of the men over his head, as they hauled at the main sheet to get the boom on board that they might take in a reef in the mainsail. Diamond felt about until he had found what seemed the most comfortable place, and there he snuggled down and lay.

Hours after hours, a great many of them, went by; and still Diamond lay there. He never felt in the least tired or impatient, for a strange pleasure filled his heart. The straining of the masts, the creaking of the boom, the singing of the ropes, the banging of the blocks as they put the vessel about, all fell in with the roaring of the wind above, the surge of the waves past her sides, and the thud with which every now and then one would strike her; while through it all Diamond could hear the gurgling, rippling, talking flow of the water against her planks, as she slipped through it, lying now on this side, now on that—like a subdued air running through the grand music his North Wind was making about him to keep him from tiring as they sped on towards the country at the back of her doorstep.

How long this lasted Diamond had no idea. He seemed to fall asleep sometimes, only through the sleep he heard the sounds going on. At length the weather seemed to get worse. The confusion and trampling of feet grew more frequent over his head; the vessel lay over more and more on her side, and went roaring through the waves, which banged and thumped at her as if in anger. All at once arose a terrible uproar. The hatch was blown off; a cold fierce wind swept in upon him; and a long arm came with it which laid hold of him and lifted him out. The same moment he saw the little vessel far below him righting herself. She had taken in all her sails and lay now tossing on the waves like a sea-bird with folded wings. A short distance to the south lay a much larger vessel, with two or three sails set, and towards it North Wind was carrying Diamond. It was a German ship, on its way to the North Pole.

"That vessel down there will give us a lift now," said North Wind; "and after that I must do the best I can."

She managed to hide him amongst the flags of the big ship, which were all snugly stowed away, and on and on they sped towards the north. At length one night she whispered in his ear, "Come on deck, Diamond"; and he got up at once and crept on deck. Everything looked very strange. Here and there on all sides were huge masses of floating ice, looking like cathedrals, and castles, and crags, while away beyond was a blue sea.

"Is the sun rising or setting?" asked Diamond.

"Neither or both, which you please. I can hardly tell which myself. If he is setting now, he will be rising the next moment."

"What a strange light it is!" said Diamond. "I have heard that the sun doesn't go to bed all the summer in these parts. Miss Coleman told me that. I suppose he feels very sleepy, and that is why the light he sends out looks so like a dream."

"That will account for it well enough for all practical purposes," said North Wind.

Some of the icebergs were drifting northward: one was passing very near the ship. North Wind seized Diamond, and with a single bound lighted on one of them—a huge thing, with sharp pinnacles and great clefts. The same instant a wind began to blow from the south. North Wind hurried Diamond down the north side of the iceberg, stepping by its jags and splintering; for this berg had never got far enough south to be melted and smoothed by the summer sun. She brought him to a cave near the water, where she entered, and, letting Diamond go, sat down as if weary on a ledge of ice.

Diamond seated himself on the other side, and for a while was enraptured with the color of the air inside the cave. It was a deep, dazzling, lovely blue, deeper than the deepest blue of the sky. The blue seemed to be in constant motion, like the blackness when you press your eyeballs with your fingers, boiling and sparkling. But when he looked across to North Wind he was frightened; her face was worn and livid.

"What is the matter with you, dear North Wind?" he said.

"Nothing much. I feel very faint. But you mustn't mind it, for I can bear it quite well. South Wind always blows me faint. If it were not for the cool of the thick ice between me and her, I should faint altogether. Indeed, as it is, I fear I must vanish."

Diamond stared at her in terror, for he saw that her form and face were growing, not small, but transparent, like something dissolving, not in water, but in light. He could see the side of the blue cave through her very heart. And she melted away till all that was left was a pale face, like the moon in the morning, with two great lucid eyes in it.

"I am going, Diamond," she said.

"Does it hurt you?" asked Diamond.

"It's very uncomfortable," she answered; "but I don't mind it, for I shall come all right again before long. I thought I should be able to go with you all the way, but I cannot. You must not be frightened though. Just go straight on, and you will come all right. You'll find me on the doorstep."

As she spoke, her face too faded quite away, only Diamond thought he could still see her eyes shining through the blue. When he went closer, however, he found that what he thought were her eyes were only two hollows in the ice. North Wind was quite gone; and Diamond would have cried, if he had not trusted her so thoroughly. So he sat still in the blue air of the cavern listening to the wash and ripple of the water all about the base of the iceberg, as it sped on and on into the open sea northwards. It was an excellent craft to go with a current, for there was twice as much of it below water as above. But a light south wind was blowing too, and so it went fast.

After a little while Diamond went out and sat on the edge of his floating island, and looked down into the ocean beneath him. The white sides of the berg reflected so much light below the water, that he could see far down into the green abyss. Sometimes he fancied he saw the eyes of North Wind looking up at him from below, but the fancy never lasted beyond the moment of its birth. And the time passed he did not know how, for he felt as if he were in a dream. When he got tired of the green water, he went into the blue cave; and when he got tired of the blue cave he went out and gazed all about him on the blue sea, ever sparkling in the sun, which kept wheeling about the sky, never going below the horizon. But he chiefly gazed northwards, to see whether any land were appearing. All this time he never wanted to eat. He broke off little bits of the berg now and then and sucked them, and he thought them very nice.

At length, one time he came out of his cave, he spied, far off upon the horizon, a shining peak that rose into the sky like the top of some tremendous iceberg; and his vessel was bearing him straight towards it. As it went on, the peak rose and rose higher and higher above the horizon; and other peaks rose after it, with sharp edges and jagged ridges connecting them. Diamond thought this must be the place he was going to; and he was right; for the mountains rose and rose, till he saw the line of the coast at their feet, and at length the iceberg drove into a little bay, all round which were lofty precipices with snow on their tops, and streaks of ice down their sides. The berg floated slowly up to a projecting rock. Diamond stepped on shore, and without looking behind him began to follow a natural path which led windingly towards the top of the precipice.

When he reached it, he found himself on a broad table of ice, along which he could walk without much difficulty. Before him, at a considerable distance, rose a lofty ridge of ice, which shot up into fantastic pinnacles and towers and battlements. The air was very cold, and seemed somehow dead, for there was not the slightest breath of wind.

In the centre of the ridge before him appeared a gap like the opening of a valley. But as he walked towards it, gazing, and wondering whether that could be the way he had to take, he saw that what had appeared a gap was the form of a woman seated against the ice front of the ridge, leaning forward with her hands in her lap, and her hair hanging down to the ground.

"It is North Wind on her doorstep," said Diamond, joyfully, and hurried on.

He soon came up to the place, and there the form sat, like one of the great figures at the door of an Egyptian temple, motionless, with drooping arms and head. Then Diamond grew frightened, because she did not move nor speak. He was sure it was North Wind, but he thought she must be dead at last. Her face was white as the snow, her eyes were blue as the air in the ice-cave, and her hair hung down straight, like icicles. She had on a greenish robe, like the color in the hollows of a glacier seen from far off.

He stood up before her, and gazed fearfully into her face for a few minutes before he ventured to speak. At length, with a great effort and a trembling voice, he faltered out—

"North Wind!"

"Well, child?" said the form, without lifting its head.

"Are you ill, dear North Wind?"

"No. I am waiting."

"What for?"

"Till I'm wanted."

"You don't care for me anymore," said Diamond, almost crying now.

"Yes, I do. Only I can't show it. All my love is down at the bottom of my heart. But I feel it bubbling there."

"What do you want me to do next, dear North Wind?" said Diamond, wishing to show his love by being obedient.

"What do you want to do yourself?"

"I want to go into the country at your back."

"Then you must go through me."

"I don't know what you mean."

"I mean just what I say. You must walk on as if I were an open door, and go right through me."

"But that will hurt you."

"Not in the least. It will hurt you, though."

"I don't mind that, if you tell me to do it."

"Do it," said North Wind.

Diamond walked towards her instantly. When he

reached her knees, he put out his hand to lay it on her, but nothing was there save an intense cold. He walked on. Then all grew white about him; and the cold stung him like fire. He walked on still, groping through the whiteness. It thickened about him. At last, it got into his heart, and he lost all sense. I would say that he fainted—only whereas in common faints all grows black about you, he felt swallowed up in whiteness. It was when he reached North Wind's heart that he fainted and fell. But as he fell, he rolled over the threshold, and it was thus that Diamond got to the back of the north wind.

Chapter X
AT THE BACK OF THE NORTH WIND

I HAVE now come to the most difficult part of my story. And why? Because I do not know enough about it. And why should I not know as much about this part as about any other part? for of course I could know nothing about the story except Diamond had told it; and why should not Diamond tell about the country at the back of the north wind, as well as about his adventures in getting there? Because, when he came back, he had forgotten a great deal, and what he did remember was very hard to tell. Things there are so different from things here! The people there do not speak the same language for one thing. Indeed, Diamond insisted that there they do not speak at all. I do not think he was right, but it may well have appeared so to Diamond. The fact is, we have different reports of the place from the most trustworthy people. Therefore we are bound to believe that it appears somewhat different to different people. All, however, agree in a general way about it.

I will tell you something of what two very different people have reported, both of whom knew more about it, I believe, than Herodotus. One of them speaks from his own experience, for he visited the country; the other from the testimony of a young peasant girl who came back from it for a month's visit to her friends. The former was a great Italian of noble family, who died more than five hundred years ago; the latter a Scotch shepherd who died not forty years ago.

The Italian, then, informs us that he had to enter that country through a fire so hot that he would have thrown himself into boiling glass to cool himself. This was not Diamond's experience, but then Durante—that was the name of the Italian, and it means Lasting, for his books will last as long as there are enough men in the world worthy of having them—Durante was an elderly man, and Diamond was a little boy, and so their experience must be a little different. The peasant girl, on the other hand, fell fast asleep in a wood, and woke in the same country.

In describing it, Durante says that the ground everywhere smelt sweetly, and that a gentle, even-tempered wind, which never blew faster or slower, breathed in his face as he went, making all the leaves point one way, not so as to disturb the birds in the tops of the trees, but, on the contrary, sounding a bass to their song. He describes also a little river which was so full that its little waves, as it hurried along, bent the grass, full of red and yellow flowers, through which it flowed. He says that the purest stream in the world beside this one would look as if it were mixed with something that did not belong to it, even although it was flowing ever in the brown shadow of the trees, and neither sun nor moon could shine upon it. He seems to imply that it is always the month of May in that country. It would be out of place to describe here the wonderful sights he saw, for the music of them is in another key from that of this story, and I shall therefore only add from the account of this traveller, that the people there are so free and so just and so healthy, that every one of them has a crown like a king and a mitre like a priest.

The peasant girl—Kilmeny was her name—could not

report such grand things as Durante, for, as the shepherd says, telling her story as I tell Diamond's—

> "Kilmeny had been she knew not where,
> And Kilmeny had seen what she could not declare;
> Kilmeny had been where the cock never crew,
> Where the rain never fell, and the wind never blew;
> But it seemed as the harp of the sky had rung,
> And the airs of heaven played round her tongue,
> When she spoke of the lovely forms she had seen,
> And a land where sin had never been;
> A land of love and a land of light,
> Withouten sun, or moon, or night;
> Where the river swayed a living stream,
> And the light a pure and cloudless beam:
> The land of vision it would seem,
> And still an everlasting dream."

The last two lines are the shepherd's own remark, and a matter of opinion. But it is clear, I think, that Kilmeny must have described the same country as Durante saw, though, not having his experience, she could neither understand nor describe it so well.

Now I must give you such fragments of recollection as Diamond was able to bring back with him.

When he came to himself after he fell, he found himself at the back of the north wind. North Wind herself was nowhere to be seen. Neither was there a vestige of snow or of ice within sight. The sun too had vanished; but that was no matter, for there was plenty of a certain still rayless light. Where it came from he never found out; but he thought it belonged to the country itself. Sometimes he thought it came out of the flowers, which were very bright, but had no strong color. He said the river—for all agree that there is a river there—flowed not only through, but over grass: its channel, instead of being rock, stones, pebbles, sand, or anything else, was of pure meadow grass, not over long. He insisted that if it did not sing tunes in people's ears, it sung tunes in their heads, in proof of which I may mention, that, in the troubles which followed, Diamond was often heard singing; and when asked what he was singing, would answer, "One of the tunes the river at the back of the north wind sung." And I may as well say at once that Diamond never told these things to any one but—no, I had better not say who it was; but whoever it was told me, and I thought it would be well to write them for my child-readers.

He could not say that he was very happy there, for he had neither his father nor mother with him, but he felt so still and quiet and patient and contented, that, as far as the mere feeling went, it was something better than mere happiness. Nothing went wrong at the back of the north wind. Neither was anything quite right, he thought. Only everything was going to be right some day. His account disagreed with that of Durante, and agreed with that of Kilmeny, in this, that he protested there was no wind there at all. I fancy he missed it. At all events *we* could not do without wind. It all depends on how big our lungs are whether the wind is too strong for us or not.

When the person he told about it asked him whether he saw anybody he knew there, he answered, "Only a little girl belonging to the gardener, who thought he had lost her, but was quite mistaken, for there she was safe enough, and was to come back some day, as I came back, if they would only wait."

"Did you talk to her, Diamond?"

"No. Nobody talks there. They only look at each other, and understand everything."

"Is it cold there?"

"No."

"Is it hot?"

"No."

"What is it then?"

"You never think about such things there."

"What a queer place it must be!"

"It's a very good place."

"Do you want to go back again?"

"No: I don't think I have ever left it; I feel it here, somewhere."

"Did the people there look pleased?"

"Yes—quite pleased, only a little sad."

"Then they didn't look glad?"

"They looked as if they were waiting to be gladder some day."

This was how Diamond used to answer questions about that country. And now I will take up the story again, and tell you how he got back to this country.

Chapter XI
HOW DIAMOND GOT HOME AGAIN

WHEN one at the back of the north wind wanted to know how things were going with anyone he loved, he had to go to a certain tree, climb the stem, and sit down in the branches. In a few minutes, if he kept very still, he would see something at least of what was going on with the people he loved.

One day when Diamond was sitting in this tree, he began to long very much to get home again, and no wonder, for he saw his mother crying. Durante says that the people there may always follow their wishes, because they never wish but what is good. Diamond's wish was to get home, and he would fain follow his wish.

But how was he to set about it? If he could only see North Wind! But the moment he had got to her back, she was gone altogether from his sight. He had never seen her back. She might be sitting on her doorstep still, looking southwards, and waiting, white and thin and blue-eyed, until she was wanted. Or she might have again become a mighty creature, with power to do that which was demanded of her, and gone far away upon many missions. She must be somewhere, however. He could not go home without her, and therefore he must find her. She could never have intended to leave him always away from his mother. If there had been any danger of that, she would have told him, and given him his choice about going. For North Wind was right honest. How to find North Wind, therefore, occupied all his thoughts.

In his anxiety about his mother, he used to climb the tree every day, and sit in its branches. However many of the dwellers there did so, they never incommoded one another; for the moment one got into the tree, he became invisible to everyone else; and it was such a wide-spreading tree that there was room for every one of the people of the country in it, without the least interference with each other. Sometimes, on getting down, two of them would meet at the root, and then they would smile to each other more sweetly than at any other time, as much as to say, "Ah, you've been up there too!"

One day he was sitting on one of the outer branches of the tree, looking southwards after his home. Far away was a blue shining sea, dotting with gleaming and sparkling specks of white. Those were the icebergs. Nearer he saw a great range of snow-capped mountains, and down below him the lovely meadow-grass of the country, with the stream flowing and flowing through it, away towards the sea. As he looked he began to wonder, for the whole country lay beneath him like a map, and that which was near him looked just as small as that which he knew to be miles away. The ridge of ice which encircled it appeared but a few yards off, and no larger than the row of pebbles with which a child will mark out the boundaries of the kingdom he has appropriated on the seashore. He thought he could distinguish the vapoury form of North Wind, seated as he had left her, on the other side. Hastily he descended the tree, and to his amazement found that the map or model of the country still lay at his feet. He stood in it. With one stride he had crossed the river; with another he had reached the ridge of ice; with the third he stepped over its peaks, and sank wearily down at North Wind's knees. For there she sat on her doorstep. The peaks of the great ridge of ice were as lofty as ever behind her, and the country at her back had vanished from Diamond's view.

North Wind was as still as Diamond had left her. Her pale face was white as the snow, and her motionless eyes were as blue as the caverns in the ice. But the instant Diamond touched her, her face began to change like that of one waking from sleep. Light began to glimmer from the blue of her eyes. A moment more, and she laid her hand on Diamond's head, and began playing with his hair. Diamond took hold of her hand, and laid his face to it. She gave a little start.

"How very alive you are, child!" she murmured. "Come nearer to me."

By the help of the stones all around he clambered up beside her, and laid himself against her bosom. She gave a great sigh, slowly lifted her arms, and slowly folded them about him, until she clasped him close. Yet a moment, and she roused herself, and came quite awake; and the cold of her bosom, which had pierced Diamond's bones, vanished.

"Have you been sitting here ever since I went through you, dear North Wind?" asked Diamond, stroking her hand.

"Yes," she answered, looking at him with her old kindness.

"Ain't you very tired?"

"No; I've often had to sit longer. Do you know how long you have been?"

"Oh! years and years," answered Diamond.

"You have just been seven days," returned North Wind.

"I thought I had been a hundred years!" exclaimed Diamond.

"Yes, I dare say," replied North Wind. "You've been away from here seven days; but how long you may have been in there is quite another thing. Behind my back and

before my face things are so different! They don't go at all
by the same rule."

"I'm very glad," said Diamond, after thinking a while.

"Why?" asked North Wind.

"Because I've been such a long time there, and such a
little while away from mother. Why, she won't be expecting me home from Sandwich yet!"

"No. But we mustn't talk any longer. I've got my orders
now, and we must be off in a few minutes."

Next moment Diamond found himself sitting alone on
the rock. North Wind had vanished. A creature like a great
humble-bee or cockchafer flew past his face; but it could
be neither, for there were no insects amongst the ice. It
passed him again and again, flying in circles around him,
and he concluded that it must be North Wind herself, no
bigger than Tom Thumb when his mother put him in the
nutshell lined with flannel. But she was no longer vapoury
and thin. She was solid, although tiny. A moment more,
and she perched on his shoulder.

"Come along, Diamond," she said in his ear, in the
smallest and highest of treble voices; "it is time we were
setting out for Sandwich."

Diamond could just see her, by turning his head towards
his shoulder as far as he could, but only with one eye, for
his nose came between her and the other.

"Won't you take me in your arms and carry me?" he
said in a whisper, for he knew she did not like a loud
voice when she was small.

"Ah! you ungrateful boy," returned North Wind, smiling, "how dare you make game of me? Yes, I will carry
you, but you shall walk a bit for your impertinence first.
Come along."

She jumped from his shoulder, but when Diamond
looked for her upon the ground, he could see nothing but
a little spider with long legs that made its way over the ice
towards the south. It ran very fast indeed for a spider, but
Diamond ran a long way before it, and then waited for it.
It was up with him sooner than he had expected, however,

and it had grown a good deal. And the spider grew and grew and went faster and faster, till all at once Diamond discovered that it was not a spider, but a weasel; and away glided the weasel, and away went Diamond after it, and it took all the run there was in him to keep up with the weasel. And the weasel grew, and grew, and grew, till all at once Diamond saw that the weasel was not a weasel but a cat. And away went the cat, and Diamond after it. And when he had run half a mile, he found the cat waiting for him, sitting up and washing her face not to lose time. And away went the cat again, and Diamond after it. But the next time he came up with the cat, the cat was not a cat, but a hunting-leopard. And the hunting-leopard grew to a jaguar, all covered with spots like eyes. And the jaguar grew to a Bengal tiger. And at none of them was Diamond afraid, for he had been at North Wind's back, and he could be afraid of her no longer whatever she did or grew. And the tiger flew over the snow in a straight line for the south, growing less and less to Diamond's eyes till it was only a black speck upon the whiteness; and then it vanished altogether. And now Diamond felt that he would rather not run any farther, and that the ice had got very rough. Besides, he was near the precipices that bounded the sea, so slackened his pace to a walk, saying aloud to himself:

"When North Wind has punished me enough for making game of her, she will come back to me; I know she will, for I can't go much farther without her."

"You dear boy! It was only in fun. Here I am!" said North Wind's voice behind him.

Diamond turned, and saw her as he liked best to see her, standing beside him, a tall lady.

"Where's the tiger?" he asked, for he knew all the creatures from a picture book that Miss Coleman had given him. "But, of course," he added, "you were the tiger. I was puzzled and forgot. I saw it such a long way off before me, and there you were behind me. It's so odd, you know."

"It must look very odd to you, Diamond: I see that. But it is no more odd to me than to break an old pine in two."

"Well, that's odd enough," remarked Diamond.

"So it is! I forgot. Well, none of these things are odder to me than it is to you to eat bread and butter."

"Well, that's odd too, when I think of it," persisted Diamond. "I should just like a slice of bread and butter! I'm afraid to say how long it is—how long it seems to me, that is—since I had anything to eat."

"Come then," said North Wind, stooping and holding out her arms. "You shall have some bread and butter very soon. I am glad to find you want some."

Diamond held up his arms to meet hers, and was safe upon her bosom. North Wind bounded into the air. Her tresses began to lift and rise and spread and stream and flow and flutter; and with a roar from her hair and an answering roar from one of the great glaciers beside them, whose slow torrent tumbled two or three icebergs at once into the waves at their feet, North Wind and Diamond went flying southwards.

Chapter XII
WHO MET DIAMOND
AT SANDWICH

AS they flew, so fast they went that the sea slid away from under them like a great web of shot silk, blue shot with grey, and green shot with purple. They went so fast that the stars themselves appeared to sail away past them overhead, "like golden boats," on a blue sea turned upside down. And they went so fast that Diamond himself went the other way as fast—I mean he went fast asleep in North Wind's arms.

When he woke, a face was bending over him; but it was not North Wind's; it was his mother's. He put out his arms to her, and she clasped him to her bosom and burst out crying. Diamond kissed her again and again to make her stop. Perhaps kissing is the best thing for crying, but it will not always stop it.

"What is the matter, mother?" he said.

"Oh, Diamond, my darling! you have been so ill!" she sobbed.

"No, mother dear. I've only been at the back of the north wind," returned Diamond.

"I thought you were dead," said his mother.

But that moment the doctor came in.

"Oh! there!" said the doctor with gentle cheerfulness; "we're better to-day, I see."

Then he drew the mother aside, and told her not to talk to Diamond, or to mind what he might say; for he must be kept as quiet as possible. And indeed Diamond was not much inclined to talk, for he felt very strange and weak, which was little wonder, seeing that all the time he had been away he had only sucked a few lumps of ice, and there could not be much nourishment in them.

Now while he is lying there, getting strong again with chicken broth and other nice things, I will tell my readers what had been taking place at his home, for they ought to be told it.

They may have forgotten that Miss Coleman was in a very poor state of health. Now there were three reasons for this. In the first place, her lungs were not strong. In the second place, there was a gentleman somewhere who had not behaved very well to her. In the third place, she had not anything particular to do. These three *nots* together are enough to make a lady very ill indeed. Of course she could not help the first cause; but if the other two causes had not existed, that would have been of little consequence; she would only have had to be a little careful. The second she could not help quite; but if she had had anything to do, and had done it well, it would have been very difficult for any man to behave badly to her. And for this third cause of her illness, if she had had anything to do that was worth doing, she might have borne his bad behavior so that even that would not have made her ill. It is not always easy, I confess, to find something to do that is worth doing, but the most difficult things are constantly being done, and she might have found something if she had tried. Her fault lay in this, that she had not tried. But, to be sure, her father and mother were to blame that they had never set her going. Only then again, nobody had told her father and mother that they ought to set her going in that direction. So as none of them would find it out of themselves, North Wind had to teach them.

We know that North Wind was very busy that night on which she left Diamond in the cathedral. She had in a sense been blowing through and through the Colemans' house the whole of the night. First, Miss Coleman's maid had left a chink of her mistress's window open, thinking she had shut it, and North Wind had wound a few of her hairs round the lady's throat. She was considerably worse the next morning. Again, the ship which North Wind had sunk that very night belonged to Mr. Coleman. Nor will my readers understand what a heavy loss this was to him until I have informed them that he had been getting poorer and poorer for some time. He was not so successful in his speculations as he had been, for he speculated a great deal more than was right, and it was time he should be pulled up. It is a hard thing for a rich man to grow poor; but it is an awful thing for him to grow dishonest, and some kinds of speculation lead a man deep into dishonesty before he thinks what he is about. Poverty will not make a man worthless—he may be worth a great deal more when he is poor than he was when he was rich; but dishonesty goes very far indeed to make a man of no value—a thing to be thrown out in the dust-hole of the creation, like a bit of a broken basin, or a dirty rag. So North Wind had to look after Mr. Coleman, and try to make an honest man of him. So she sank the ship which was his last venture, and he was what himself and his wife and the world called ruined.

Nor was this all yet. For on board that vessel Miss Coleman's lover was a passenger; and when the news came that the vessel had gone down, and that all on board had perished, we may be sure she did not think the loss of their fine house and garden and furniture the greatest misfortune in the world.

Of course, the trouble did not end with Mr. Coleman and his family. Nobody can suffer alone. When the cause of suffering is most deeply hidden in the heart, and nobody knows anything about it but the man himself, he must be a great and a good man indeed, such as few of us have known, if the pain inside him does not make him behave so as to cause all about him to be more or less uncomfortable. But when a man brings money-troubles on himself by making haste to be rich, then most of the people he has to do with must suffer in the same way with himself. The elm-tree which North Wind blew down that very night, as if small and great trials were to be gathered in one heap, crushed Miss Coleman's pretty summerhouse: just so the fall of Mr. Coleman crushed the little family that lived over his coach-house and stable. Before Diamond was well enough to be taken home, there was no home for him to go to. Mr. Coleman—or his creditors, for I do not know the particulars—had sold house, carriage, horses, furniture, and everything. He and his wife and daughter and Mrs. Crump had gone to live in a small house in Hoxton, where he would be unknown, and whence he could walk to his place of business in the City. For he was not an old man, and hoped yet to retrieve his fortunes. Let us hope that he lived to retrieve his honesty, the tail of which had slipped through his fingers to the very last joint, if not beyond it.

Of course, Diamond's father had nothing to do for a time, but it was not so hard for him to have nothing to do as it was for Miss Coleman. He wrote to his wife that, if her sister would keep her there till he got a place, it would be better for them, and he would be greatly obliged to her. Meantime, the gentleman who had bought the house had allowed his furniture to remain where it was for a little while.

Diamond's aunt was quite willing to keep them as long as she could. And indeed Diamond was not yet well enough to be moved with safety.

When he had recovered so far as to be able to go out, one day his mother got her sister's husband, who had a little pony-cart, to carry them down to the sea-shore, and leave them there for a few hours. He had some business to do further on at Ramsgate, and would pick them up as he returned. A whiff of the sea-air would do them both good, she said, and she thought besides she could best tell Diamond what had happened if she had him quite to herself.

Chapter XIII
THE SEASIDE

DIAMOND and his mother sat down upon the edge of the rough grass that bordered the sand. The sun was just far enough past its highest not to shine in their eyes when they looked eastward. A sweet little wind blew on their left side, and comforted the mother without letting her know what it was that comforted her. Away before them stretched the sparkling waters of the ocean, every wave of which flashed out its own delight back in the face of the great sun, which looked down from the stillness of its blue house with gloriously silent face upon its flashing children. On each hand the shore rounded outwards, forming a little bay. There were no white cliffs here, as further north and south, and the place was rather dreary, but the sky got at them so much the better. Not a house, not a creature was within sight. Dry sand was about their feet, and under them thin wiry grass, that just managed to grow out of the poverty-stricken shore.

"Oh dear!" said Diamond's mother, with a deep sigh, "it's a sad world!"

"Is it?" said Diamond; "I didn't know."

"How should you know, child? You've been too well taken care of, I trust."

"Oh yes, I have," returned Diamond. "I'm so sorry! I thought you were taken care of too. I thought my father took care of you. I will ask him about it. I think he must have forgotten."

"Dear boy!" said his mother; "your father's the best man in the world."

"So I thought!" returned Diamond with triumph. "I was sure of it!—Well, doesn't he take very good care of you?"

"Yes, yes, he does," answered his mother, bursting into tears. "But who's to take care of him? And how is he to take care of us if he's got nothing to eat himself?"

"Oh dear!" said Diamond with a gasp; "hasn't he got anything to eat? Oh! I must go home to him."

"No, no, child. He's not come to that yet. But what's to become of us, I don't know."

"Are you very hungry, mother? There's the basket. I thought you put something to eat in it."

"O you darling stupid! I didn't say I was hungry," returned his mother, smiling through her tears.

"Then I don't understand you at all," said Diamond. "Do tell me what's the matter."

"There *are* people in the world who have nothing to eat, Diamond."

"Then I suppose they don't stop in it any longer. They—they—what you call—die—don't they?"

"Yes, they do. How would you like that?"

"I don't know. I never tried. But I suppose they go where they get something to eat."

"Like enough they don't want it," said his mother petulantly.

"That's all right then," said Diamond, thinking I dare say more than he chose to put in words.

"Is it though? Poor boy! how little *you* know about things! Mr. Coleman's lost all his money, and your father has nothing to do, and we shall have nothing to eat by and by."

"Are you sure, mother?"

"Sure of what?"

"Sure that we shall have nothing to eat."

"No, thank Heaven! I'm not sure of it. I hope not."

"Then I *can't* understand it, mother. There's a piece of gingerbread in the basket, I know."

"O you little bird! You have no more sense than a sparrow that picks what it wants, and never thinks of the winter and the frost and the snow."

"Ah—yes—I see. But the birds get through the winter, don't they?"

"Some of them fall dead on the ground."

"They must die some time. They wouldn't like to be birds always. Would you, mother?"

What a child it is! thought his mother, but she said nothing.

"Oh! now I remember," Diamond went on. "Father told me that day I went to Epping Forest with him, that the rose-bushes, and the may-bushes, and the holly-bushes were the birds' barns, for there were the hips, and the haws, and the holly-berries, all ready for the winter."

"Yes; that's all very true. So you see the birds are provided for. But there are no such barns for you and me, Diamond."

"Ain't there?"

"No. We've got to work for our bread."

"Then let's go and work," said Diamond, getting up.

"It's no use. We've not got anything to do."

"Then let's wait."

"Then we shall starve."

"No. There's the basket. Do you know, mother, I think I shall call that basket the barn."

"It's not a very big one. And when it's empty—where are we then?"

"At auntie's cupboard," returned Diamond promptly.

"But we can't eat auntie's things all up and leave her to starve."

"No, no. We'll go back to father before that. He'll have found a cupboard somewhere by that time."

"How do you know that?"

"I don't know it. But *I* haven't got even a cupboard, and I've always had plenty to eat. I've heard you say I had too much, sometimes."

"But I tell you that's because I've had a cupboard for you, child."

"And when yours was empty, auntie opened hers."

"But that can't go on."

"How do you know? I think there must be a big cupboard somewhere, out of which the little cupboards are filled, you know, mother."

"Well, I wish I could find the door of that cupboard," said his mother. But the same moment she stopped, and was silent for a good while. I cannot tell whether Diamond knew what she was thinking, but I think I know. She had heard something at church the day before, which came back upon her—something like this, that she hadn't to eat for to-morrow as well as for to-day; and that what was not wanted couldn't be missed. So, instead of saying anything more, she stretched out her hand for the basket, and she and Diamond had their dinner.

And Diamond did enjoy it. For the drive and the fresh air had made him quite hungry; and he did not, like his mother, trouble himself about what they should dine off that day week. The fact was he had lived so long without any food at all at the back of the north wind, that he knew quite well that food was not essential to existence; that in fact, under certain circumstances, people could live without it well enough.

His mother did not speak much during their dinner. After it was over she helped him to walk about a little, but he was not able for much and soon got tired. He did not get fretful, though. He was too glad of having the sun and the wind again, to fret because he could not run about. He lay down on the dry sand, and his mother covered him with a shawl. She then sat by his side, and took a bit of work from her pocket. But Diamond felt rather sleepy, and turned on his side and gazed sleepily over the sand. A few yards off he saw something fluttering.

"What is that, mother?" he said.

"Only a bit of paper," she answered.

"It flutters more than a bit of paper would, I think," said Diamond.

"I'll go and see if you like," said his mother. "My eyes are none of the best."

So she rose and went and found that they were both right, for it was a little book, partly buried in the sand. But several of its leaves were clear of the sand, and these the wind kept blowing about in a very flutterful manner. She took it up and brought it to Diamond.

"What is it, mother?" he asked.

"Some nursery rhythms, I think," she answered.

"I'm too sleepy," said Diamond. "Do read some of them to me."

"Yes, I will," she said, and began one.—"But this is such nonsense!" she said again. "I will try to find a better one."

She turned the leaves searching, but three times, with sudden puffs, the wind blew the leaves rustling back to the same verses.

"Do read that one," said Diamond, who seemed to be of the same mind as the wind. "It sounded very nice. I am sure it is a good one."

So his mother thought it might amuse him, though she couldn't find any sense in it. She never thought he might understand it, although she could not.

Now I do not exactly know what the mother read, but this is what Diamond heard, or thought afterwards that he had heard. He was, however as I have said, very sleepy, and when he thought he understood the verses he may have been only dreaming better ones. This is how they went—

I know a river
whose waters run asleep
run run ever
singing in the shallows
dumb in the hollows
sleeping so deep
and all the swallows
that dip their feathers
in the hollows
or in the shallows
are the merriest swallows of all
for the nests they bake
with the clay they cake
with the water they shake
from their wings that rake
the water out of the shallows
or the hollows
will hold together
in any weather
and so the swallows
are the merriest fellows
and have the merriest children
and are built so narrow
like the head of an arrow
to cut the air
and go just where
the nicest water is flowing
and the nicest dust is blowing
for each so narrow
like head of an arrow
is only a barrow
to carry the mud he makes
from the nicest water flowing
and the nicest dust that is blowing
to build his nest
for her he loves best
with the nicest cakes
which the sunshine bakes

all for their merry children
all so callow
with beaks that follow
gaping and hollow
wider and wider
after their father
or after their mother
the food-provider
who brings them a spider
or a worm the poor hider
down in the earth
so there's no dearth
for their beaks as yellow
as the buttercups growing
beside the flowing
of the singing river
always and ever
growing and blowing
for fast as the sheep
awake or asleep
crop them and crop them
they cannot stop them
but up they creep
and on they go blowing
and so with the daisies
the little white praises
they grow and they blow
and they spread out their crown
and they praise the sun
and when he goes down
their praising is done
and they fold up their crown
and they sleep every one
till over the plain
he's shining amain
and they're at it again
praising and praising
such low songs raising

that no one hears them
but the sun who rears them
and the sheep that bite them
are the quietest sheep
awake or asleep
with the merriest bleat
and the little lambs
are the merriest lambs
they forget to eat
for the frolic in their feet
and the lambs and their dams
are the whitest sheep
with the woolliest wool·
and the longest wool
and the trailingest tails
and they shine like snow
in the grasses that grow
by the singing river
that sings for ever
and the sheep and the lambs
are merry for ever
because the river
sings and they drink it
and the lambs and their dams
are quiet
and white
because of their diet
for what they bite
is buttercups yellow
and daisies white
and grass as green
as the river can make it
with wind as mellow
to kiss it and shake it
as never was seen
but here in the hollows
beside the river
where all the swallows

are merriest of fellows
for the nests they make
with the clay they cake
in the sunshine bake
till they are like bone
as dry in the wind
as a marble stone
so firm they bind
the grass in the clay
that dries in the wind
the sweetest wind
that blows by the river
flowing for ever
but never you find
whence comes the wind
that blows on the hollows
and over the shallows
where dip the swallows
alive it blows
the life as it goes
awake or asleep
into the river
that sings as it flows
and the life it blows
into the sheep
awake or asleep
with the woolliest wool
and the trailingest tails
and it never fails
gentle and cool
to wave the wool
and to toss the grass
as the lambs and the sheep
over it pass
and tug and bite
with their teeth so white
and then with the sweep
of their trailing tails

smooth it again
and it grows amain
and amain it grows
and the wind as it blows
tosses the swallows
over the hollows
and down on the shallows
till every feather
doth shake and quiver
and all their feathers
go all together
blowing the life
and the joy so rife
into the swallows
that skim the shallows
and have the yellowest children
for the wind that blows
is the life of the river
flowing for ever
that washes the grasses
still as it passes
and feeds the daisies
the little white praises
and buttercups bonny
so golden and sunny
with butter and honey
that whiten the sheep
awake or asleep
that nibble and bite
and grow whiter than white
and merry and quiet
on the sweet diet
fed by the river
and tossed for ever
by the wind that tosses
the swallow that crosses
over the shallows
dipping his wings

to gather the water
and bake the cake
that the wind shall make
as hard as a bone
as dry as a stone
it's all in the wind
that blows from behind
and all in the river
that flows for ever
and all in the grasses
and the white daisies
and the merry sheep
awake or asleep
and the happy swallows
skimming the shallows
and it's all in the wind
that blows from behind

Here Diamond became aware that his mother had stopped reading.

"Why don't you go on, mother dear?" he asked.

"It's such nonsense!" said his mother. "I believe it would go on for ever."

"That's just what it did," said Diamond.

"What did?" she asked.

"Why, the river. That's almost the very tune it used to sing."

His mother was frightened, for she thought the fever was coming on again. So she did not contradict him.

"Who made that poem?" asked Diamond.

"I don't know," she answered. "Some silly woman for her children, I suppose—and then thought it good enough to print."

"She must have been at the back of the north wind some time or other, anyhow," said Diamond. "She couldn't have got a hold of it anywhere else. That's just how it went." And he began to chants bits of it here and there; but his mother said nothing for fear of making him worse; and she was very glad indeed when she saw her brother-in-law jogging along in his little cart. They lifted Diamond in, and got up themselves, and away they went, "home again, home again, home again," as Diamond sang. But he soon grew quiet, and before they reached Sandwich he was fast asleep and dreaming of the country at the back of the north wind.

Chapter XIV
OLD DIAMOND

AFTER this Diamond recovered so fast, that in a few days he was quite able to go home as soon as his father had a place for them to go to. Now his father having saved a little money, and finding that no situation offered itself, had been thinking over a new plan. A strange occurrence it was which turned his thoughts in that direction. He had a friend in the Bloomsbury region, who lived by letting out cabs and horses to the cabmen. This man, happening to meet him one day as he was returning from an unsuccessful application, said to him:

"Why don't you set up for yourself now—in the cab line, I mean?"

"I haven't enough for that," answered Diamond's father.

"You must have saved a goodish bit, I should think. Just come home with me now and look at a horse I can let you have cheap. I bought him only a few weeks ago, thinking he'd do for a Hansom, but I was wrong. He's got bone enough for a waggon, but a waggon ain't a Hansom. He ain't got go enough for a Hansom. You see, parties as takes Hansoms wants to go like the wind, and he ain't got wind enough, for he ain't so young as he once was. But for a four-wheeler as takes families and their luggages, he's the very horse. He'd carry a small house any day. I bought him cheap, and I'll sell him cheap."

"Oh, I don't want him," said Diamond's father. "A body must have time to think over an affair of so much importance. And there's the cab too. That would come to a deal of money."

"I could fit you there, I dare say," said his friend. "But come and look at the animal, anyhow."

"Since I lost my own old pair, as was Mr. Coleman's," said Diamond's father, turning to accompany the cab-master, "I ain't almost got the heart to look a horse in the face. It's a thousand pities to part man and horse."

"So it is," returned his friend sympathetically.

But what was the ex-coachman's delight, when, on going into the stable where his friend led him, he found the horse he wanted him to buy was no other than his own old Diamond, grown very thin and bony and long-legged, as if they had been doing what they could to fit him for Hansom work!

"*He* ain't a Hansom horse," said Diamond's father indignantly.

"Well, you're right. He ain't handsome, but he's a good un," said his owner.

"Who says he ain't handsome? He's one of the handsomest horses a gentleman's coachman ever druv," said Diamond's father; remarking to himself under his breath—"thought I says it as shouldn't"—for he did not feel inclined all at once to confess that his own old horse could have sunk so low.

"Well," said his friend, "all I say is—There's a animal for you, as strong as a church; an' 'll go like a train, least-ways a parly," he added, correcting himself.

But the coachman had a lump in his throat and tears in his eyes. For the old horse, hearing his voice, had turned his long neck, and when his old friend went up to him and laid his hand on his side, he whinnied for joy, and laid his big head on his master's breast. This settled the matter. The coachman's arms were round the horse's neck in a moment, and he fairly broke down and cried. The cabmaster had never been so fond of a horse himself as to hug him like that, but he saw in a moment how it was. And he must have been a good-hearted fellow, for I never heard of such an idea coming into the head of any other man with a horse to sell: instead of putting something on to the price because he was now pretty sure of selling him, he actually took a pound off what he had meant to ask for him, saying to himself it was a shame to part old friends.

Diamond's father, as soon as he came to himself, turned and asked how much he wanted for the horse.

"I see you're old friends," said the owner.

"It's my own old Diamond. I liked him far the best of the pair, though the other was good. You ain't got him too, have you?"

"No; nothing in the stable to match *him* there."

"I believe you," said the coachman. "But you'll be wanting a long price for *him*, I know."

"No, not so much. I bought him cheap, and as I say, he ain't for my work."

The end of it was that Diamond's father bought old Diamond again, along with a four-wheeled cab. And as there were some rooms to be had over the stable, he took them, wrote to his wife to come home, and set up as a cabman.

Chapter XV
THE MEWS

IT was late in the afternoon when Diamond and his mother and the baby reached London. I was so full of Diamond that I forgot to tell you a baby had arrived in the meantime. His father was waiting for them with his own cab, but they had not told Diamond who the horse was; for his father wanted to enjoy the pleasure of his surprise when he found it out. He got in with his mother without looking at the horse, and his father having put up Diamond's carpetbag and his mother's little trunk, got upon the box himself and drove off; and Diamond was quite proud of riding home in his father's own carriage. But when he got to the mews, he could not help being a little dismayed at first; and if he had never been to the back of the north wind, I am afraid he would have cried a little. But instead of that, he said to himself it was a fine thing all the old furniture was there. And instead of helping his mother to be miserable at the change, he began to find out all the advantages of the place; for every place has some advantages, and they are always better worth knowing than the disadvantages. Certainly the weather was depressing, for a thick dull persistent rain was falling by the time they reached home. But happily the weather is very changeable; and besides, there was a good fire burning in the room, which their neighbor with the drunken husband had attended to for them; and the tea-things were put out, and the kettle was boiling on the fire. And with a good fire, and tea and bread and butter, things cannot be said to be miserable.

Diamond's father and mother were, notwithstanding, *rather* miserable, and Diamond began to feel a kind of darkness beginning to spread over his own mind. But the same moment he said to himself, "This will never do. I can't give in to this. I've been to the back of the north wind. Things go right there, and so I must try to get things to go right here. I've got to fight the miserable things. They shan't make me miserable if I can help it." I do not mean that he thought these very words. They are perhaps too grown-up for him to have thought, but they represent the kind of thing that was in his heart and his head. And when heart and head go together, nothing can stand before them.

"What nice bread and butter this is!" said Diamond.

"I'm glad you like it, my dear," said his father. "I bought the butter myself at the little shop around the corner."

"It's very nice, thank you, father. Oh, there's baby waking! I'll take him."

"Sit still, Diamond," said his mother. "Go on with your bread and butter. You're not strong enough to lift him yet."

So she took the baby herself, and set him on her knee. Then Diamond began to amuse him, and went on till the little fellow was shrieking with laughter. For the baby's world was his mother's arms; and the drizzling rain, and the dreary mews, and even his father's troubled face could not touch him. What cared baby for the loss of a hundred situations? Yet neither father nor mother thought him hardhearted because he crowed and laughed in the middle of their troubles. On the contrary, his crowing and laughing were infectious. His little heart was so full of merriment that it could not hold it all, and it ran over into theirs. Father and mother began to laugh too, and Diamond laughed till he had a fit of coughing which frightened his mother, and made them all stop. His father took the baby, and his mother put him to bed.

But it was indeed a change to them all, not only from Sandwich, but from their old place. Instead of the great river where the huge barges with their mighty brown and yellow sails went tacking from side to side like little pleasure-skiffs, and where the long thin boats shot past with eight and sometimes twelve rowers, their windows now looked out upon a dirty paved yard. And there was no more garden for Diamond to run into when he pleased, with gay flowers about his feet, and solemn sun-filled trees over his head. Neither was there a wooden wall at the back of his bed with a hole in it for North Wind to come in at when she liked. Indeed, there was such a high wall, and there were so many houses about the mews, that North Wind seldom got into the place at all, except when something *must* be done, and she had a grand cleaning out like other housewives; while the partition at the head of Diamond's new bed only divided it from the room occupied by a cabman who drank too much beer, and came home chiefly to quarrel with his wife and pinch his children. It was dreadful to Diamond to hear the scolding and the crying. But it could not make him miserable, because he had been at the back of the north wind.

If my reader find it hard to believe that Diamond should be so good, he must remember that he had been to the back of the north wind. If he never knew a boy so good, did he ever know a boy that had been to the back of the north wind? It was not in the least strange of Diamond to behave as he did; on the contrary, it was thoroughly sensible of him.

We shall see how he got on.

Chapter XVI
DIAMOND MAKES A BEGINNING

THE wind blew loud, but Diamond slept a deep sleep, and never heard it. My own impression is that every time when Diamond slept well and remembered nothing about it in the morning, he had been all that night at the back of the north wind. I am almost sure that was how he woke so refreshed, and felt so quiet and hopeful all the day. Indeed he said this much, though not to me,—that always when he woke from such a sleep there was a something in his mind, he could not tell what—could not tell whether it was the last far-off sounds of the river dying away in the distance, or some of the words of the endless song his mother had read to him on the seashore. Sometimes he thought it must have been the twittering of the swallows—over the shallows, you know; but it *may* have been the chirping of the dingy sparrows picking up their breakfast in the yard—how can I tell? I don't know what I know, I only know what I think; and to tell the truth, I am more for the swallows than the sparrows. When he knew he was coming awake, he would sometimes try hard to keep hold of the words of what seemed a new song, one he had not heard before—a song in which the words and the music somehow appeared to be all one; but even when he thought he had got them well fixed in his mind, even as he came *awaker*—as he would say—one line faded away out of it, and then another, and then another, till at last there was nothing left but some lovely picture of water or grass or daisies, or something else very common, but with all the commonness polished off it, and the lovely soul of it, which people so seldom see, and, alas! yet seldomer believe in, shining out. But after that he would sing the oddest, loveliest little songs to the baby—of his own making, his mother said; but Diamond said he did not make them; they were made somewhere inside him, and he knew nothing about them till they were coming out.

When he woke that first morning he got up at once, saying to himself, "I've been ill long enough, and have given a great deal of trouble; I must try and be of use now, and help my mother." When he went into her room he found her lighting the fire, and his father just getting out of bed. They had only the one room, besides the little one, not much more than a closet, in which Diamond slept. He began at once to set things to rights, but the baby waking up, he took him, and nursed him till his mother had got the breakfast ready. She was looking gloomy, and his father was silent; and indeed except Diamond had done all he possibly could to keep out the misery that was trying to get in at the doors and windows, he too would have grown miserable, and then they would have been all miserable together. But to try to make others comfortable is the only way to get right comfortable ourselves, and that comes partly of not being able to think so much about ourselves when we are helping other people. For our Selves will always do pretty well if we don't pay them too much attention. Our Selves are like some little children who will be happy enough so long as they are left to their own games, but when we begin to interfere with them, and make them presents of too nice playthings, or too many sweet things, they begin at once to fret and spoil.

"Why, Diamond, child!" said his mother at last, "you're as good to your mother as if you were a girl—nursing the baby, and toasting the bread, and sweeping up the hearth! I declare a body would think you had been among the fairies."

Could Diamond have had greater praise or greater pleasure? You see when he forgot his Self his mother took care of his Self, and loved and praised his Self. Our own praises poison our Selves, and puff and swell them up, till they lose all shape and beauty, and become like great toadstools. But the praises of father or mother do our Selves good, and comfort them and make them beautiful. *They* never do them any harm. If they do any harm, it comes of our mixing some of our own praises with them, and that turns them nasty and slimy and poisonous.

When his father had finished his breakfast, which he did rather in a hurry, he got up and went down into the yard to get out his horse and put him to the cab.

"Won't you come and see the cab, Diamond?" he said.

"Yes, *please* father—if mother can spare me a minute," answered Diamond.

"Bless the child! I don't want him," said his mother cheerfully.

But as he was following his father out of the door, she called him back.

"Diamond, just hold the baby one minute. I have something to say to your father."

So Diamond sat down again, took the baby in his lap, and began poking his face into its little body, laughing and singing all the while, so that the baby crowed like a little bantam. And what he sang was something like this—such nonsense to those that couldn't understand it! but not to the baby, who got all the good in the world out of it:—

> baby's a-sleeping
> wake up baby

for all the swallows
are the merriest fellows
and have the yellowest children
who would go sleeping
and snore like a gaby
disturbing his mother
and father and brother
and all a-boring
their ears with his snoring
snoring snoring
for himself and no other
for himself in particular
wake up baby
sit up perpendicular
hark to the gushing
hark to the rushing
where the sheep are the woolliest
and the lambs are the unruliest
and their tails the whitest
and their eyes the brightest
and baby's the bonniest
and baby's the funniest
and baby's the shiniest
and baby's the tiniest
and baby's the merriest
and baby's the worriest
of all the lambs
that plague their dams
and mother's the whitest
of all the dams
that feed the lambs
that go crop-cropping
without stop-stopping
and father's the best
of all the swallows
that build their nest
out of the shining shallows
and he has the merriest children

that's baby and Diamond
and Diamond and baby
and baby and Diamond
and Diamond and baby

Here Diamond's knees went off in a wild dance which
tossed the baby about and shook the laughter out of him in
immoderate peals. His mother had been listening at the
door to the last few lines of his song, and came in with the
tears in her eyes. She took the baby from him, gave him
a kiss, and told him to run to his father.

By the time Diamond got into the yard, the horse was
between the shafts, and his father was looping the traces
on. Diamond went round to look at the horse. The sight of
him made him feel very queer. He did not know much
about different horses, and all other horses than their own
were very much the same to him. But he could not make
it out. This was Diamond and it wasn't Diamond. Diamond didn't hang his head like that; yet the head that was
hanging was very like the one that Diamond used to hold
so high. Diamond's bones didn't show through his skin
like that; but the skin they pushed out of shape so was
very like Diamond's skin; and the bones might be Diamond's bones, for he had never seen the shape of *them*.
But when he came round in front of the old horse, and he
put out his long neck, and began sniffing at him and rubbing his upper lip and his nose on him, then Diamond saw
it *could* be no other than old Diamond, and he did just as
his father had done before—put his arms round his neck
and cried—but not much.

"Ain't it jolly, father?" he said. "Was there ever anybody so lucky as me? Dear old Diamond!"

And he hugged the horse again, and kissed both his big
hairy cheeks. He could only manage one at a time
however—the other cheek was so far off on the other side
of his big head.

His father mounted the box with just the same air, as
Diamond thought, with which he had used to get upon the

coachbox, and Diamond said to himself, "Father's as grand as ever anyhow." He had kept his brown livery-coat, only his wife had taken the silver buttons off and put brass ones instead, because they did not think it polite to Mr. Coleman in his fallen fortunes to let his crest be seen upon the box of a cab. Old Diamond had kept just his collar; and that had the silver crest upon it still, for his master thought nobody would notice that, and so let it remain for a memorial of the better days of which it reminded him— not unpleasantly, seeing it had been by no fault either of his or of the old horse's that they had come down in the world together.

"Oh, father, do let me drive a bit," said Diamond, jumping up on the box beside him.

His father changed places with him at once, putting the reins into his hands. Diamond gathered them up eagerly.

"Don't pull at his mouth," said his father; "just feel at it gently to let him know you're there and attending to him. That's what I call talking to him through the reins."

"Yes, father, I understand," said Diamond. Then to the horse he said, "Go on, Diamond." And old Diamond's ponderous bulk began at once to move to the voice of the little boy.

But before they had reached the entrance of the mews, another voice called after young Diamond, which, in his turn, he had to obey, for it was that of his mother. "Diamond! Diamond!" it cried; and Diamond pulled the reins, and the horse stood still as a stone.

"Husband," said his mother, coming up, "you're never going to trust *him* with the reins—a baby like that?"

"He must learn some day, and he can't begin too soon. I see already he's a born coachman," said his father proudly. "And I don't see well how he could escape it, for my father and my grandfather, that's his great-grandfather, was all coachmen, I'm told; so it must come natural to him, any one would think. Besides, you see, old

Diamond's as proud of him as we are our own selves, wife. Don't you see how he's turning round his ears, with the mouths of them open, for the first word he speaks to tumble in? He's too well bred to turn his head, you know."

"Well, but, husband, I can't do without him to-day. Everything's got to be done, you know. It's my first day here. And there's that baby!"

"Bless you, wife! I never meant to take him away—only to the bottom of Endell Street. He can watch his way back."

"No, thank you, father; not to-day," said Diamond. "Mother wants me. Perhaps she'll let me go another day."

"Very well, my man," said his father, and took the reins which Diamond was holding out to him.

Diamond got down, a little disappointed of course, and went in with his mother, who was too pleased to speak. She only took hold of his hand as tight as if she had been afraid of his running away instead of glad that he would not leave her.

Now, although they did not know it, the owner of the stables, the same man who had sold the horse to his father, had been standing just inside one of the stable-doors, with his hands in his pockets, and had heard and seen all that passed; and from that day John Stonecrop took a great fancy to the little boy. And this was the beginning of what came of it.

That same evening, just as Diamond was feeling tired of the day's work, and wishing his father would come home, Mr. Stonecrop knocked at the door. His mother went and opened it.

"Good evening, ma'am," said he. "Is little master in?"

"Yes, to be sure he is—at your service, I'm sure, Mr. Stonecrop," said his mother.

"No, no, ma'am; it's I'm at his service. I'm just a-going out with my own cab, and if he likes to come with me, he shall drive my old horse till he's tired."

"It's getting rather late for him," said his mother thoughtfully. "You see he's been an invalid."

Diamond thought, what a funny thing! How could he have been an invalid when he did not even know what the word meant? But, of course, his mother was right.

"Oh, well," said Mr. Stonecrop, "I can just let him drive through Bloomsbury Square, and then he shall run home again."

"Very good, sir. And I'm much obliged to you," said his mother. And Diamond, dancing with delight, got his cap, put his hand in Mr. Stonecrop's, and went with him to the yard where the cab was waiting. He did not think the horse looked nearly so nice as Diamond, nor Mr. Stonecrop nearly so grand as his father; but he was none the less pleased. He got up on the box, and his new friend got up beside him.

"What's the horse's name?" whispered Diamond, as he took the reins from the man.

"It's not a nice name," said Mr. Stonecrop. "You needn't call him by it. I didn't give it him. He'll go well enough without it. Give the boy a whip, Jack. I never carries one when I drives old—"

He didn't finish the sentence. Jack handed Diamond a whip, with which, by holding it half down the stick, he managed just to flack the haunches of the horse; and away he went.

"Mind the gate," said Mr. Stonecrop; and Diamond did mind the gate, and guided the nameless horse through it in safety, pulling him this way and that according as was necessary. Diamond learned to drive all the sooner that he had been accustomed to do what he was told, and could obey the smallest hint in a moment. Nothing helps one to get on like that. Some people don't know how to do what they are told; they have not been used to it, and they neither understand quickly nor are able to turn what they do understand into action quickly. With an obedient mind one learns the rights of things fast enough;

for it is the law of the universe, and to obey is to understand.

"Look out!" cried Mr. Stonecrop, as they were turning the corner into Bloomsbury Square.

It was getting dusky now. A cab was approaching rather rapidly from the opposite direction, and Diamond pulling aside, and the other driver pulling up, they only just escaped a collision. Then they knew each other.

"Why, Diamond, it's a bad beginning to run into your own father," cried the driver.

"But, father, wouldn't it have been a bad ending to run into your own son?" said Diamond in return; and the two men laughed heartily.

"This is very kind of you, I'm sure, Stonecrop," said his father.

"Not a bit. He's a brave fellow, and'll be fit to drive on his own hook in a week or two. But I think you'd better let him drive you home now, for his mother don't like his having over much of the night air, and I promised not to take him farther than the square."

"Come along then, Diamond," said his father, as he brought his cab up to the other, and moved off the box to the seat beside it. Diamond jumped across, caught at the reins, said "Good night, and thank you, Mr. Stonecrop," and drove away home, feeling more of a man than he had ever yet had a chance of feeling in all his life. Nor did his father find it necessary to give him a single hint as to his driving. Only I suspect the fact that it was old Diamond, and old Diamond on his way to his stable, may have had something to do with young Diamond's success.

"Well, child," said his mother, when he entered the room, "you've not been long gone."

"No, mother; here I am. Give me the baby."

"The baby's asleep," said his mother.

"Then give him to me, and I'll lay him down."

But as Diamond took him, he woke up and began to laugh. For he was indeed one of the merriest children. And

no wonder, for he was as plump as a plum-pudding, and
had never had an ache or a pain that lasted more than five
minutes at a time. Diamond sat down with him and began
to sing to him.

> baby baby babbing
> your father's gone a-cabbing
> to catch a shilling for its pence
> to make the baby babbing dance
> for old Diamond's a duck
> they say he can swim
> but the duck of diamonds
> is baby that's him
> and of all the swallows
> the merriest fellows
> that bake their cake
> with the water they shake
> out of the river
> flowing for ever
> and make dust into clay
> on the shiniest day
> to build their nest
> father's the best
> and mother's the whitest
> and her eyes are the brightest
> of all the dams
> that watch their lambs
> cropping the grass
> where the waters pass
> singing for ever
> and of all the lambs
> with the shakingest tails
> and the jumpingest feet
> baby's the funniest
> baby's the bonniest
> and he never wails
> and he's always sweet
> and Diamond's his nurse

and Diamond's his nurse
and Diamond's his nurse

When Diamond's rhymes grew scarce, he always began dancing the baby. Some people wondered that such a child could rhyme as he did, but his rhymes were not very good, for he was only trying to remember what he had heard the river sing at the back of the north wind.

Chapter XVII
DIAMOND GOES ON

DIAMOND became a great favorite with all the men about the mews. Some may think it was not the best place in the world for him to be brought up in; but it must have been, for there he was. At first, he heard a good many rough and bad words; but he did not like them, and so they did him little harm. He did not know in the least what they meant, but there was something in the very sound of them, and in the tone of voice in which they were said, which Diamond felt to be ugly. So they did not even stick to him, not to say get inside him. He never took any notice of them, and his face shone pure and good in the middle of them, like a primrose in a hailstorm. At first, because his face was so quiet and sweet, with a smile always either awake or asleep in his eyes, and because he never heeded their ugly words and rough jokes, they said he wasn't all there, meaning that he was half an idiot, whereas he was a great deal more there than they had the sense to see. And before long the bad words found themselves ashamed to come out of the men's mouths when Diamond was near. The one would nudge the other to remind him that the boy was within hearing, and the words choked themselves before they got any farther. When they talked to him nicely he had always a good answer, sometimes a smart one, ready, and that helped much to make them change their minds about him.

One day Jack gave him a curry-comb and a brush to try his hand upon old Diamond's coat. He used them so deftly, so gently, and yet so thoroughly, as far as he could reach, that the man could not help admiring him.

"You must make haste and grow," he said. "It won't do to have a horse's belly clean and his back dirty, you know."

"Give me a leg," said Diamond, and in a moment he was on the old horse's back with the comb and brush. He sat on his withers, and reaching forward as he ate his hay, he curried and he brushed, first at one side of his neck, and then at the other. When that was done he asked for a dressing-comb, and combed his mane thoroughly. Then he pushed himself on to his back, and did his shoulders as far down as he could reach. Then he sat on his croup, and did his back and sides; then he turned round like a monkey, and attacked his hind-quarters, and combed his tail. This last was not so easy to manage, for he had to lift it up, and every now and then old Diamond would whisk it out of his hands, and once he sent the comb flying out of the stable door, to the great amusement of the men. But Jack fetched it again, and Diamond began once more, and did not leave off till he had done the whole business fairly well, if not in a first-rate, experienced fashion. All the time the old horse went on eating his hay, and, but with an occasional whisk of his tail when Diamond tickled or scratched him, took no notice of the proceeding. But that was all a pretence, for he knew very well who it was that was perched on his back, and rubbing away at him with the comb and the brush. So he was quite pleased and proud, and perhaps said to himself something like this,—

"I'm a stupid old horse, who can't brush his own coat; but there's my young godson on my back, cleaning me like an angle."

I won't vouch for what the old horse was thinking, for it is very difficult to find out what any old horse is thinking.

"Oh dear!" said Diamond when he had done, "I'm so tired!"

And he laid himself down at full length on old Diamond's back.

By this time all the men in the stable were gathered about the two Diamonds, and all much amused. One of them lifted him down, and from that time he was a greater favorite than before. And if ever there was a boy who had a chance of being a prodigy at cab-driving, Diamond was that boy, for the strife came to be who should have him out with him on the box.

His mother, however, was a little shy of the company for him, and besides she could not always spare him. Also his father liked to have him himself when he could; so that he was more desired than enjoyed among the cabmen.

But one way and another he did learn to drive all sorts of horses, and to drive them well, and that through the most crowded streets in London city. Of course there was the man always on the box-seat beside him, but before long there was seldom the least occasion to take the reins out of his hands. For one thing he never got frightened, and consequently was never in too great a hurry. Yet when the moment came for doing something sharp, he was always ready for it. I must once more remind my readers that he had been to the back of the north wind.

One day, which was neither washing-day nor cleaning-day, nor marketing-day, nor Saturday, nor Monday—upon which consequently Diamond could be spared from the baby—his father took him on his own cab. After a stray job or two by the way, they drew up in the row upon the stand between Cockspur Street and Pall Mall. They waited a long time, but nobody seemed to want to be carried anywhere. By and by ladies would be going home from the Academy exhibition, and then there would be a chance of a job.

"Though, to be sure," said Diamond's father—with what truth I cannot say, but he believed what he said—"some ladies is very hard, and keeps you to the bare sixpence a mile, when every one knows that ain't enough to keep a family *and* a cab upon. To be sure it's the law; but mayhap they may get more law than they like some day themselves."

As it was very hot, Diamond's father got down to have a glass of beer himself, and give another to the old waterman. He left Diamond on the box.

A sudden noise got up and Diamond looked round to see what was the matter.

There was a crossing near the cab-stand, where a girl was sweeping. Some rough young imps had picked a quarrel with her, and were now hauling at her broom to get it away from her. But as they did not pull all together, she was holding it against them, scolding and entreating alternately.

Diamond was off his box in a moment, and running to the help of the girl. He got hold of the broom at her end and pulled along with her. But the boys proceeded to rougher measures, and one of them hit Diamond on the nose, and made it bleed; and as he could not let go the broom to mind his nose, he was soon a dreadful figure. But presently his father came back, and missing Diamond, looked about. He had to look twice, however, before he could be sure that that was his boy in the middle of the tumult. He rushed in, and sent the assailants flying in all directions. The girl thanked Diamond, and began sweeping as if nothing had happened, while his father led him away. With the help of old Tom, the waterman, he was soon washed into decency, and his father set him on the box again, perfectly satisfied with the account he gave of the cause of his being in a fray.

"I couldn't let them behave so to a poor girl—could I, father?" he said.

"Certainly not, Diamond," said his father, quite pleased, for Diamond's father was a gentleman.

A moment after, up came the girl, running, with her broom over her shoulder, and calling, "Cab, there! cab!"

Diamond's father turned instantly, for he was the foremost in the rank, and followed the girl. One or two other passing cabs heard the cry, and made for the place, but the girl had taken care not to call till she was near enough to give her friends the first chance. When they reached the curbstone—who should it be waiting for the cab but Mrs. and Miss Coleman! They did not look at the cabman, however. The girl opened the door for them; they gave her the address, and a penny; she told the cabman, and away they drove.

When they reached the house, Diamond's father got down and rang the bell. As he opened the door of the cab, he touched his hat as he had been wont to do. The ladies both stared for a moment, and then exclaimed together:

"Why, Joseph! can it be you?"

"Yes, ma'am; yes, miss;" answered he, again touching his hat, with all the respect he could possibly put into the action. "It's a lucky day which I see you once more upon it."

"Who would have thought it?" said Mrs. Coleman. "It's changed times for both of us, Joseph, and it's not very often we can have a cab even; but you see my daughter is still very poorly, and she can't bear the motion of the omnibuses. Indeed we meant to walk a bit first before we took a cab, but just at the corner, for as hot as the sun was, a cold wind came down the street, and I saw that Miss Coleman must not face it. But to think we should have fallen upon you, of all the cabmen in London! I didn't know you had got a cab."

"Well, you see, ma'am, I had a chance of buying the old horse, and I couldn't resist *him*. There he is, looking at you, ma'am. Nobody knows the sense in that head of his."

The two ladies went near to pat the horse, and then they noticed Diamond on the box.

"Why you've got both Diamonds with you," said Miss Coleman. "How do you do, Diamond?"

Diamond lifted his cap, and answered politely.

"He'll be fit to drive himself before long," said his father, proudly. "The old horse is a-teaching of him."

"Well, he must come and see us, now you've found us out. Where do you live?"

Diamond's father gave the ladies a ticket with his name and address printed on it; and then Mrs. Coleman took out her purse, saying:

"And what's your fare, Joseph?"

"No, thank you, ma'am," said Joseph. "It was your own old horse as took you; and me you paid long ago."

He jumped on his box before she could say another word, and with a parting salute drove off, leaving them on the pavement, with the maid holding the door for them.

It was a long time now since Diamond had seen North Wind, or even thought much about her. And as his father drove along, he was thinking not about her, but about the crossing-sweeper, and was wondering what made him feel as if he knew her quite well, when he could not remember anything of her. But a picture arose in his mind of a little girl running before the wind and dragging her broom after her; and from that, by degrees, he recalled the whole adventure of the night when he got down from North Wind's back in a London street. But he could not quite satisfy himself whether the whole affair was not a dream which he had dreamed when he was a very little boy. Only he had been to the back of the north wind since—there could be no doubt of that; for when he woke every morning, he always knew that he had been there again. And as he thought and thought, he recalled another thing that had happened that morning, which, although it seemed a mere accident, might have something to do with what had happened since. His father had intended going on the stand at King's Cross that morning, and had turned into Gray's Inn Lane to drive there, when they found the way blocked up, and upon inquiry were informed that a stack of chimneys had been blown down in the night, and had fallen across the road. They were just clearing the rubbish away. Diamond's father turned, and made for Charing Cross.

That night the father and mother had a great deal to talk about.

"Poor things!" said the mother; "it's worse for them than it is for us. You see they've been used to such grand things, and for them to come down to a little poky house like that—it breaks my heart to think of it."

"I don't know," said Diamond thoughtfully, "whether Mrs. Coleman had bells on her toes."

"What do you mean, child?" said his mother.

"She had rings on her fingers anyhow," returned Diamond.

"Of course she had, as any lady would. What has that to do with it?"

"When we were down at Sandwich," said Diamond, "you said you would have to part with your mother's ring, now we were poor."

"Bless the child! he forgets nothing," said his mother. "Really, Diamond, a body would need to mind what they say to you."

"Why?" said Diamond. "I only think about it."

"That's just why," said the mother.

"Why is that why?" persisted Diamond, for he had not yet learned that grown-up people are not often so much grown up that they never talk like children—and spoilt ones too.

"Mrs. Coleman is none so poor as all that yet. No, thank Heaven! she's not come to that."

"Is it a *great* disgrace to be poor?" asked Diamond, because of the tone in which his mother had spoken.

But his mother, whether conscience-stricken I do not know, hurried him away to bed, where after various attempts to understand her, resumed and resumed again in spite of invading sleep, he was conquered at last, and gave in, murmuring over and over to himself, "Why is why?" but getting no answer to the question.

Chapter XVIII
THE DRUNKEN CABMAN

A FEW nights after this, Diamond woke up suddenly, believing he heard the North Wind thundering along. But it was something quite different. South Wind was moaning round the chimneys, to be sure, for she was not very happy that night, but it was not her voice that had wakened Diamond. Her voice would only have lulled him the deeper asleep. It was a loud, angry voice, now growling like that of a beast, now raving like that of a madman; and when Diamond came a little wider awake, he knew that it was the voice of the drunken cabman, the wall of whose room was at the head of his bed. It was anything but pleasant to hear, but he could not help hearing it. At length there came a cry from the woman, and then a scream from the baby. Thereupon Diamond thought it time that somebody did something, and as himself was the only somebody at hand, he must go and see whether he could not do the something. So he got up and put on part of his clothes, and went down the stair, for the cabman's room did not open upon their stair, and he had to go out into the yard, and in at the next door. This, fortunately the cabman, being drunk, had left open. By the time he reached their stair, all was still except the voice of the crying baby, which guided him to the right door. He opened it softly, and peeped in. There, leaning back in a chair, with his arms hanging down by his sides, and his legs stretched out before him and supported on his heels, sat the drunken cabman. His wife lay in her clothes upon the bed, sobbing, and the baby was wailing in the cradle. It was very miserable altogether.

Now the way most people do when they see anything very miserable is to turn away from the sight, and try to forget it. But Diamond began as usual to try to destroy the misery. The little boy was just as much one of God's messengers as if he had been an angel with a flaming sword, going out to fight the devil. The devil he had to fight just then was Misery. And the way he fought him was the very best. Like a wise soldier, he attacked him first in his weakest point—that was the baby; for Misery can never get such a hold of a baby as of a grown person. Diamond was knowing in babies, and he knew he could do something to make the baby happy; for although he had only known one baby as yet, and although not one baby is the same as another, yet they are so very much alike in some things, and he knew that one baby so thoroughly, that he had good reason to believe he could do something for any other. I have known people who would have begun to fight the devil in a very different and a very stupid way. They would have begun by scolding the idiotic cabman; the next they would make his wife angry by saying it must be her fault as well as his, and by leaving ill-bred though well-meant shabby little books for them to read, which they were sure to hate the sight of; while all the time they would not have put out a finger to touch the wailing baby. But Diamond had him out of the cradle in a moment, set him up on his knee, and told him to look at the light. Now all the light there was came only from a lamp in the yard, and it was a very dingy and yellow light, for the glass of the lamp was dirty, and the gas was bad; but the light that came from it was, notwithstanding, as certainly light as if it had come from the sun itself, and the baby knew that, and smiled to it; and although it was indeed a wretched room which that lamp lighted—so dreary, and dirty, and empty, and hopeless!—there in the middle of it sat Diamond on a stool, smiling to the baby, and the baby on his knees smiling to the lamp. The father of him sat staring at nothing, neither asleep nor awake, not quite lost in stupidity either, for through it all he was dimly angry with himself, he did not know why. It was that he had struck his wife. He had forgotten it, but was miserable about it, notwithstanding. And this misery was the voice of the great Love that had made him and his wife and the baby and Diamond, speaking in his heart, and telling him to be good. For that great Love speaks in the most wretched and dirty hearts; only the tone of its voice depends on the echoes of the place in which it sounds. On Mount Sinai, it was thunder; in the cabman's heart it was *misery*; in the soul of St. John it was perfect blessedness.

By and by he became aware that there was a voice of singing in the room. This, of course, was the voice of Diamond singing to the baby—song after song, every one as foolish as another to the cabman, for he was too tipsy to part one word from another: all the words mixed up in his ear in a gurgle without division or stop; for such was the way he spoke himself, when he was in this horrid condition. But the baby was more than content with Diamond's songs, and Diamond himself was so contented with what the songs were all about, that he did not care a bit about the songs themselves, if only baby liked them. But they did the cabman good as well as the baby and Diamond, for they put him to sleep, and the sleep was busy all the time it lasted, smoothing the wrinkles out of his temper.

At length Diamond grew tired of singing, and began to talk to the baby instead. And as soon as he stopped singing, the cabman began to wake up. His brain was a little clearer now, his temper a little smoother, and his heart not quite so dirty. He began to listen and he went on listening, and heard Diamond saying to the baby something like this, for he thought the cabman was asleep:

"Poor daddy! Baby's daddy takes too much beer and gin, and that makes him somebody else, and not his own self at all. Baby's daddy would never hit baby's mammy if he didn't take too much beer. He's very fond of baby's mammy, and works from morning to night to get her breakfast and dinner and supper, only at night he forgets, and pays the money away for beer. And they put nasty stuff in the beer, I've heard my daddy say, that drives all the good out, and lets all the bad in. Daddy says when a man takes to drink, there's a thirsty devil creeps into his inside, because he knows he will always get enough there. And the devil is always crying out for more drink, and that makes the man thirsty, and so he drinks more and more, till he kills himself with it. And then the ugly devil creeps out of him, and crawls about on his belly, looking for some other cabman to get into, that he may drink, drink, drink. That's what *my* daddy says, baby. And he says, too, the only way to make the devil come out, is to give him plenty of cold water and tea and coffee, and nothing at all that comes from the public-house; for the devil can't abide that kind of stuff, and creeps out pretty soon, for fear of being drowned in it. But your daddy *will* drink the nasty stuff, poor man! I wish he wouldn't, for it makes mammy cross with him, and no wonder! and then when mammy's cross, he's crosser, and there's nobody in the house to take care of them but baby; and you *do* take care of them, baby—don't you, baby? I know you do. Babies always take care of their fathers and mothers—don't they, baby? That's what they come for—isn't it, baby? And when daddy stops drinking beer and nasty gin with turpentine in it, father says, then mammy *will* be so happy, and look so pretty! and daddy will be so good to baby! and baby will be as happy as a swallow, which is the merriest fellow! And Diamond will be so happy too! And when Diamond's a man, he'll take baby out with him on the box, and teach him to drive a cab."

He went on with chatter like this till baby was asleep, by which time he was tired, and father and mother were both wide awake,—only rather confused—the one from the beer, the other from the blow—and staring, the one from his chair, the other from her bed, at Diamond. But he was quite unaware of their notice, for he sat half-asleep, with his eyes wide open, staring in his turn, though without knowing it, at the cabman, while the cabman could not withdraw his gaze from Diamond's white face and big eyes. For Diamond's face was always rather pale, and now it was paler than usual with sleeplessness, and the light of the street-lamp upon it. At length he found himself nodding, and he knew then it was time to put the baby down, lest he should let him fall. So he rose from the little three-legged stool, and laid the baby in the cradle, and covered him up—it was well it was a warm night, and he did not want much covering—and then he all but staggered out of the door, he was so tipsy himself with sleep.

"Wife," said the cabman, turning towards the bed, "I do somehow believe that wur an angel just gone. Did you see him, wife? He warn't wery big, and he hadn't got none o' them wingses, you know. It wur one o' them baby-angels you sees on the gravestones, you know."

"Nonsense, hubby!" said his wife; "but it's just as good. I might say better, for you can ketch hold of *him* when you like. That's little Diamond as everybody knows, and a duck o' diamonds he is! No woman could wish for a better child than he be."

"I ha' heerd on him in the stable, but I never see the brat afore. Come, old girl, let bygones be bygones, and gie us a kiss, and we'll go to bed."

The cabman kept his cab in another yard, although he had his room in this. He was often late in coming home, and was not one to take notice of children, especially when he was tipsy, which was oftener than not. Hence, if he had ever seen Diamond, he did not know him. But his wife knew him well enough, as did every one else who lived all day in the yard. She was a good-natured woman. It was she who had got the fire lighted and the tea ready for them when Diamond and his mother came home from Sandwich. And her husband was not an ill-natured man either, and when in the morning he recalled not only Diamond's visit, but how he himself had behaved to his wife, he was very vexed with himself, and gladdened his poor wife's heart by telling her how sorry he was. And for a whole week after, he did not go near the public-house, hard as it was to avoid it, seeing a certain rich brewer had built one, like a trap to catch souls and bodies in, at almost every corner he had to pass on his way home. Indeed, he was never quite so bad after that, though it was some time before he began really to reform.

Chapter XIX
DIAMOND'S FRIENDS

ONE day when old Diamond was standing with his nose in his bag between Pall Mall and Cockspur Street, and his master was reading the newspaper on the box of his cab, which was the last of a good many in the row, little Diamond got down for a run, for his legs were getting cramped with sitting. And first of all he strolled with his hands in his pockets up to the crossing, where the girl and her broom were to be found in all weathers. Just as he was going to speak to her, a tall gentleman stepped upon the crossing. He was pleased to find it so clean, for the streets were muddy, and he had nice boots on; so he put his hand in his pocket, and gave the girl a penny. But when she gave him a sweet smile in return, and made him a pretty courtesy, he looked at her again, and said:

"Where do you live, my child?"

"Paradise Row," she answered; "next door to the Adam and Eve—down the area."

"Whom do you live with?" he asked.

"My wicked old grannie," she replied.

"You shouldn't call your grannie wicked," said the gentleman.

"But she is," said the girl, looking up confidently in his face. "If you don't believe me, you can come and take a look at her."

The words sounded rude, but the girl's face looked so simple that the gentleman saw she did not mean to be rude, and became still more interested in her.

"Still you shouldn't say so," he insisted.

"Shouldn't I? Everybody calls her wicked old grannie— even them that's as wicked as her. You should hear her swear. There's nothing like it in the Row. Indeed, I assure you, sir, there's ne'er a one of them can shut my grannie up once she begins and gets right a-going. You must put her in a passion first, you know. It's no good till you do that—she's so old now. How she *do* make them laugh, to be sure!"

Although she called her wicked, the child spoke so as plainly to indicate pride in her grannie's pre-eminence in swearing.

The gentleman looked very grave to hear her, for he was sorry that such a nice little girl should be in such bad keeping. But he did not know what to say next, and stood for a moment with his eyes on the ground. When he lifted them, he saw the face of Diamond looking up in his.

"Please, sir," said Diamond, "her grannie's very cruel to her sometimes, and shuts her out in the streets at night, if she happens to be late."

"Is this your brother?" asked the gentleman of the girl.

"No, sir."

"How does he know your grandmother, then? He does not look like one of her sort."

"Oh no, sir! He's a good boy—quite."

Here she tapped her forehead with her finger in a significant manner.

"What do you mean by that?" asked the gentleman, while Diamond looked on smiling.

"The cabbies call him God's baby," she whispered. "He's not right in the head, you know. A tile loose."

Still Diamond, though he heard every word, and understood it too, kept on smiling. What could it matter what people called him, so long as he did nothing he ought not to do? And, besides, *God's baby* was surely the best of names!

"Well, my little man, and what can you do?" asked the gentleman, turning towards him—just for the sake of saying something.

"Drive a cab," said Diamond.

"Good; and what else?" he continued; for, accepting what the girl had said, he regarded the still sweetness of Diamond's face as a sign of silliness, and wished to be kind to the poor little fellow.

"Nurse a baby," said Diamond.

"Well—and what else?"

"Clean father's boots, and make him a bit of toast for his tea."

"You're a useful little man," said the gentleman. "What else can you do?"

"Not much that I know of," said Diamond. "I can't curry a horse, except somebody puts me on his back. So I don't count that."

"Can you read?"

"No; but mother can and father can, and they're going to teach me some day soon."

"Well, here's a penny for you."

"Thank you, sir."

"And when you have learned to read, come to me, and I'll give you sixpence and a book with fine pictures in it."

"Please, sir, where am I to come?" asked Diamond, who was too much a man of the world not to know that he must have the gentleman's address before he could go and see him.

"You're no such silly!" thought he, as he put his hand in his pocket, and brought out a card. "There," he said, "your father will be able to read that, and tell you where to go."

"Yes, sir. Thank you, sir," said Diamond, and put the card in his pocket.

The gentleman walked away, but turning round a few paces off, saw Diamond give his penny to the girl, and, walking slower, heard him say:

"I've got a father, and a mother, and little brother, and you've got nothing but a wicked old grannie. You may have my penny."

The girl put it beside the other in her pocket, the only trustworthy article of dress she wore. Her grandmother always took care that she had a stout pocket.

"Is she as cruel as ever?" asked Diamond.

"Much the same. But I gets more coppers now than I used to, and I can get summats to eat, and take browns enough home besides to keep her from grumbling. It's a good thing she's so blind, though."

"Why?" asked Diamond.

" 'Cause if she was as sharp in the eyes as she used to be, she would find out I never eats her broken wittles, and then she'd know as I must get something somewheres."

"Doesn't she watch you, then?"

"O' course she do. Don't she just! But I make believe and drop it in my lap, and then hitch it into my pocket."

"What would she do if she found you out?"

"She'd never give me no more."

"But you don't want it!"

"Yes, I do want it."

"What do you do with it, then?"

"Give it to cripple Jim."

"Who's cripple Jim?"

"A boy in the Row. His mother broke his leg when he wur a kid, so he's never come to much; but he's a good boy, is Jim, and I love Jim dearly. I always keeps off a penny for Jim—leastways as often as I can.—But there, I must sweep again, for them busses makes no end o' dirt."

"Diamond! Diamond!" cried his father, who was afraid he might get no good by talking to the girl; and Diamond obeyed, and got up again upon the box. He told his father about the gentleman, and what he had promised him if he would learn to read, and showed him the gentleman's card.

"Why, it's not many doors from the Mews!" said his father, giving him back the card. "Take care of it, my boy, for it may lead to something. God knows, in these hard times a man wants as many friends as he's ever likely to get."

"Haven't you got friends enough, father?" asked Diamond.

"Well, I have no right to complain; but the more the better, you know."

"Just let me count," said Diamond.

And he took his hands from his pockets, and spreading out the fingers of his left hand, began to count, beginning at the thumb.

"There's mother first; and then baby, and then me. Next there's old Diamond—and the cab—no, I won't count the cab, for it never looks at you, and when Diamond's out of the shafts, it's nobody. Then there's the man that drinks next door, and his wife, and his baby."

"They're no friends of mine," said his father.

"Well, they're friends of mine," said Diamond.

His father laughed.

"Much good they'll do you!" he said.

"How do you know they won't?" returned Diamond.

"Well, go on," said his father.

"Then there's Jack and Mr. Stonecrop, and, deary me! not to have mentioned Mr. Coleman and Mrs. Coleman, and Miss Coleman, and Mrs. Crump. And then there's the clergyman that spoke to me in the garden that day the tree was blown down."

"What's his name?"

"I don't know his name."

"Where does he live?"

"I don't know."

"How can you count him, then?"

"He did talk to me, and very kindlike too."

His father laughed again.

"Why, child, you're just counting everybody you know. That don't make 'em friends."

"Don't it? I thought it did. Well, but they shall be my friends. I shall make 'em."

"How will you do that?"

"They can't help themselves then, if they would. If I choose to be their friend, you know, they can't prevent me. Then there's that girl at the crossing."

"A fine set of friends you do have, to be sure, Diamond!"

"Surely *she's* a friend anyhow, father. If it hadn't been for her, you would never have got Mrs. Coleman and Miss Coleman to carry home."

His father was silent, for he saw that Diamond was right, and was ashamed to find himself more ungrateful than he had thought.

"Then there's the new gentleman," Diamond went on.

"If he do as he say," interposed his father.

"And why shouldn't he? I daresay sixpence ain't too much for him to spare. But I don't quite understand, father: is nobody your friend but the one that does something for you?"

"No, I won't say that, my boy. You would have to leave out baby then."

"Oh no, I shouldn't. Baby can laugh in your face, and crow in your ears, and make you feel so happy. Call you that nothing, father?"

The father's heart was fairly touched now. He made no

answer to this last appeal, and Diamond ended off with saying:

"And there's the best of mine to come yet—and that's you, daddy—except it be mother, you know. You're my friend, daddy, ain't you? And I'm your friend, ain't I?"

"And God for us all," said his father, and then they were both silent, for that was very solemn.

Chapter XX
DIAMOND LEARNS TO READ

THE question of the tall gentleman as to whether Diamond could read or not, set his father thinking it was high time he could; and as soon as old Diamond was suppered and bedded, he began the task that very night. But it was not much of a task to Diamond, for his father took for his lesson-book those very rhymes his mother had picked up on the sea-shore; and as Diamond was not beginning too soon, he learned very fast indeed. Within a month he was able to spell out most of the verses for himself.

But he had never come upon the poem he thought he had heard his mother read from that day. He had looked through and through the book several times after he knew the letters and a few words, fancying he could tell the look of it, but had always failed to find one more like it than another. So he wisely gave up the search till he could really read. Then he resolved to begin at the beginning, and read them all straight through. This took him nearly a fortnight. When he had almost reached the end, he came upon the following verses, which took his fancy much, although they were certainly not very like those he was in search of.

LITTLE BOY BLUE

Little Boy Blue lost his way in a wood.
  Sing apples and cherries, roses and honey;
He said, "I would not go back if I could,
  It's all so jolly and funny."

He sang, "This wood is all my own,
  Apples and cherries, roses and honey;
So here I'll sit, like a king on my throne,
  All so jolly and funny."

A little snake crept out of the tree,
  Apples and cherries, roses and honey;
"Lie down at my feet, little snake," said he,
  All so jolly and funny.

A little bird sang in the tree overhead,
  Apples and cherries, roses and honey;
"Come and sing your song on my finger instead,
  All so jolly and funny."

The snake coiled up; and the bird flew down,
And sang him the song of Birdie Brown.

Little Boy Blue found it tiresome to sit,
And he thought he had better walk on a bit.

So up he got, his way to take,
And he said, "Come along, little bird and snake."

And waves of snake o'er the damp leaves passed,
And the snake went first and Birdie Brown last;

By Boy Blue's head, with flutter and dart,
Flew Birdie Brown with its song in its heart.

He came where the apples grew red and sweet;
"Tree, drop me an apple down at my feet."

He came where the cherries hung plump and red;
"Come to my mouth, sweet kisses," he said,

And the boughs bow down, and the apples they dapple
The grass, too many for him to grapple.

And the cherriest cherries, with never a miss,
Fall to his mouth, each a full-grown kiss.

He met a little brook singing a song.
He said, "Little brook, you are going wrong.

"You must follow me, follow me, follow, I say,
Do as I tell you, and come this way."

And the song-singing, sing-songing forest brook
Leaped from its bed and after him took,

Followed him, followed. And pale and wan,
The dead leaves rustled as the water ran.

And every bird high up on the bough,
And every creature low down below,

He called and the creatures obeyed the call,
Took their legs and their wings and followed him all;

Squirrels that carried their tails like a sack,
Each on his own little humpy brown back;

Householder snails, and slugs all tails,
And butterflies, flutterbies, ships all sails;

And weasels, and ousels, and mice, and larks,
And owls, and rere-mice, and harkydarks.

All went running, and creeping, and flowing,
After the merry boy fluttering and going;

The dappled fawns fawning, the fallow-deer following,
The swallows and flies, flying and swallowing;

Cockchafers, henchafers, cockioli-birds,
Cockroaches, henroaches, cuckoos in herds.

The spider forgot and followed him spinning,
And lost all his thread from end to beginning.

The gay wasp forgot his rings and his waist,
He never had made such undignified haste.

The dragon-flies melted to mist with their hurrying.
The mole in his moleskins left his barrowing burrowing.

The bees went buzzing, so busy and beesy,
And the midges in columns so upright and easy.

But Little Boy Blue was not content,
Calling for followers still as he went,

Blowing his horn, and beating his drum,
And crying aloud, "Come all of you, come!"

He said to the shadows, "Come after me";
And the shadows began to flicker and flee,

And they flew through the wood all flattering and fluttering
Over the dead leaves flickering and muttering.

And he said to the wind, "Come, follow; come, follow,
With whistle and pipe, and rustle and hollo."

And the wind wound round at his desire,
As if he had been the gold cock on the spire.

And the cock itself flew down from the church,
And left the farmers all in the lurch.

They run and they fly, they creep and they come,
Everything, everything, all and some.

The very trees they tugged at their roots,
Only their feet were too fast in their boots,

After him leaning and straining and bending,
As on through their boles he kept walking and wendling,

Till out of the wood he burst on a lea,
Shouting and calling, "Come after me!"

And then they rose with a leafy hiss,
And stood as if nothing had been amiss.

Little Boy Blue sat down on a stone,
And the creatures came round him every one.

And he said to the clouds, "I want you there";
And down they sank through the thin blue air.

And he said to the sunset far in the west,
"Come here; I want you; I know best."

And the sunset came and stood up on the wold,
And burned and glowed in purple and gold.

Then Little Boy Blue began to ponder:
"What's to be done with them all, I wonder."

Then Little Boy Blue, he said, quite low,
"What to do with you all I am sure I don't know."

Then the clouds clodded down till dismal it grew;
The snake sneaked close; round Birdie Brown flew;

The brook sat up like a snake on it tail;
And the wind came up with a *what-will-you* wail;

And all the creatures sat and stared;
The mole opened his very eyes and glared;

And for rats and bats and the world and his wife,
Little Boy Blue was afraid of his life.

Then Birdie Brown began to sing,
And what he sang was the very thing:

"You have brought us all hither, Little Boy Blue,
Pray what do you want us all to do?"

"Go away! go away!" said Little Boy Blue;
"I'm sure I don't want you—get away—do."

No, no; no, no; no, yes, and no, no,"
Sang Birdie Brown, "it mustn't be so.

"We cannot for nothing come here, and away.
Give us some work, or else we stay."

"Oh dear! and oh dear!" with sob and with sigh,
Said Little Boy Blue, and began to cry.

But before he got far, he thought of a thing;
And up he stood, and spoke like a king.

"Why do you hustle and jostle and bother?
Off with you all! Take me back to my mother."

The sunset stood at the gates of the west.
"Follow *me*, follow *me*," came from Birdie Brown's breast.

"I am going that way as fast as I can,"
Said the brook, as it sank and turned and ran.

Back to the woods fled the shadows like ghosts;
"If we stay, we shall all be missed from our posts."

Said the wind with a voice that had changed its cheer,
"I was just going there, when you brought me here."

"That's where I live," said the sack-backed squirrel,
And he turned his sack with a swing and a swirl.

Said the cock of the spire, "His father's churchwarden."
Said the brook running faster, "I run through his garden."

Said the mole, "Two hundred worms—there I caught 'em
Last year, and I'm going again next autumn."

Said they all, "If that's where you want us to steer for,
What in earth or in water did you bring us here for?"

"Never you mind," said Little Boy Blue;
"That's what I tell you. If that you won't do,

"I'll get up at once, and go home without you.
I think I will; I begin to doubt you."

He rose; and up rose the snake on its tail,
And hissed three times, half a hiss, half a wail.

Little Boy Blue he tried to go past him;
But wherever he turned, sat the snake and faced him.

"If you don't get out of my way," he said,
"I tell you, snake, I will break your head."

The snake he neither would go nor come;
So he hit him hard with the stick of his drum.

The snake fell down as if he were dead,
And Little Boy Blue set his foot on his head.

And all the creatures they marched before him,
And marshalled him home with a high cockolorum.

And Birdie Brown sang Twirrrr twitter twirrrr twee—
  Apples and cherries, rose and honey;
Little Boy Blue has listened to me—
  All so jolly and funny.

Chapter XXI
SAL'S NANNY

DIAMOND managed with many blunders to read this rhyme to his mother.

"Isn't it nice, mother?" he said.

"Yes, it's pretty," she answered.

"I think it means something," returned Diamond.

"I'm sure I don't know what," she said.

"I wonder if it's the same boy—yes, it must be the same—Little Boy Blue, you know. Let me see—how does that rhyme go?"

` Little Boy Blue, come blow me your horn—

Yes, of course it is—for this one went 'blowing his horn and beating his drum.' He had a drum too.

Little Boy Blue, come blow me your horn;
The sheep's in the meadow, the cow's in the corn.

He had to keep them out, you know. But he wasn't minding his work. It goes—

Where's the little boy that looks after the sheep?
He's under the haystack, fast asleep.

There, you see, mother! And then, let me see—

Who'll go and wake him? No, not I;
For if I do, he'll be sure to cry.

So I suppose nobody did wake him. He was a rather cross little boy, I dare say, when woke up. And when he did wake of himself, and saw the mischief the cow had done to the corn, instead of running home to his mother, he ran away into the wood and lost himself. Don't you think that's very likely, mother?"

"I shouldn't wonder," she answered.

"So you see he was naughty; for even when he lost himself he did not want to go home. Any of the creatures would have shown him the way if he had asked it—all but the snake. He followed the snake, you know, and he took him farther away. I suppose it was a young one of the same serpent that tempted Adam and Eve. Father was telling us about it last Sunday, you remember." '

"Bless the child!" said his mother to herself; and then added aloud, finding that Diamond did not go on, "Well, what next?"

"I don't know, mother. I'm sure there's a great deal more, but what it is I can't say. I only know that he killed the snake. I suppose that's what he had a drumstick for. He couldn't do it with his horn."

"But surely you're not such a silly as to take it all for true, Diamond?"

"I think it must be. It looks true. That killing of the snake looks true. It's what *I've* got to do so often."

His mother looked uneasy. Diamond smiled full in her face, and added—

"When baby cries and won't be happy, and when father and you talk about your troubles, I mean."

This did little to reassure his mother; and lest my reader should have his qualms about it too, I venture to remind him once more that Diamond had been to the back of the north wind.

Finding she made no reply, Diamond went on—

"In a week or so, I shall be able to go to the tall gentleman and tell him I can read. And I'll ask him if he can help me to understand the rhyme."

But before the week was out, he had another reason for going to Mr. Raymond.

For three days, on each of which, at one time or other, Diamond's father was on the same stand near the National Gallery, the girl was not at her crossing, and Diamond got quite anxious about her, fearing she must be ill. On the fourth day, not seeing her yet, he said to his father, who had that moment shut the door of his cab upon a fare—

"Father, I want to go and look after the girl. She can't be well."

"All right," said his father. "Only take care of yourself, Diamond."

So saying he climbed on his box and drove off.

He had great confidence in his boy, you see, and would trust him anywhere. But if he had known the kind of place in which the girl lived, he would perhaps have thought twice before he allowed him to go alone. Diamond, who did know something of it, had not, however, any fear. From talking to the girl he had a good notion of where about it was, and he remembered the address well enough; so by asking his way some twenty times, mostly of policemen, he came at length pretty near the place. The last policeman he questioned looked down upon him from the summit of six feet two inches, and replied with another question, but kindly:

"What do you want there, my small kid? It ain't where you was bred, I guess."

"No, sir," answered Diamond. "I live in Bloomsbury."

"That's a long way off," said the policeman.

"Yes, it's a good distance," answered Diamond; "but I find my way about pretty well. Policemen are always kind to me."

"But what on earth do you want here?"

Diamond told him plainly what he was about, and of course the man believed him, for nobody ever disbelieved Diamond. People might think he was mistaken, but they never thought he was telling a story.

"It's an ugly place," said the policeman.

"Is it far off?" asked Diamond.

"No. It's next door almost. But it's not safe."

"Nobody hurts me," said Diamond.

"I must go with you, I suppose."

"Oh, no! please not," said Diamond. "They might think I was going to meddle with them, and I ain't, you know."

"Well, do as you please," said the man, and gave him full directions.

Diamond set off, never suspecting that the policeman, who was a kind-hearted man, with children of his own, was following him close, and watching him round every corner. As he went on, all at once he thought he remembered the place, and whether it really was so, or only that he had laid up the policeman's instructions well in his mind, he went straight for the cellar of old Sal.

"He's a sharp little kid, anyhow, for as simple as he looks," said the man to himself. "Not a wrong turn does he take! But old Sal's a rum un for such a child to pay a morning visit to. She's worse when she's sober than when she's half drunk. I've seen her when she'd have torn him in pieces."

Happily then for Diamond, old Sal had gone out to get some gin. When he came to her door at the bottom of the area-stair and knocked, he received no answer. He laid his ear to the door, and thought he heard a moaning within. So he tried the door, and found it was not locked. It was a dreary place indeed,—and very dark, for the window was below the level of the street, and covered with mud, while over the grating which kept people from falling into the area, stood a chest of drawers, placed there by a dealer in second-hand furniture, which shut out almost all the light. And the smell in the place was dreadful. Diamond stood still for a while, for he could see next to nothing, but he heard the moaning plainly enough now. When he got used to the darkness, he discovered his friend lying with closed eyes and a white suffering face on a heap of little better than rags in a corner of the den. He went up to her and spoke, but she made him no answer. Indeed, she was not in the least aware of his presence, and Diamond saw that he could do nothing for her without help. So taking a lump of barley-sugar from his pocket, which he had bought for her as he came along, and laying it beside her, he left the place, having already made up his mind to go and see the tall gentleman,. Mr. Raymond, and ask him to do something for Sal's Nanny, as the girl was called.

By the time he got up the area-steps, three or four women who had seen him go down were standing together at the top waiting for him. They wanted his clothes for their children; but they did not follow him down lest Sal should find them there. The moment he appeared, they laid their hands on him, and all began talking at once, for each wanted to get some advantage over her neighbours. He told them quite quietly, for he was not frightened, that he had come to see what was the matter with Nanny.

"What do you know about Nanny?" said one of them fiercely. "Wait till old Sal comes home, and you'll catch it, for going prying into her house when she's out. If you don't give me your jacket directly, I'll go and fetch her."

"I can't give you my jacket," said Diamond. "It belongs to my father and mother, you know. It's not mine to give. Is it now? You would not think it right to give away what wasn't yours—would you now?"

"Give it away! No, that I wouldn't; I'd keep it," she said with a rough laugh. "But if the jacket ain't yours, what right have you to keep it? Here, Cherry, make haste. It'll be one go apiece."

They all began to tug at the jacket, while Diamond stooped and kept his arms bent to resist them. Before they had done him or the jacket any harm, however, suddenly they all scampered away; and Diamond, looking in the opposite direction, saw the tall policeman coming towards him.

"You had better have let me come with you, little man," he said, looking down in Diamond's face, which was flushed with his resistance.

"You came just in the right time, thank you," returned Diamond. "They've done me no harm."

"They would have if I hadn't been at hand, though."

"Yes; but you were at hand, you know, so they couldn't."

Perhaps the answer was deeper in purport than either Diamond or the policeman knew. They walked away together, Diamond telling his friend how ill poor Nanny was, and that he was going to let the tall gentleman know. The policeman put him in the nearest way for Bloomsbury, and stepping out in good earnest, Diamond reached Mr. Raymond's door in less than an hour. When he asked if he was at home, the servant, in return, asked what he wanted.

"I want to tell him something."

"But I can't go and trouble him with such a message as that."

"He told me to come to him—that is, when I could read—and I can."

"How am I to know that?"

Diamond stared with astonishment for one moment, then answered:

"Why, I've just told you. That's how you know it."

But this man was made of coarser grain that the policeman, and instead of seeing that Diamond could not tell a lie, he put his answer down as impudence, and saying, "Do you think I'm going to take your word for it?" shut the door in his face.

Diamond turned and sat down on the doorstep, thinking with himself that the tall gentleman must either come in or come out, and he was therefore in the best possible position for finding him. He had not waited long before the door opened again; but when he looked round, it was only the servant once more.

"Get away," he said. "What are you doing on the doorstep?"

"Waiting for Mr. Raymond," answered Diamond, getting up.

"He's not at home."

"Then I'll wait till he comes," returned Diamond, sitting down again with a smile.

What the man would have done next I do not know, but a step sounded from the hall, and when Diamond looked round again, there was the tall gentleman.

"Who's this, John?" he asked.

"I don't know, sir. An imperent little boy as will sit on the doorstep."

"Please, sir," said Diamond, "he told me you weren't at home, and I sat down to wait for you."

"Eh, what!" said Mr. Raymond. "John! John! This won't do. Is it a habit of yours to turn away my visitors? There'll be some one else to turn away, I'm afraid, if I find any more of this kind of thing. Come in, my little man. I suppose you've come to claim your sixpence?"

"No, sir, not that."

"What! can't you read yet?"

"Yes, I can now, a little. But I'll come for that next time. I came to tell you about Sal's Nanny."

"Who's Sal's Nanny?"

"The girl at the crossing you talked to the same day."

"Oh, yes; I remember. What's the matter? Has she got run over?"

Then Diamond told him all.

Now Mr. Raymond was one of the kindest men in London. He sent at once to have the horse put to the brougham, took Diamond with him, and drove to the Children's Hospital. There he was well known to everybody, for he was not only a large subscriber, but he used to go and tell the children stories of an afternoon. One of the doctors promised to go and find Nanny, and do what could be done—have her brought to the hospital, if possible.

That same night they sent a litter for her, and as she could be of no use to old Sal until she was better, she did not object to having her removed. So she was soon lying in the fever ward—for the first time in her life in a nice clean bed. But she knew nothing of the whole affair. She was too ill to know anything.

Chapter XXII
MR. RAYMOND'S RIDDLE

MR. RAYMOND took Diamond home with him, stopping at the Mews to tell his mother that he would send him back soon. Diamond ran in with the message himself, and when he reappeared he had in his hand the torn and crumpled book which North Wind had given him.

"Ah! I see," said Mr. Raymond: "you are going to claim your sixpence now."

"I wasn't thinking of that so much as of another thing," said Diamond. "There's a rhyme in this book I can't quite understand. I want you to tell me what it means, if you please."

"I will if I can," answered Mr. Raymond. "You shall read it to me when we get home, and then I shall see."

Still with a good many blunders, Diamond did read it after a fashion. Mr. Raymond took the little book and read it over again.

Now Mr. Raymond was a poet himself, and so, although he had never been at the back of the north wind, he was able to understand the poem pretty well. But before saying anything about it, he read it over aloud, and Diamond thought he understood it much better already.

"I'll tell you what I think it means," he then said. "It means that people may have their way for a while, if they like, but it will get them into such troubles they'll wish they hadn't had it."

"I know, I know!" said Diamond. "Like the poor cabman next door. He drinks too much."

"Just so," returned Mr. Raymond. "But when people want to do right, things about them will try to help them. Only they must kill the snake, you know."

"I was sure the snake had something to do with it," cried Diamond triumphantly.

A good deal more talk followed, and Mr. Raymond gave Diamond his sixpence.

"What will you do with it?" he asked.

"Take it home to my mother," he answered. "She has a teapot—such a black one!—with a broken spout, and she keeps all her money in it. It ain't much; but she saves it up to buy shoes for me. And there's baby coming on famously, and he'll want shoes soon. And every sixpence is something—ain't it, sir?"

"To be sure, my man. I hope you'll always make as good a use of your money."

"I hope so, sir," said Diamond.

"And here's a book for you, full of pictures and stories and poems. I wrote it myself, chiefly for the children of the hospital where I hope Nanny is going. I don't mean I printed it, you know. I made it," added Mr. Raymond, wishing Diamond to understand that he was the author of the book.

"I know what you mean. I make songs myself. They're awfully silly, but they please baby, and that's all they're meant for."

"Couldn't you let me hear one of them now?" said Mr. Raymond.

"No, sir, I couldn't. I forget them as soon as I've done with them. Besides, I couldn't make a line without baby on my knee. We make them together, you know. They're just as much baby's as mine. It's he that pulls them out of me."

"I suspect the child's a genius," said the poet to himself, "and that's what makes people think him silly."

Now if any of my child readers want to know what a genius is—shall I try to tell them, or shall I not? I will give them one very short answer: it means one who understands things without any other body telling him what they mean. God makes a few such now and then to teach the rest of us.

"Do you like riddles?" asked Mr. Raymond, turning over the leaves of his own book.

"I don't know what a riddle is," said Diamond.

"It's something that means something else, and you've got to find out what the something else is."

Mr. Raymond liked the old-fashioned riddle best, and had written a few—one of which he now read.

I have only one foot, but thousands of toes;
My one foot stands, but never goes.
I have many arms, and they're mighty all;
And hundreds of fingers, large and small.
From the ends of my fingers my beauty grows.
I breathe with my hair, and I drink with my toes.
I grow bigger and bigger about the waist,
And yet I am always very tight laced.
None e'er saw me eat—I've no mouth to bite;
Yet I eat all day in the full sunlight.
In the summer with song I shake and quiver,
But in winter I fast and groan and shiver.

"Do you know what that means, Diamond?" he asked, when he finished.

"No, indeed, I don't," answered Diamond.

"Then you can read it for yourself, and think over it, and see if you can find it out," said Mr. Raymond, giving him the book. "And now you had better go home to your mother. When you've found the riddle, you can come again."

If Diamond had had to find out the riddle in order to see Mr. Raymond again, I doubt if he would ever have seen him.

"Oh then," I think I hear some little reader say, "he could not have been a genius, for a genius finds out things without being told."

I answered, "Genius finds out truths, not tricks." And if you do not understand that, I am afraid you must be content to wait till you grow older and know more.

Chapter XXIII
THE EARLY BIRD

WHEN Diamond got home he found his father at home already, sitting by the fire and looking rather miserable, for his head ached and he felt sick. He had been doing night work of late, and it had not agreed with him, so he had given it up, but not in time, for he had taken some kind of fever. The next day he was forced to keep his bed, and his wife nursed him, and Diamond attended to the baby. If he had not been ill, it would have been delightful to have him at home; and the first day Diamond sang more songs than ever to the baby, and his father listened with some pleasure. But the next he could not bear even Diamond's sweet voice, and was very ill indeed; so Diamond took the baby into his own room, and had no end of quiet games with him there. If he did pull all his bedding on the floor, it did not matter, for he kept baby very quiet, and made the bed himself again, and slept in it with baby all the next night, and many nights after.

But long before his father got well, his mother's savings were all but gone. She did not say a word about it in the hearing of her husband, lest she should distress him; and one night, when she could not help crying, she came into Diamond's room that his father might not hear her. She thought Diamond was asleep, but he was not. When he heard her sobbing, he was frightened, and said—

"Is father worse, mother?"

"No, Diamond," she answered, as well as she could; "he's a good bit better."

"Then what are you crying for, mother?"

"Because my money is almost all gone," she replied.

"O mammy, you make me think of a little poem baby and I learned out of North Wind's book to-day. Don't you remember how I bothered you about some of the words?"

"Yes, child," said his mother heedlessly, thinking only of what she should do after to-morrow.

Diamond began and repeated the poem, for he had a wonderful memory.

A little bird sat on the edge of her nest;
  Her yellow-beaks slept as sound as tops;
That day she had done her very best,
  And had filled every one of their little crops.
She had filled her own just over-full,
And hence she was feeling a little dull.

'Oh dear!' she sighed, as she sat with her head
  Sunk in her chest, and no neck at all,
While her crop stuck out like a feather bed
  Turned inside out, and rather small;
'What shall I do if things don't reform?
I don't know where there's a single worm.

'I've had twenty to-day, and the children five each,
  Besides a few flies, and some very fat spiders;
No one will say I don't do as I preach—
  I'm not of the best of bird-providers;
But where's the use? We want a storm—
I don't know where there's a single worm.'

'There's five in my crop,' said a wee, wee bird,
   Which woke at the voice of his mother's pain;
'I know where there's five.' And with the word
   He tucked in his head, and went off again.
'The folly of childhood,' sighed his mother,
'Has always been my especial bother.'

The yellow-beaks they slept on and on—
   And never had heard of the bogy To-morrow;
But the mother sat outside, making her moan—
   She'll soon have to beg, or steal, or borrow;
For she never can tell the night before
Where she shall find one red worm more.

The fact, as I say, was, she'd had too many;
   She couldn't sleep, and she called it virtue,
Motherly foresight, affection, any
   Name you may call it that will not hurt you;
So it was late ere she tucked her head in,
And she slept so late it was almost a sin.

But the little fellow who knew of five,
   Nor troubled his head about any more,
Woke very early, felt quite alive,
   And wanted a sixth to add to his store;
He pushed his mother, the greedy elf,
Then thought he had better try for himself.

When his mother awoke and had rubbed her eyes,
   Feeling less like a bird, and more like a mole,
She saw him—fancy with what surprise—
   Dragging a huge worm out of a hole!
'Twas of his same hero the proverb took form:
'Tis the early bird that catches the worm.

  "There, mother!" said Diamond, as he finished; "ain't it
funny?"

"I wish you were like that little bird, Diamond, and could catch worms for yourself," said his mother, as she rose to go and look after her husband.

Diamond lay awake for a few minutes, thinking what he could to do to catch worms. It was very little trouble to make up his mind, however, and still less to go to sleep after it.

Chapter XXIV
ANOTHER EARLY BIRD

H E got up in the morning as soon as he heard the men moving in the yard. He tucked in his little brother so that he could not tumble out of bed, and then went out, leaving the door open, so that if he should cry his mother might hear him at once. When he got into the yard he found the stable-door just opened.

"I'm the early bird, I think," he said to himself. "I hope I shall catch the worm."

He would not ask any one to help him, fearing his project might meet with disapproval and opposition. With great difficulty, but with the help of a broken chair he brought down from his bedroom, he managed to put the harness on Diamond. If the old horse had had the least objection to the proceeding, of course he could not have done it; but even when it came to the bridle, he opened his mouth for the bit, just as if he had been taking the apple which Diamond sometimes gave him. He fastened the cheek-strap very carefully, just in the usual hole, for fear of choking his friend, or else letting the bit get amongst his teeth. It was a job to get the saddle on; but with the chair he managed it. If old Diamond had had an education in physics to equal that of the camel, he would have knelt down to let him put it on his back, but that was more than could be expected of him, and then Diamond had to creep quite under him to get hold of the girth. The collar was almost the worst part of the business; but there Diamond could help Diamond. He held his head very low till his little master had got it over and turned it round, and then he lifted his head, and shook it on to his shoulders. The yoke was rather difficult; but when he had laid the traces over the horse's neck, the weight was not too much for him. He got him right at last, and led him out of the stable.

By this time there were several of the men watching him, but they would not interfere, they were so anxious to see how he would get over the various difficulties. They followed him as far as the stable-door, and there stood watching him again as he put the horse between the shafts, got them up one after the other into the loops, fastened the traces, the belly-band, the breeching, and the reins.

Then he got his whip. The moment he mounted the box, the men broke into a hearty cheer of delight at his success. But they would not let him go without a general inspection of the harness; and although they found it right, for not a buckle had to be shifted, they never allowed him to do it for himself again all the time his father was ill.

The cheer brought his mother to the window, and there she saw her little boy setting out alone with the cab in the gray of the morning. She tugged at the window, but it was stiff; and before she could open it, Diamond, who was in a great hurry, was out of the mews, and almost out of the street. She called, "Diamond! Diamond!" but there was no answer except from Jack.

"Never fear for him, ma'am," said Jack. "It'ud be only a devil as would hurt him, and there ain't so many o' them as some folk 'ud have you believe. A boy o' Diamond's size as can 'arness a 'oss o' t'other Diamond's size, and put him to, right as a trivet—if he do upset the keb—'ll fall on *his* feet, ma'am."

"But he won't upset the cab, will he, Jack?"

"Not he, ma'am. Leastways, he won't go for to do it."

"I know as much as that myself. What do you mean?"

"I mean he's as little likely to do it as the oldest man in the stable. How's the gov'nor to-day, ma'am?"

"A good deal better, thank you," she answered, closing the window in some fear lest her husband should have been made anxious by the news of Diamond's expedition. He knew pretty well, however, what his boy was capable of, and although not quite easy was less anxious than his mother. But as the evening drew on, the anxiety of both of them increased, and every sound of wheels made his father raise himself in his bed, and his mother peep out of the window.

Diamond had resolved to go straight to the cabstand where he was best known, and never to crawl for fear of getting annoyed by idlers. Before he got across Oxford Street, however, he was hailed by a man who wanted to catch a train, and was in too great a hurry to think about the driver. Having carried him to King's Cross in good time, and got a good fare in return, he set off again in great spirits, and reached the stand in safety. He was the first there after all.

As the men arrived they all greeted him kindly, and inquired after his father.

"Ain't you afraid of the old 'oss running away with you?" asked one.

"No, he wouldn't run away with *me*," answered Diamond. "He knows I'm getting the shillings for father. Or if he did he would only run home."

"Well, you're a plucky one, for all your girl's looks!" said the man; "and I wish ye luck."

"Thank you, sir," said Diamond. "I'll do what I can. I came to the old place, you see, because I knew you would let me have my turn here."

In the course of the day one man did try to cut him out,

but he was a stranger; and the shout the rest of them raised let him see it would not do, and made him so far ashamed besides, that he went away crawling.

Once, in a block, a policeman came up to him, and asked him for his number. Diamond showed him his father's badge, saying with a smile:

"Father's ill at home, and so I came out with the cab. There's no fear of me. I can drive. Besides, the old horse could go alone."

"Just as well, I dare say. You're a pair of 'em. But you *are* a rum 'un for a cabby—ain't you now?" said the policeman. "I don't know as I ought to let you go."

"I ain't done nothing," said Diamond. "It's not my fault I'm no bigger. I'm big enough for my age."

"That's where it is," said the man. "You ain't fit."

"How do you know that?" asked Diamond, with his usual smile, and turning his head like a little bird.

"Why, how are you to get out of this ruck now, when it begins to move?"

"Just you get up on the box," said Diamond, "and I'll show you. There, that van's a-moving now. Jump up."

The policeman did as Diamond told him, and was soon satisfied that the little fellow could drive.

"Well," he said, as he got down again, "I don't know as I should be right to interfere. Good luck to you, my little man!"

"Thank you, sir," said Diamond, and drove away.

In a few minutes a gentleman hailed him.

"Are you the driver of this cab?" he asked.

"Yes, sir," said Diamond, showing his badge, of which he was proud.

"You're the youngest cabman I ever saw. How am I to know you won't break all my bones?"

"I would rather break all my own," said Diamond. "But if you're afraid, never mind me; I shall soon get another fare."

"I'll risk it," said the gentleman; and, opening the door himself, he jumped in.

He was a going a good distance, and soon found that Diamond got him over the ground well. Now when Diamond had only to go straight ahead, and had not to mind so much what he was about, his thoughts always turned to the riddle Mr. Raymond had set him; and this gentleman looked so clever that he fancied he must be able to read it for him. He had given up all hope of finding it out for himself, and he could not plague his father about it when he was ill. He had thought of the answer himself, but fancied it could not be the right one, for to see how it all fitted required some knowledge of physiology. So, when he reached the end of his journey, he got down very quickly, and with his head just looking in at the window, said, as the gentleman gathered his gloves and newspapers:

"Please, sir, can you tell me the meaning of a riddle?"

"You must tell me the riddle first," answered the gentleman, amused.

Diamond repeated the riddle.

"Oh! that's easy enough," he returned. "It's a tree."

"Well, it ain't got no mouth, sure enough; but how then does it eat all day long?"

"It sucks in its food through the tiniest holes in its leaves," he answered. "It's breath is its food. And it can't do it except in the daylight."

"Thank you, sir, thank you," returned Diamond. "I'm sorry I couldn't find it out myself; Mr. Raymond would have been better pleased with me."

"But you needn't tell him any one told you."

Diamond gave him a stare which came from the very back of the north wind, where that kind of thing is unknown.

"That would be cheating," he said at last.

"Ain't you a cabby, then?"

"Cabbies don't cheat."

"Don't they? I am of a different opinion."

"I'm sure my father don't."

"What's you fare, young innocent?"

"Well, I think the distance is a good deal over three

miles—that's two shillings. Only father says sixpence a
mile is too little, though we can't ask for more."

"You're a deep one. But I think you're wrong. It's over
four miles—not much, but it is."

"Then that's half-a-crown," said Diamond.

"Well, here's three shillings. Will that do?"

"Thank you kindly, sir. I'll tell my father how good you
were to me—first to tell me my riddle, then to put me
right about the distance, and then to give me sixpence
over. It'll help father to get well again, it will."

"I hope it may, my man. I shouldn't wonder if you're as
good as you look, after all."

As Diamond returned, he drew up at a stand he had never
been on before: it was time to give Diamond his bag of
chopped beans and oats. The men got about him, and began
to chaff him. He took it all good-humouredly, until one of
them, who was an ill-conditioned fellow, began to tease old
Diamond by poking him roughly in the ribs, and making
general game of him. That he could not bear, and the tears
came to his eyes. He undid the nose-bag, put it in the boot,
and was just going to mount and drive away, when the fellow interfered, and would not let him get up. Diamond en-
deavored to persuade him, and was very civil, but he would
have his fun out of him, as he said. In a few minutes a
group of idle boys had assembled, and Diamond found himself in a very uncomfortable position. Another cab drew up
at the stand, and the driver got off and approached the as-
semblage.

"What's up here?" he asked, and Diamond knew the
voice. It was that of the drunken cabman.

"Do you see this young oyster? He pretends to drive a
cab," said his enemy.

"Yes, I do see him. And I sees you too. You'd better
leave him alone. He ain't no oyster. He's an angel come
down on his own business. You be off, or I'll be nearer
you than quite agreeable."

The drunken cabman was a tall, stout man, who did not
look one to take liberties with.

"Oh! if he's a friend of yours," said the other, drawing back.

Diamond got out the nose-bag again. Old Diamond should have his feed out now.

"Yes, he is a friend o' mine. One o' the best I ever had. It's a pity he ain't a friend o' yourn. You'd be the better for it, but it ain't no fault of hisn."

When Diamond went home at night, he carried with him one pound one shilling and sixpence, besides a few coppers extra, which had followed some of the fares.

His mother had got very anxious indeed—so much so that she was almost afraid, when she did hear the sound of his cab, to go and look, lest she should be again disappointed, and should break down before her husband. But there was the old horse, and there was the cab all right, and there was Diamond on the box, his pale face looking triumphant as a full moon in the twilight.

When he drew up at the stable-door, Jack came out, and after a good many friendly questions and congratulations, said:

"You go in to your mother, Diamond. I'll put up the old 'oss. I'll take care on him. He do deserve some small attention, he do."

"Thank you, Jack," said Diamond, and bounded into the house, and into the arms of his mother, who was waiting for him at the top of the stair.

The poor, anxious woman led him into his own room, sat down on his bed, took him on her lap as if he had been a baby, and cried.

"How's father?" asked Diamond, almost afraid to ask.

"Better, my child," she answered, "but uneasy about you, my dear."

"Didn't you tell him I was the early bird gone out to catch the worm?"

"*That* was what put it in your head, was it, you monkey?" said his mother, beginning to get better.

"That or something else," answered Diamond, so very

quietly that his mother held his head back and stared in his face.

"Well! of all children!" she said, and said no more.

"And here's my worm," resumed Diamond.

But to see her face as he poured the shillings and six-pences and pence into her lap! She burst out crying a second time, and ran with the money to her husband.

And how pleased he was! It did him no end of good. But while he was counting the coins, Diamond turned to baby, who was lying awake in his cradle, sucking his precious thumb, and took him up, saying:

"Baby, baby! I haven't seen you for a whole year."

And then he began to sing to him as usual. And what he sang was this, for he was too happy either to make a song of his own or to sing sense. It was one out of Mr. Raymond's book.

THE TRUE HISTORY OF THE CAT AND THE FIDDLE

> Hey, diddle, diddle!
> The cat and the fiddle!
> He played such a merry tune,
> That the cow went mad
> With the pleasure she had,
> And jumped right over the moon.
> But then, don't you see?
> Before that could be,
> The moon had come down and listened.
> The little dog hearkened,
> So loud that he barkened,
> "There's nothing like it, there isn't."
>
> Hey, diddle, diddle!
> Went the cat and the fiddle,
> Hey diddle, diddle, dee, dee!
> The dog laughed at the sport
> Till his cough cut him short,
> It was hey diddle, diddle, oh me!

  And back came the cow
  With a merry, merry low,
For she'd humbled the man in the moon.
  The dish got excited,
  The spoon was delighted,
And the dish waltzed away with the spoon.

  But the man in the moon,
  Coming back too soon
From the famous town of Norwich,
  Caught up the dish,
  Said, "It's just what I wish
To hold my cold plum-porridge!"
  Gave the cow a rat-tat,
  Flung water on the cat,
And sent him away like a rocket.
  Said, "O Moon, there you are!"
  Got into her car,
And went off with the spoon in his pocket.

  Hey ho! diddle, diddle!
  The wet cat and wet fiddle,
They made such a caterwauling,
  That the cow in a fright
  Stood bolt upright
Bellowing now, and bawling;
  And the dog on his tail,
  Stretched his neck with a wail.
But "Ho! ho!" said the man in the moon—
  "No more in the South
  Shall I burn my mouth,
For I've found a dish and a spoon."

Chapter XXV
DIAMOND'S DREAM

"THERE, baby!" said Diamond; "I'm so happy that I can only sing nonsense. Oh, father, think if you had been a poor man, and hadn't had a cab and old Diamond! What should I have done?"

"I don't know indeed what you could have done," said his father from the bed.

"We should have all starved, my precious Diamond," said his mother, whose pride in her boy was even greater than her joy in the shillings. Both of them together made her heart ache, for pleasure can do that as well as pain.

"Oh no! we shouldn't," said Diamond. "I could have taken Nanny's crossing 'till she came back; and then the money, instead of going for Old Sal's gin, would have gone for father's beef-tea. I wonder what Nanny will do when she gets well again. Somebody else will be sure to have taken the crossing by that time. I wonder if she will fight for it, and whether I shall have to help her. I won't bother my head about that. Time enough yet! Hey diddle! hey diddle! hey diddle diddle! I wonder whether Mr.

Raymond would take me to see Nanny. Hey diddle! hey diddle! hey diddle diddle! The baby and fiddle! O, mother, I'm such a silly! But I can't help it. I wish I could think of something else, but there's nothing will come into my head but *hey diddle diddle! the cat and the fiddle!* I wonder what the angels do—when they're extra happy, you know—when they've been driving cabs all day and taking home the money to their mothers. Do you think they ever sing nonsense, mother?"

"I dare say they've got their own sort of it," answered his mother, "else they wouldn't be like other people."

She was thinking more of her twenty-one shillings and six pence, and of the nice dinner she would get for her sick husband next day, than of the angels and their nonsense, when she said it. But Diamond found her answer all right.

"Yes, to be sure," he replied. "They wouldn't be like other people it they hadn't their nonsense sometimes. But it must be very pretty nonsense, and not like that silly hey diddle diddle! the cat and the fiddle! I wish I could get it out of my head. I wonder what the angels' nonsense is like. Nonsense is a very good thing, ain't it, mother?—a little of it now and then; more of it for baby, and not so much for grown people like cabmen and their mothers? It's like the pepper and salt that goes in the soup—that's it—isn't it, mother? There's baby fast asleep! Oh, what a nonsense baby it is—to sleep so much! Shall I put him down, mother?"

Diamond chattered away. What rose in his happy little heart ran out of his mouth, and did his father and mother good. When he went to bed, which he did early, being more tired, as you may suppose, than usual, he was still thinking what the nonsense could be like which the angels sang when they were too happy to sing sense. But before coming to any conclusion he fell fast asleep. And no wonder, for it must be acknowledged a difficult question.

That night he had a very curious dream which I think my readers would like to have told them. They would, at least, if they are as fond of nice dreams as I am, and don't have enough of them of their own.

He dreamed that he was running about in the twilight in the old garden. He thought he was waiting for North Wind, but she did not come. So he would run down to the back gate, and see if she were there. He ran and ran. It was a good long garden out of his dream, but in his dream it had grown so long and spread out so wide that the gate he wanted was nowhere. He ran and ran, but instead of coming to the gate found himself in a beautiful country, not like any country he had even been in before. There were no trees of any size; nothing bigger in fact than hawthorns, which were full of may-blossom. The place in which they grew was wild and dry, mostly covered with grass, but having patches of heath. It extended on every side as far as he could see. But although it was so wild, yet wherever in an ordinary heath you might have expected furze bushes, or holly, or broom, there grew roses—wild and rare—all kinds. On every side, far and near, roses were glowing. There too was the gum-cistus, whose flowers fall every night and come again the next morning, lilacs and syringas and laburnums, and many shrubs besides, of which he did not know the names; but the roses were everywhere. He wandered on and on, wondering when it would come to an end. It was of no use going back, for there was no house to be seen anywhere. But he was not frightened, for you know Diamond was used to things that were rather out of the way. He threw himself down under a rose-bush, and fell asleep.

He woke, not out of his dream, but into it, thinking he heard a child's voice, calling "Diamond, Diamond!" He jumped up, but all was still about him. The rose-bushes were pouring out their odors in clouds. He could see the scent like mists of the same color as the rose, issuing like a slow fountain and spreading in the air till it joined the thin rosy vapor which hung over all the wilderness. But again came the voice calling him, and it seemed to come from over his head. He looked up, but saw only the deep

blue sky full of stars—more brilliant, however, than he had
seen them before; and both sky and stars looked nearer to
the earth.

While he gazed up, again he heard the cry. At the same
moment he saw one of the biggest stars over his head give
a kind of twinkle and jump, as if it went out and came in
again. He threw himself on his back, and fixed his eyes
upon it. Nor had he gazed long before it went out, leaving
something like a scar in the blue. But as he went on gazing
he saw a face where the star had been—a merry face, with
bright eyes. The eyes appeared not only to see Diamond,
but to know that Diamond had caught sight of them, for the
face withdrew the same moment. Again came the voice,
calling "Diamond, Diamond"; and in jumped the star to its
place.

Diamond called as loud as he could, right up into the
sky:

"Here's Diamond, down below you. What do you want
him to do?"

The next instant many of the stars round about that one
went out, and many voices shouted from the sky,—

"Come up; come up. We're so jolly! Diamond! Diamond!"

This was followed by a peal of the merriest, kindliest
laughter, and all the stars jumped into their places again.

"How am I to come up?" shouted Diamond.

"Go round the rose-bush. It's got its foot in it," said the
first voice.

Diamond got up at once, and walked to the other side of
the rose-bush.

There he found what seemed the very opposite of what
he wanted—a stair down into the earth. It was of turf and
moss. It did not seem to promise well for getting into the
sky, but Diamond had learned to look through the look of
things. The voice must have meant that he was to go down
this stair; and down this stair Diamond went, without waiting to think more about it.

It was such a nice stair, so cool and soft—all the sides

as well as the steps grown with moss and grass and ferns! Down and down Diamond went—a long way, until at last he heard the gurgling and splashing of a little stream; nor had he gone much farther before he met it—yes, met it coming up the stairs to meet him, running up just as naturally as if it had been doing the other thing. Neither was Diamond in the least surprised to see it pitching itself from one step to another as it climbed towards him; he never thought it was odd—and no more it was, there. It would have been odd here. It made a merry tune as it came, and its voice was like the laughter he had heard from the sky. This appeared promising; and he went on, down and down the stair, and up and up the stream, till at last he came where it hurried out from under a stone, and the stair stopped altogether. And as the stream bubbled up, the stone shook and swayed with its force; and Diamond thought he would try to lift it. Lightly it rose to his hand, forced up by the stream from below; and, by what would have seemed an unaccountable perversion of things had he been awake, threatened to come tumbling upon his head. But he avoided it, and when it fell, got upon it. He now saw that the opening through which the water came pouring in was over his head, and with the help of the stone he scrambled out by it, and found himself on the side of a grassy hill which rounded away from him in every direction, and down which came the brook which vanished in the hole. But scarcely had he noticed so much as this before a merry shouting and laughter burst upon him, and a number of naked little boys came running, every one eager to get to him first. At the shoulders of each fluttered two little wings, which were of no use for flying, as they were mere buds; only being made for it they could not help fluttering as if they were flying. Just as the foremost of the troop reached him, one or two of them fell, and the rest with shouts of laughter came tumbling over them till they heaped up a mound of struggling merriment. One after another they extricated themselves, and each as he got free threw his arms round Diamond and kissed him. Diamond's heart was ready to melt within him from clear delight. When they had all embraced him,—

"Now let us have some fun," cried one, and with a shout they all scampered hither and thither, and played the wildest gambols on the grassy slopes. They kept constantly coming back to Diamond, however, as the centre of their enjoyment, rejoicing over him as if they had found a lost playmate.

There was a wind on the hillside which blew like the very embodiment of living gladness. It blew into Diamond's heart, and made him so happy that he was forced to sit down and cry.

"Now let's go and dig for stars," said one who seemed to be the captain of the troop.

They all scurried away, but soon returned, one after another, each with a pickaxe on his shoulder and a spade in his hand. As soon as they were gathered, the captain led them in a straight line to another part of the hill. Diamond rose and followed.

"Here is where we begin our lesson for to-night," he said. "Scatter and dig."

There was no more fun. Each went by himself, walking slowly with bent shoulders and his eyes fixed on the ground. Every now and then one would stop, kneel down, and look intently, feeling with his hands and parting the grass. One would get up and walk on again, another spring to his feet, catch eagerly at his pickaxe and strike it into the ground once and again, then throw it aside, snatch up his spade, and commence digging at the loosened earth. Now one would sorrowfully shovel the earth into the hole again, trample it down with his little bare white feet, and walk on. But another would give a joyful shout, and after much tugging and loosening would draw from the hole a lump as big as his head, or no bigger than his fist; when the under side of it would pour such a blaze of golden or bluish light into Diamond's eyes that he was quite dazzled. Gold and blue were the commoner colors: the jubilation was greater over red or green or purple. And every time a star was dug up all the little angels dropped their tools and crowded about it, shouting and dancing and fluttering their wing-buds.

When they had examined it well, they would kneel down one after the other and peep through the hole; but they always stood back to give Diamond the first look. All that Diamond could report, however, was, that through the star-holes he saw a great many things and places and people he knew quite well, only somehow they were different—there was something marvellous about them—he could not tell what. Every time he rose from looking through a star-hole, he felt as if his heart would break for joy; and he said that if he had not cried, he did not know what would have become of him.

As soon as all had looked, the star was carefully fitted in again, a little mould was strewn over it, and the rest of the heap left as a sign that that star had been discovered.

At length one dug up a small star of a most lovely colour—a colour Diamond had never seen before. The moment the angel saw what it was, instead of showing it about, he handed it to one of his neighbours, and seated himself on the edge of the hole, saying:

"This will do for me. Good-bye. I'm off."

They crowded about him, hugging and kissing him; then stood back with a solemn stillness, their wings lying close to their shoulders. The little fellow looked round on them once with a smile, and then shot himself headlong through the starhole. Diamond, as privileged, threw himself on the ground to peep after him, but he saw nothing.

"It's no use," said the captain. "I never saw anything more of one that went that way."

"His wings can't be much use," said Diamond, concerned and fearful, yet comforted by the calm looks of the rest.

"That's true," said the captain. "He's lost them by this time. They all do that go that way. You haven't got any, you see."

"No," said Diamond. "I never did have any."

"Oh! didn't you?" said the captain.

"Some people say," he added, after a pause, "that they come again. I don't know. I've never found the color I care about myself. I suppose I shall some day."

Then they looked again at the star, put it carefully into its hole, danced round it and over it—but solemnly, and called it by the name of the finder.

"Will you know it again?" asked Diamond.

"Oh yes. We never forget a star that's been made a door of."

Then they went on with their searching and digging.

Diamond having neither pickaxe nor spade, had the more time to think.

"I don't see any little girls," he said at last.

The captain stopped his shovelling, leaned on his spade, rubbed his forehead thoughtfully with his left hand—the little angels were all left-handed—repeated the words "little girls," and then, as if a thought had struck him, resumed his work, saying—

"I think I know what you mean. I've never seen any of them, of course; but I suppose that's the sort you mean. I'm told—but mind I don't say it is so, for I don't know—that when we fall asleep, a troop of angels very like ourselves, only quite different, goes round to all the stars we have discovered, and discovers them after us. I suppose with our shovelling and handling we spoil them a bit; and I dare say the clouds that come up from below make them smoky and dull sometimes. They say—mind, I say *they say*—these other angels take them out one by one, and pass each round as we do, and breathe over it, and rub it with their white hands, which are softer than ours, because they don't do any pick-and-spade work, and smile at it, and put it in again; and that is what keeps them from growing dark."

"How jolly!" thought Diamond. "I should like to see *them* at their work too.—When do you go to sleep?" he asked the captain.

"When we grow sleepy," answered the captain. "They

do say—but mind I say *they say*—that it is when those others—what do you call them? I don't know if that is their name; I am only guessing that may be the sort you mean—when they are on their rounds and come near any troop of us we fall asleep. They live on the west side of the hill. None of *us* have ever been to the top of it yet."

Even as he spoke, he dropped his spade. He tumbled down beside it, and lay fast asleep. One after the other each of the troop dropped his pickaxe or shovel from his listless hands, and lay fast asleep by his work.

"Ah!" thought Diamond to himself, with delight, "now the girl-angels are coming, and I, not being an angel, shall not fall asleep like the rest, and I shall see the girl-angels."

But the same moment he felt himself growing sleepy. He struggled hard with the invading power. He put up his fingers to his eyelids and pulled them open. But it was of no use. He thought he saw a glimmer of pale rosy light far up the green hill, and ceased to know.

When he awoke, all the angels were starting up wide awake too. He expected to see them lift their tools, but no, the time for play had come. They looked happier than ever, and each began to sing where he stood. He had not heard them sing before.

"Now," he thought, "I shall know what kind of nonsense the angles sing when they are merry. They don't drive cabs, I see, but they dig for stars, and they work hard enough to be merry after it."

And he did hear some of the angels' nonsense; for if it was all sense to them, it had only just as much sense to Diamond as made good nonsense of it. He tried hard to set it down in his mind, listening as closely as he could, now to one, now to another, and now to all together. But while they were yet singing he began, to his dismay, to find that he was coming awake—faster and faster. And as he came awake, he found that, for all the goodness of his memory, verse after verse of the angels' nonsense vanished from it. He always thought he could keep the last, but as the next began he lost the one before it, and at length awoke, struggling to keep hold of the last verse of all. He felt as if the effort to keep from forgetting that one verse of the vanishing song nearly killed him. And yet by the time he was wide awake he could not be sure of that even. It was something like this:

> White hands of whiteness
>   Wash the stars' faces,
> Till glitter, glitter, glit, goes their brightness
>   Down to poor places.

This, however, was so near sense that he thought it could not be really what they did sing.

Chapter XXVI
DIAMOND TAKES A FARE THE WRONG
WAY RIGHT

THE next morning Diamond was up almost as early as before. He had nothing to fear from his mother now, and made no secret of what he was about. By the time he reached the stable, several of the men were there. They asked him a good many questions as to his luck the day before, and he told them all they wanted to know. But when he proceeded to harness the old horse, they pushed him aside with rough kindness, called him a baby, and began to do it all for him. So Diamond ran in and had another mouthful of tea and bread and butter; and although he had never been so tired as he was the night before, he started quite fresh this morning. It was a cloudy day, and the wind blew hard from the north—so hard sometimes that, perched on the box with just his toes touching the ground, Diamond wished that he had some kind of strap to fasten himself down with lest he should be blown away. But he did not really mind it.

His head was full of the dream he had dreamed; but it did not make him neglect his work, for his work was not to dig stars but to drive old Diamond and pick up fares. There are not many people who can think about beautiful things and do common work at the same time. But then there are not many people who have been to the back of the north wind.

There was not much business doing. And Diamond felt rather cold, notwithstanding his mother had herself put on his comforter and helped him with his greatcoat. But he was too well aware of his dignity to get inside his cab as some do. A cabman ought to be above minding the weather—at least so Diamond thought. At length he was called to a neighbouring house, where a young woman with a heavy box had to be taken to Wapping for a coast-steamer.

He did not find it at all pleasant, so far east and so near the river; for the roughs were in great force. However, there being no block, not even in Nightingale Lane, he reached the entrance of the wharf, and set down his passenger without annoyance. But as he turned to go back, some idlers, not content with chaffing him, showed a mind to the fare the young woman had given him. They were just pulling him off the box, and Diamond was shouting for the police, when a pale-faced man, in very shabby clothes, but with the look of a gentleman somewhere about him, came up, and making good use of his stick, drove them off.

"Now, my little man," he said, "get on while you can. Don't lose any time. This is not a place for you."

But Diamond was not in the habit of thinking only of himself. He saw that his new friend looked weary, if not ill, and very poor.

"Won't you jump in, sir?" he said. "I will take you wherever you like."

"Thank you, my man; but I have no money; so I can't."

"Oh! I don't want any money. I shall be much happier if you will get in. You have saved me all I had. I owe you a lift, sir."

"Which way are you going?"

"To Charing Cross; but I don't mind where I go."

"Well, I am very tired. If you will take me to Charing Cross, I shall be greatly obliged to you. I have walked from Gravesend, and had hardly a penny left to get through the tunnel."

So saying, he opened the door and got in, and Diamond drove away.

But as he drove he could not help fancying he had seen the gentleman—for Diamond knew he was a gentleman—before. Do all he could, however, he could not recall where or when. Meantime his fare, if we may call him such, seeing he was to pay nothing, whom the relief of being carried had made less and less inclined to carry himself, had been turning over things in his mind, and, as they passed the Mint, called to Diamond, who stopped his horse, got down, and went to the window.

"If you didn't mind taking me to Chiswick, I should be able to pay you when we got there. It's a long way, but you shall have the whole fare from the Docks—and something over."

"Very well, sir," said Diamond. "I shall be most happy."

He was just climbing up again, when the gentleman put his head out of the window and said—

"It's The Wilderness—Mr. Coleman's place; but I'll direct you when we come into the neighbourhood."

It flashed upon Diamond who he was. But he got upon his box to arrange his thoughts before making any reply.

The gentleman was Mr. Evans, to whom Miss Coleman was to have been married, and Diamond had seen him several times with her in the garden. I have said that he had not behaved very well to Miss Coleman. He had put off their marriage more than once in a cowardly fashion, merely because he was ashamed to marry upon a small income, and live in a humble way. When a man thinks of what people will say in such a case, he may love, but his love is but a poor affair. Mr. Coleman took him into the firm as a junior partner, and it was in a measure through his influence that he entered upon those speculations which ruined him. So his love had not been a blessing. The ship which North Wind had sunk was their last venture, and Mr. Evans had gone out with it in the hope of turning its cargo to the best advantage. He was one of the single boat-load which managed to reach a desert island, and he had gone through a great many hardships and sufferings since then. But he was not past being taught, and his troubles had done him no end of good, for they had made him doubt himself, and begin to think, so that he had come to see that he had been foolish as well as wicked. For, if he had had Miss Coleman with him in the desert island, to build her a hut, and hunt for her food, and make clothes for her, he would have thought himself the most fortunate of men; and when he was at home, he would not marry till he could afford a man-servant. Before he got home again, he had even begun to understand that no man can make haste to be rich without going against the will of God, in which case it is the one frightful thing to be successful. So he had come back a more humble man, and longing to ask Miss Coleman to forgive him. But he had no idea what ruin had fallen upon them, for he had never made himself thoroughly acquainted with the firm's affairs. Few speculative people do know their own affairs. Hence he never doubted he should find matters much as he left them, and expected to see them all at The Wilderness as before. But if he had not fallen in with Diamond, he would not have thought of going there first.

What was Diamond to do? He had heard his father and mother drop some remarks concerning Mr. Evans which made him doubtful of him. He understood that he had not been so considerate as he might have been. So he went rather slowly till he should make up his mind. It was, of course, of no use to drive Mr. Evans to Chiswick. But if he should tell him what had befallen them, and where they lived now, he might put off going to see them, and he was certain that Miss Coleman, at least, must want very much to see Mr. Evans. He was pretty sure also that the best thing in any case was to bring them together, and let them set matters right for themselves.

The moment he came to this conclusion, he changed his course from westward to northward, and went straight for Mr. Coleman's poor little house in Hoxton. Mr. Evans was too tired and too much occupied with his thoughts to take the least notice of the streets they passed through, and had no suspicion, therefore, of the change of direction.

By this time the wind had increased almost to a hurricane, and as they had often to head it, it was no joke for either of the Diamonds. The distance, however, was not great. Before they reached the street where Mr. Coleman lived it blew so tremendously, that when Miss Coleman, who was going out a little way, opened the door, it dashed against the wall with such a bang, that she was afraid to venture, and went in again. In five minutes after, Diamond drew up at the door. As soon as he had entered the street, however, the wind blew right behind them, and when he pulled up, old Diamond had so much ado to stop the cab against it, that the breeching broke. Young Diamond jumped off his box, knocked loudly at the door, then turned to the cab and said—before Mr. Evans had quite begun to think something must be amiss:

"Please, sir, my harness has given way. Would you mind stepping in here for a few minutes? They're friends of mine. I'll take you where you like after I've got it mended. I shan't be many minutes, but you can't stand in this wind."

Half stupid with fatigue and want of food Mr. Evans yielded to the boy's suggestion, and walked in at the door which the maid held with difficulty against the wind. She took Mr. Evans for a visitor, as indeed he was, and showed him into the room on the ground-floor. Diamond, who had followed into the hall, whispered to her as she closed the door—

"Tell Miss Coleman. It's Miss Coleman he wants to see."

"I don't know," said the maid. "He don't look much like a gentleman."

"He is, though; and I know him, and so does Miss Coleman."

The maid could not but remember Diamond, having seen him when he and his father brought the ladies home. So she believed him, and went to do what he told her.

What passed in the little parlour when Miss Coleman came down does not belong to my story, which is all about Diamond. If he had known that Miss Coleman thought Mr. Evans was dead, perhaps he would have managed it differently. There was a cry and a running to and fro in the house, and then all was quiet again.

Almost as soon as Mr. Evans went in, the wind began to cease, and was now still. Diamond found that by making the breeching just a little tighter than was quite comfortable for the old horse he could do very well for the present; and, thinking it better to let him have his bag in this quiet place, he sat on the box till the old horse should have eaten his dinner. In a little while Mr. Evans came out, and asked him to come in. Diamond obeyed, and to his delight Miss Coleman put her arms round him and kissed him, and there was payment for him! not to mention the five precious shillings she gave him, which he could not refuse because his mother wanted them so much at home for his father. He left them nearly as happy as they were themselves.

The rest of the day he did better, and, although he had not so much to take home as the day before, yet on the whole the result was satisfactory. And what a story he had to tell his father and mother about his adventures, and how he had done, and what was the result! They asked him such a multitude of questions! some of which he could answer, and some of which he could not answer; and his father seemed ever so much better from finding that his boy was already not only useful to his family but useful to other people, and quite taking his place as a man who judged what was wise, and did work worth doing.

For a fortnight Diamond went on driving his cab, and keeping his family. He had begun to be known about some parts of London, and people would prefer taking his cab because they liked what they heard of him. One gentleman who lived near the mews, engaged him to carry him to the City every morning at a certain hour; and Diamond was punctual as clockwork—though to effect that, required a good deal of care, for his father's watch was not much to be depended on, and had to be watched itself by the clock of St. George's church. Between the two, however, he did make a success of it.

After that fortnight, his father was able to go out again. Then Diamond went to make inquiries about Nanny, and this led to something else.

Chapter XXVII
THE CHILDREN'S HOSPITAL

THE first day his father resumed his work, Diamond went with him as usual. In the afternoon, however, his father, having taken a fare to the neighbourhood, went home, and Diamond drove the cab the rest of the day. It was hard for old Diamond to do all the work, but they could not afford to have another horse. They contrived to save him as much as possible, and fed him well, and he did bravely.

The next morning his father was so much stronger that Diamond thought he might go and ask Mr. Raymond to take him to see Nanny. He found him at home. His servant had grown friendly by this time, and showed him in without any cross-questioning. Mr. Raymond received him with his usual kindness, consented at once, and walked with him to the Hospital, which was close at hand. It was a comfortable old-fashioned house, built in the reign of Queen Anne, and in her day, no doubt, inhabited by rich and fashionable people; now it was a home for poor sick children, who were carefully tended for love's sake. There are regions in London where a hospital in every other street might be full of such children, whose fathers and mothers are dead, or unable to take care of them.

When Diamond followed Mr. Raymond into the room where those children who had got over the worst of their illness and were growing better lay, he saw a number of little iron bedsteads, with their heads to the walls, and in every one of them a child, whose face was a story in itself. In some, health had begun to appear in a tinge upon the cheeks, and a doubtful brightness in the eyes, just as out of the cold dreary winter the spring comes in blushing buds and bright crocuses. In others there were more of the signs of winter left. Their faces reminded you of snow and keen cutting winds, more than of sunshine and soft breezes and butterflies; but even in them the signs of suffering told that the suffering was less, and that if the spring-time had but arrived, it had yet arrived.

Diamond looked all round, but could see no Nanny. He turned to Mr. Raymond with a question in his eyes.

"Well?" said Mr. Raymond.

"Nanny's not here," said Diamond.

"Oh, yes, she is."

"I don't see her."

"I do, though. There she is."

He pointed to a bed right in front of where Diamond was standing.

"That's not Nanny," he said.

"It *is* Nanny. I have seen her many times since you have. Illness makes a great difference."

Why, that girl must have been to the back of the north wind! thought Diamond, but he said nothing, only stared; and as he stared, something of the old Nanny began to dawn through the face of the new Nanny. The old Nanny, though a good girl, and a friendly girl, had been rough, blunt in her speech, and dirty in her person. Her face would always have reminded one who had already been to the back of the north wind of something he had seen in the best of company, but it had been coarse notwithstanding, partly from the weather, partly from her living amongst low people, and partly from having to defend herself: now it was so sweet, and gentle, and refined, that she might have had a lady and gentleman for a father and mother. And Diamond could not help thinking of words which he had heard in the church the day before: "Surely it is good to be afflicted"; or something like that. North Wind, somehow or other, must have had to do with her! She had grown from a rough girl into a gentle maiden.

Mr. Raymond, however, was not surprised, for he was used to see such lovely changes—something like the change which passes upon the crawling, many-footed creature, when it turns sick and ill, and revives a butterfly, with two wings instead of many feet. Instead of her having to take care of herself, kind hands ministered to her, making her comfortable and sweet and clean, soothing her aching head, and giving her cooling drink when she was thirsty; and kind eyes, the stars of the kingdom of heaven, had shone upon her; so that, what with the fire of the fever and the dew of tenderness, that which was coarse in her had melted away, and her whole face had grown so refined and sweet that Diamond did not know her. But as he gazed, the best of the old face, all the true and good part of it, that which was Nanny herself, dawned upon him, like the moon coming out of a cloud, until at length, instead of only believing Mr. Raymond that this was she, he saw for himself that it was Nanny indeed—very worn, but grown beautiful.

He went up to her. She smiled. He had heard her laugh, but had never seen her smile before.

"Nanny, do you know me?" said Diamond.

She only smiled again, as if the question was amusing.

She was not likely to forget him; for although she did not yet know it was he who had got her there, she had dreamed of him often, and had talked much about him when delirious. Nor was it much wonder, for he was the only boy except Joe who had ever shown her kindness.

Meantime Mr. Raymond was going from bed to bed,

talking to the little people. Every one knew him, and every one was eager to have a look, and a smile, and a kind word from him. Diamond sat down on a stool at the head of Nanny's bed. She laid her hand in his. No one else of her old acquaintance had been near her.

Suddenly a little voice called aloud—

"Won't Mr. Raymond tell us a story?"

"Oh, yes, please do! please do!" cried several little voices which also were stronger than the rest. For Mr. Raymond was in the habit of telling them a story when he went to see them, and they enjoyed it far more than the other nice things which the doctor permitted him to give them.

"Very well," said Mr. Raymond, "I will. What sort of a story shall it be?"

"A true story," said one little girl.

"A fairy tale," said a little boy.

"Well," said Mr. Raymond, "I suppose, as there is a difference, I may choose. I can't think of any true story just at this moment, so I will tell you a sort of a fairy one."

"Oh, jolly!" exclaimed the little boy who had called out for a fairy tale.

"It came into my head this morning as I got out of bed," continued Mr. Raymond; "and if it turns out pretty well, I will write it down, and get somebody to print it for me, and then you shall read it when you like."

"Then nobody ever heard it before?" asked one older child.

"No, nobody."

"Oh!" exclaimed several, thinking it very grand to have the first telling; and I dare say there might be a peculiar freshness about it, because everything would be nearly as new to the story-teller himself as to the listeners.

Some were only sitting up and some were lying down, so there could not be the same busy gathering, and bustling, and shifting to and fro with which children generally prepare themselves to hear a story; but their faces, and the turning of their heads, and many feeble exclamations of expected pleasure, showed that all such preparations were making within them.

Mr. Raymond stood in the middle of the room, that he might turn from side to side, and give each a share of seeing him. Diamond kept his place by Nanny's side, with her hand in his. I do not know how much of Mr. Raymond's story the smaller children understood; indeed, I don't quite know how much there was in it to be understood, for in such a story every one has just to take what he can get. But they all listened with apparent satisfaction, and certainly with great attention. Mr. Raymond wrote it down afterwards, and here it is—somewhat altered, no doubt, for a good story-teller tries to make his stories better every time he tells them. I cannot myself help thinking that he was somewhat indebted for this one to the old story of The Sleeping Beauty.

Chapter XXVIII
LITTLE DAYLIGHT

NO house of any pretension to be called a palace is in the least worthy of the name, except it has a wood near it—very near it—and the nearer the better. Not all round it—I don't mean that, for a palace ought to be open to the sun and wind, and stand high and brave, with weathercocks glittering and flags flying; but on one side of every palace there must be a wood. And there was a very grand wood indeed beside the palace of the king who was going to be Daylight's father; such a grand wood, that nobody yet had ever got to the other end of it. Near the house it was kept very trim and nice, and it was free of brushwood for a long way in; but by degrees it got wild, and it grew wilder, and wilder, and wilder, until some said wild beasts at last did what they liked in it. The king and his courtiers often hunted, however, and this kept the wild beasts far away from the palace.

One glorious summer morning, when the wind and sun were out together, when the vanes were flashing and the flags frolicking against the blue sky, little Daylight made her appearance from somewhere—nobody could tell where—a beautiful baby, with such bright eyes that she might have come from the sun, only by and by she showed such lively ways that she might equally well have come out of the wind. There was great jubilation in the palace, for this was the first baby the queen had had, and there is as much happiness over a new baby in a palace as in a cottage.

But there is one disadvantage of living near a wood; you do not know quite who your neighbors may be. Everybody knew there were in it several fairies, living within a few miles of the palace, who always had had something to do with each new baby that came; for fairies live so much longer than we, that they can have business with a good many generations of human mortals. The curious houses they lived in were well known also,—one, a hollow oak; another, a birch-tree, though nobody could ever find how that fairy made a house of it; another, a hut of growing trees intertwined, and patched up with turf and moss. But there was another fairy who had lately come to the place, and nobody even knew she was a fairy except the other fairies. A wicked old thing she was, always concealing her power, and being as disagreeable as she could, in order to tempt people to give her offence, that she might have the pleasure of taking vengeance upon them. The people about thought she was a witch, and those who knew her by sight were careful to avoid offending her. She lived in a mud house, in a swampy part of the forest.

In all history we find that fairies give their remarkable gifts to prince or princess, or any child of sufficient importance in their eyes, always at the christening. Now this we can understand, because it is an ancient custom amongst human beings as well; and it is not hard to explain why wicked fairies should choose the same time to do unkind things; but it is difficult to understand how they should be able to do them, for you would fancy all wicked creatures would be powerless on such an occasion. But I never knew of any interference on the part of a wicked fairy that did not turn out a good thing in the end. What a good thing, for instance, it was that one princess should sleep for a hundred years! Was she not saved from all the plague of young men who were not worthy of her? And did she not come awake exactly at the right moment when the right prince kissed her? For my part, I cannot help wishing a good many girls would sleep till just the same fate overtook them. It would be happier for them, and more agreeable to their friends.

Of course all the known fairies were invited to the christening. But the king and queen never thought of inviting an old witch. For the power of the fairies they have by nature; whereas a witch gets her power by wickedness. The other fairies, however, knowing the danger thus run, provided as well as they could against accidents from her quarter. But they could neither render her powerless, nor could they arrange their gifts in reference to hers beforehand, for they could not tell what those might be.

Of course the old hag was there without being asked. Not to be asked was just what she wanted, that she might have a sort of a reason for doing what she wished to do. For somehow even the wickedest of creatures likes a pretext for doing the wrong thing.

Five fairies had one after the other given the child such gifts as each counted best, and the fifth had just stepped back to her place in the surrounding splendor of ladies and gentlemen, when, mumbling a laugh between her toothless gums, the wicked fairy hobbled out into the middle of the circle, and at the moment when the archbishop was handing the baby to the lady at the head of the nursery department of state affairs, addressed him thus, giving a bite or two to every word before she could part with it:

"Please your Grace, I'm very deaf: would your Grace mind repeating the princess's name?"

"With pleasure, my good woman," said the archbishop, stooping to shout in her ear; "the infant's name is little Daylight."

"And little daylight it shall be," cried the fairy, in the

tone of a dry axle, "and little good shall any of her gifts do her. For I bestow upon her the gift of sleeping all day long, whether she will or not. Ha, ha! He, he! Hi, hi!"

Then out started the sixth fairy, who, of course, the others had arranged should come after the wicked one, in order to undo as much as she might.

"If she sleep all day," she said, mournfully, "she shall, at least, wake all night."

"A nice prospect for her mother and me!" thought the poor king; for they loved her far too much to give her up to nurses, especially at night, as most kings and queens do—and are sorry for it afterwards.

"You spoke before I had done," said the wicked fairy. "That's against the law. It gives me another chance."

"I beg your pardon," said the other fairies, all together.

"She did. I hadn't done laughing," said the crone. "I had only got to Hi, hi! and I had to go through Ho, ho! and Hu, hu! So I decree that if she wakes all night she shall wax and wane with its mistress the moon. And what that may mean I hope her royal parents will live to see. Ho, ho! Hu, hu!"

But out stepped another fairy, for they had been wise enough to keep two in reserve, because every fairy knew the trick of one.

"Until," said the seventh fairy, "a prince comes who shall kiss her without knowing it."

The wicked fairy made a horror noise like an angry cat, and hobbled away. She could not pretend that she had not finished her speech this time, for she had laughed Ho, ho! and Hu, hu!

"I don't know what that means," said the poor king to the seventh fairy.

"Don't be afraid. The meaning will come with the thing itself," said she.

The assembly broke up, miserable enough—the queen, at least, prepared for a good many sleepless nights, and the lady at the head of the nursery department anything but comfortable in the prospect before her, for of course the

queen could not do it all. As for the king, he made up his
mind, with what courage he could summon, to meet the
demands of the case, but wondered whether he could with
any propriety require the First Lord of the Treasury to take
a share of the burden laid upon him.

I will not attempt to describe what they had to go
through for some time. But at last the household settled
into a regular system—a very irregular one in some re-
spects. For at certain seasons the palace rang all night with
bursts of laughter from little Daylight, whose heart the old
fairy's curse could not reach; she was Daylight still, only
a little in the wrong place, for she always dropped asleep
at the first hint of dawn in the east. But her merriment was
of short duration. When the moon was at the full, she was
in glorious spirits, and as beautiful as it was possible for
a child of her age to be. But as the moon waned, she
faded, until at last she was wan and withered like the poor-
est, sickliest child you might come upon in the streets of
a great city in the arms of a homeless mother. Then the
night was quiet as the day, for the little creature lay in her
gorgeous cradle night and day with hardly a motion, and
indeed at last without even a moan, like one dead. At first
they often thought she was dead, but at last they got used
to it, and only consulted the almanac to find the moment
when she would begin to revive, which, of course, was
with the first appearance of the silver thread of the crescent moon. Then she would move her lips, and they would
give her a little nourishment; and she would grow better
and better and better, until for a few days she was splen-
didly well. When well, she was always merriest out in the
moonlight; but even when near her worst, she seemed better when, in warm summer nights, they carried her cradle
out into the light of the waning moon. Then in her sleep
she would smile the faintest, most pitiful smile.

For a long time very few people ever saw her awake. As
she grew older she became such a favorite, however, that
about the palace there were always some who would contrive to keep awake at night, in order to be near her. But

she soon began to take every chance of getting away from her nurses and enjoying her moonlight alone. And thus things went on until she was nearly seventeen years of age. Her father and mother had by that time got so used to the odd state of things that they had ceased to wonder at them. All their arrangements had reference to the state of the Princess Daylight, and it is amazing how things contrive to accommodate themselves. But how any prince was ever to find and deliver her, appeared inconceivable.

As she grew older she had grown more and more beautiful, with the sunniest hair and the loveliest eyes of heavenly blue, brilliant and profound as the sky of a June day. But so much more painful and sad was the change as her bad time came on. The more beautiful she was in the full moon, the more withered and worn did she become as the moon waned. At the time at which my story has now arrived, she looked, when the moon was small or gone, like an old woman exhausted with suffering. This was the more painful that her appearance was unnatural; for her hair and eyes did not change. Her wan face was both drawn and wrinkled, and had an eager hungry look. Her skinny hands moved as if wishing, but unable, to lay hold of something. Her shoulders were bent forward, her chest went in, and she stooped as if she were eighty years old. At last she had to be put to bed, and there await the flow of the tide of life. But she grew to dislike being seen, still more being touched by any hands, during this season. One lovely summer evening, when the moon lay all but gone upon the verge of the horizon, she vanished from her attendants, and it was only after searching for her a long time in great terror, that they found her fast asleep in the forest, at the foot of a silver birch, and carried her home.

A little way from the palace there was a great open glade, covered with the greenest and softest grass. This was her favorite haunt; for here the full moon shone free and glorious, while through a vista in the trees she could generally see more or less of the dying moon as it crossed the opening. Here she had a little rustic house built for her, and here she mostly resided. None of the court might go there without leave, and her own attendants had learned by this time not to be officious in waiting upon her, so that she was very much at liberty. Whether the good fairies had anything to do with it or not I cannot tell, but at last she got into the way of retreating further into the wood every night as the moon waned, so that sometimes they had great trouble in finding her; but as she was always very angry if she discovered they were watching her, they scarcely dared to do so. At length one night they thought they had lost her altogether. It was morning before they found her. Feeble as she was, she had wandered into a thicket a long way from the glade, and there she lay—fast asleep, of course.

Although the fame of her beauty and sweetness had gone abroad, yet as everybody knew she was under a bad spell, no king in the neighborhood had any desire to have her for a daughter-in-law. There were serious objections to such a relation.

About this time in a neighboring kingdom, in consequence of the wickedness of the nobles, an insurrection took place upon the death of the old king, the greater part of the nobility was massacred, and the young prince was compelled to flee for his life, disguised like a peasant. For some time, until he got out of the country, he suffered much from hunger and fatigue; but when he got into that ruled by the princess's father, and had no longer any fear of being recognized, he fared better, for the people were kind. He did not abandon his disguise, however. One tolerable reason was that he had no other clothes to put on, and another that he had very little money, and did not know where to get any more. There was no good in telling everybody he met that he was a prince, for he felt that a prince ought to be able to get on like other people, else his rank only made a fool of him. He had read of princes setting out upon adventure; and here he was out in similar case, only without having had a choice in the matter. He would go on, and see what would come of it.

For a day or two he had been walking through the palace-wood, and had had next to nothing to eat, when he came upon the strangest little house, inhabited by a very nice tidy motherly old woman. This was one of the good fairies. The moment she saw him she knew quite well who he was and what was going to come of it; but she was not at liberty to interfere with the orderly march of events. She received him with the kindness she would have shown to any other traveller, and gave him bread and milk, which he thought the most delicious food he had ever tasted, wondering that they did not have it for dinner at the palace sometimes. The old woman pressed him to stay all night. When he awoke he was amazed to find how well and strong he felt. She would not take any of the money he offered, but begged him, if he found occasion of continuing in the neighborhood, to return and occupy the same quarters.

"Thank you much, good mother," answered the prince; "but there is little chance of that. The sooner I get out of this wood the better."

"I don't know that," said the fairy.

"What do you mean?" asked the prince.

"Why how *should* I know?" returned she.

"I can't tell," said the prince.

"Very well," said the fairy.

"How strangely you talk!" said the prince.

"Do I?" said the fairy.

"Yes, you do," said the prince.

"Very well," said the fairy.

The prince was not used to be spoken to in this fashion, so he felt a little angry, and turned and walked away. But this did not offend the fairy. She stood at the door of her little house looking after him till the trees hid him quite. Then she said "At last!" and went in.

The prince wandered and wandered, and got nowhere. The sun sank and sank and went out of sight, and he seemed no nearer the end of the wood than ever. He sat down on a fallen tree, ate a bit of bread the old woman had given him, and waited for the moon; for, although he was not much of an astronomer, he knew the moon would rise some time, because she had risen the night before. Up she came, slow and slow, but of a good size, pretty nearly round indeed; whereupon, greatly refreshed with his piece of bread, he got up and went—he knew not whither.

After walking a considerable distance, he thought he was coming to the outside of the forest; but when he reached what he thought the last of it, he found himself only upon the edge of a great open space in it, covered with grass. The moon shone very bright, and he thought he had never seen a more lovely spot. Still it looked dreary because of its loneliness, for he could not see the house at the other side. He sat down weary again, and gazed into the glade. He had not seen so much room for several days.

All at once he spied something in the middle of the grass. What could it be? It moved; it came nearer. Was it a human creature, gliding across—a girl dressed in white, gleaming in the moonshine? She came nearer and nearer. He crept behind a tree and watched, wondering. It must be some strange being of the wood—a nymph whom the moonlight and the warm dusky air had enticed from her tree. But when she came close to where he stood, he no longer doubted she was human—for he had caught sight of her sunny hair, and her clear blue eyes, and the loveliest face and form that he had ever seen. All at once she began singing like a nightingale, and dancing to her own music, with her eyes ever turned towards the moon. She passed close to where he stood, dancing on by the edge of the trees and away in a great circle towards the other side, until he could see but a spot of white in the yellowish green of the moonlit grass. But when he feared it would vanish quite, the spot grew, and became a figure once more. She approached him again, singing and dancing and waving her arms over her head, until she had completed the circle. Just opposite his tree she stood, ceased her song, dropped her arms, and broke out into a long clear laugh, musical as a brook. Then, as if tired, she threw herself on the grass, and lay gazing at the moon. The prince was almost afraid to breathe lest he should startle her, and she should vanish from his sight. As to venturing near her, that never came into his head.

She had lain for a long hour or longer, when the prince began again to doubt concerning her. Perhaps she was but a vision of his own fancy. Or was she a spirit of the wood, after all? If so, he too would haunt the wood, glad to have lost kingdom and everything for the hope of being near her. He would build him a hut in the forest, and there he would live for the pure chance of seeing her again. Upon nights like this at least she would come out and bask in the moonlight, and make his soul blessed. But while he thus dreamed she sprang to her feet, turned her face full to the moon, and began singing as if she would draw her down from the sky by the power of her entrancing voice. She looked more beautiful than ever. Again she began dancing to her own music, and danced away into the distance. Once more she returned in a similar manner; but although he was watching as eagerly as before, what with fatigue and what with gazing, he fell fast asleep before she came near him. When he awoke it was broad daylight, and the princess was nowhere.

He could not leave the place. What if she should come the next night! He would gladly endure a day's hunger to see her again: he would buckle his belt quite tight. He walked round the glade to see if he could discover any prints of her feet. But the grass was so short, and her steps had been so light, that she had not left a single trace behind her.

He walked half-way round the wood without seeing anything to account for her presence. Then he spied a lovely little house, with thatched roof and low eaves, surrounded by an exquisite garden, with doves and peacocks walking in it. Of course this must be where the gracious lady who loved the moonlight lived. Forgetting his appearance, he walked towards the door, determined to make inquiries, but as he passed a little pond full of gold and silver fishes, he caught sight of himself and turned to find the door to the kitchen. There he knocked, and asked for a piece of bread. The good-natured cook brought him in, and gave him an excellent breakfast, which the prince found nothing the worse for being served in the kitchen. While he ate, he talked with his entertainer, and learned that this was the favorite retreat of the Princess Daylight. But he learned nothing more, both because he was afraid of seeming inquisitive, and because the cook did not choose to be heard talking about her mistress to a peasant lad who had begged for his breakfast.

As he rose to take his leave, it occurred to him that he might not be so far from the old woman's cottage as he had thought, and he asked the cook whether she knew anything of such a place, describing it as well as he could. She said she knew it well enough, adding with a smile—

"It's there you're going, is it?"

"Yes, if it's not far off."

"It's not more than three miles. But mind what you are about, you know."

"Why do you say that?"

"If you're after any mischief, she'll make you repent it."

"The best thing that could happen under the circumstances," remarked the prince.

"What do you mean by that?" asked the cook.

"Why, it stands to reason," answered the prince, "that if you wish to do anything wrong, the best thing for you is to be made to repent of it."

"I see," said the cook. "Well, I think you may venture. She's a good old soul."

"Which way does it lie from here?" asked the prince.

She gave him full instructions; and he left her with many thanks.

Being now refreshed, however, the prince did not go back to the cottage that day: he remained in the forest, amusing himself as best he could, but waiting anxiously for the night, in the hope that the princess would again appear. Nor was he disappointed, for, directly the moon rose, he spied a glimmering shape far across the glade. As it drew nearer, he saw it was she indeed—not dressed in white as before: in a pale blue like the sky, she looked lovelier still. He thought it was that the blue suited her better than the white; he did not know that she was really more beautiful because the moon was nearer the full. In fact the next night was full moon, and the princess would then be at the zenith of her loveliness.

The prince feared for some time that she was not coming near his hiding-place that night; but the circles in her dance ever widened as the moon rose, until at last they embraced the whole glade, and she came still closer to the trees where he was hiding than she had come the night before. He was entranced with her loveliness, for it was indeed a marvellous thing. All night long he watched her, but dared not go near her. He would have been ashamed of watching her too, had he not become almost incapable of thinking of anything but how beautiful she was. He watched the whole night long, and saw that as the moon went down she retreated in smaller and smaller circles, until at last he could see her no more.

Weary as he was, he set out for the old woman's cottage, where he arrived just in time for her breakfast, which she shared with him. He then went to bed, and slept for many hours. When he awoke, the sun was down, and he departed in great anxiety lest he should lose a glimpse of the lovely vision. But, whether it was by the machinations of the swamp-fairy, or merely that it is one thing to go and another to return by the same road, he lost his way. I shall not attempt to describe his misery when the moon rose, and he saw nothing but trees, trees, trees. She was high in the heavens before he reached the glade. Then indeed his troubles vanished, for there was the princess coming dancing towards him, in a dress that shone like gold, and with shoes that glimmered through the grass like fire-flies. She was of course still more beautiful than before. Like an embodied sunbeam she passed him, and danced away into the distance.

Before she returned in her circle, clouds had begun to gather about the moon. The wind rose, the trees moaned, and their lighter branches leaned all one way before it. The prince feared that the princess would go in, and he should see her no more that night. But she came dancing on more jubilant than ever, her golden dress and her sunny hair streaming out upon the blast, waving her arms towards the moon, and in the exuberance of her delight ordering the clouds away from off her face. The prince could hardly believe she was not a creature of the elements, after all.

By the time she had completed another circle, the clouds had gathered deep, and there were growlings of distant thunder. Just as she passed the tree where he stood, a flash of lightning blinded him for a moment, and when he saw again, to his horror, the princess lay on the ground. He darted to her, thinking she had been struck; but when she heard him coming, she was on her feet in a moment.

"What do you want?" she asked.

"I beg your pardon. I thought—the lightning—" said the prince, hesitating.

"There is nothing the matter," said the princess, waving him off rather haughtily.

The poor prince turned and walked towards the wood.

"Come back," said Daylight: "I like you. You do what you are told. Are you good?"

"Not so good as I should like to be," said the prince.

"Then go and grow better," said the princess.

Again the disappointed prince turned and went.

"Come back," said the princess.

He obeyed, and stood before her waiting.

"Can you tell me what the sun is like?" she asked.

"No," he answered. "But where's the good of asking what you know?"

"But I don't know," she rejoined.

"Why, everybody knows."

"That's the very thing: I'm not everybody. I've never seen the sun."

"Then you can't know what it's like till you do see it."

"I think you must be a prince," said the princess.

"Do I look like one?" said the prince.

"I can't quite say that."

"Then why do you think so?"

"Because you both do what you are told and speak the truth.—Is the sun so very bright?"

"As bright as the lightning."

"But it doesn't go out like that, does it?"

"Oh no. It shines like the moon, rises and sets like the moon, is much the same shape as the moon, only so bright that you can't look at it for a moment."

"But I *would* look at it," said the princess.

"But you couldn't," said the prince.

"But I could," said the princess.

"Why don't you, then?"

"Because I can't."

"Why can't you?"

"Because I can't wake. And I never shall wake until—"
Here she hid her face in her hands, turned away, and walked in the slowest, stateliest manner towards the house. The prince ventured to follow her at a little distance, but she turned and made a repellent gesture, which, like a true gentleman-prince, he obeyed at once. He waited a long time, but as she did not come near him again, and as the night had now cleared, he set off at last for the old woman's cottage.

It was long past midnight when he reached it, but, to his surprise, the old woman was paring potatoes at the door. Fairies are fond of doing odd things. Indeed, however they may dissemble, the night is always their day. And so it is with all who have fairy blood in them.

"Why, what are you doing there, this time of the night, mother?" said the prince; for that was the kind way in which any young man in his country would address a woman who was much older than himself.

"Getting your supper ready, my son," she answered.

"Oh! I don't want any supper," said the prince.

"Ah! you've seen Daylight," said she.

"I've seen a princess who never saw it," said the prince.

"Do you like her?" asked the fairy.

"Oh! don't I?" said the prince. "More than you would believe, mother."

"A fairy can believe anything that ever was or ever could be," said the old woman.

"Then are you a fairy?" asked the prince.

"Yes," said she.

"Then what do you do for things not to believe?" asked the prince.

"There's plenty of them—everything that never was nor ever could be."

"Plenty, I grant you," said the prince. "But do you believe there could be a princess who never saw the daylight? Do you believe that, now?"

This the prince said, not that he doubted the princess, but that he wanted the fairy to tell him more. She was too old a fairy, however, to be caught so easily.

"Of all people, fairies must not tell secrets. Besides, she's a princess."

"Well, I'll tell *you* a secret. I'm a prince."

"I know that."

"How do you know it?"

"By the curl of the third eyelash on your left eyelid."

"Which corner do you count from?"

"That's a secret."

"Another secret? Well, at least, if I am a prince, there can be no harm in telling me about a princess."

"It's just princes I can't tell."

"There ain't any more of them—are there?" said the prince.

"What! you don't think you're the only prince in the world, do you?"

"Oh, dear, no! not at all. But I know there's one too many just at present, except the princess——"

"Yes, yes, that's it," said the fairy.

"What's *it*?" asked the prince.

But he could get nothing more out of the fairy, and had to go to bed unanswered, which was something of a trial.

Now wicked fairies will not be bound by the laws which the good fairies obey, and this always seems to give the bad the advantage over the good, for they use means to gain their ends which the others will not. But it is all of no consequence, for what they do never succeeds; nay, in the end it brings about the very thing they are trying to prevent. So you see that somehow, for all their cleverness, wicked fairies are dreadfully stupid, for, although from the beginning of the world they have really helped instead of thwarting the good fairies, not one of them is a bit the wiser for it. She will try the bad thing just as they all did before her; and succeeds no better of course.

The prince had so far stolen a march upon the swamp-fairy that she did not know he was in the neighborhood until after he had seen the princess those three times. When she knew it, she consoled herself by thinking that the princess must be far too proud and too modest for any young man to venture even to speak to her before he had seen her six times at least. But there was even less danger than the wicked fairy thought; for, however much the princess might desire to be set free, she was dreadfully afraid of the wrong prince. Now, however, the fairy was going to do all she could.

She so contrived it by her deceitful spells, that the next night the prince could not by any endeavour find his way to the glade. It would take me too long to tell her tricks. They would be amusing to us, who know that they could not do any harm, but they were something other than amusing to the poor prince. He wandered about the forest till daylight, and then fell fast asleep. The same thing occurred for seven following days, during which neither could he find the good fairy's cottage. After the third quarter of the moon, however, the bad fairy thought she might be at ease about the affair for a fortnight at least, for there was no chance of the prince wishing to kiss the princess during that period. So the first day of the fourth quarter he did find the cottage, and the next day he found the glade. For nearly another week he haunted it. But the princess never came. I have little doubt she was on the farther edge of it some part of every night, but at this period she always wore black, and, there being little or no light, the prince never saw her. Nor would he have known her if he had seen her. How could he have taken the worn decrepit creature she was now, for the glorious Princess Daylight?

At last, one night when there was no moon at all, he ventured near the house. There he heard voices talking, although it was past midnight; for her women were in considerable uneasiness, because the one whose turn it was to watch her had fallen asleep, and had not seen which way she went, and this was a night when she would probably wander very far, describing a circle which did not touch the open glade at all, but stretched away from the back of the house, deep into that side of the forest—a part of which the prince knew nothing. When he understood from what they said that she had disappeared, and that she must have gone somewhere in the said direction, he plunged at once into the wood to see if he could find her. For hours he roamed with nothing to guide him but the vague notion of a circle which on one side bordered on the house, for so much had he picked up from the talk he had overheard.

It was getting towards the dawn, but as yet there was no streak of light in the sky, when he came to a great birch-tree, and sat down weary at the foot of it. While he sat— very miserable, you may be sure—full of fear for the princess, and wondering how her attendants could take it so quietly, he bethought himself that it would not be a bad plan to light a fire, which, if she were anywhere near, would attract her. This he managed with a tinder-box, which the good fairy had given him. It was just beginning to blaze up, when he heard a moan, which seemed to come from the other side of the tree. He sprung to his feet, but his heart throbbed so that he had to lean for a moment against the tree before he could move. When he got round, there lay a human form in a little dark heap on the earth.

There was light enough from his fire to show that it was not the princess. He lifted it in his arms, hardly heavier than a child, and carried it to the flame. The countenance was that of an old woman, but it had a fearfully strange look. A black hood concealed her hair, and her eyes were closed. He laid her down as comfortably as he could, chafed her hands, put a little cordial from a bottle, also the gift of the fairy, into her mouth; took off his coat and wrapped it about her, and in short did the best he could. In a little while she opened her eyes and looked at him—so pitifully! The tears rose and flowed down her gray wrinkled cheeks, but she said never a word. She closed her eyes again, but the tears kept on flowing, and her whole appearance was so utterly pitiful that the prince was very near crying too. He begged her to tell him what was the matter, promising to do all he could to help her; but still she did not speak. He thought she was dying, and took her in his arms again to carry her to the princess's house, where he thought the good-natured cook might be able to do something for her. When he lifted her, the tears flowed faster, and she gave such a sad moan that it went to his very heart.

"Mother, mother!" he said—"Poor mother!" and kissed her on the withered lips.

She started; and what eyes they were that opened upon him! But he did not see them, for it was still very dark, and he had enough to do to make his way through the trees towards the house.

Just as he approached the door, feeling more tired than he could have imagined possible—she was such a little thin old thing—she began to move, and became so restless that, unable to carry her a moment longer, he thought to lay her on the grass. But she stood upright on her feet. Her hood had dropped, and her hair fell about her. The first gleam of the morning was caught on her face: that face was bright as the never-aging Dawn, and her eyes were lovely as the sky of darkest blue. The prince recoiled in over-mastering wonder. It was Daylight herself whom he had brought from the forest! He fell at her feet, nor dared look up until she laid her hand upon his head. He rose then.

"You kissed me when I was an old woman: there! I kiss you when I am a young princess," murmured Daylight.— "Is that the sun coming?"

Chapter XXIX
RUBY

THE children were delighted with the story, and made many amusing remarks upon it. Mr. Raymond promised to search his brain for another, and when he had found one to bring it to them. Diamond having taken leave of Nanny, and promised to go and see her again soon, went away with him.

Now Mr. Raymond had been turning over in his mind what he could do both for Diamond and for Nanny. He had therefore made some acquaintance with Diamond's father, and had been greatly pleased with him. But he had come to the resolution, before he did anything so good as he would like to do for them, to put them all to a certain test. So as they walked away together, he began to talk with Diamond as follows:—

"Nanny must leave the hospital soon, Diamond."

"I'm glad of that, sir."

"Why? Don't you think it's a nice place?"

"Yes, very. But it's better to be well and doing something, you know, even if it's not quite so comfortable."

"But they can't keep Nanny so long as they would like. They can't keep her till she's *quite* strong. There are always so many sick children they want to take in and make better. And the question is, What will she do when they send her out again?"

"That's just what I can't tell, though I've been thinking of it over and over, sir. Her crossing was taken long ago, and I couldn't bear to see Nanny fighting for it, especially with such a poor fellow as has taken it. He's quite lame, sir."

"She doesn't look much like fighting, now, does she, Diamond?"

"No, sir. She looks too like an angel. Angels don't fight—do they, sir?"

"Not to get things for themselves, at least," said Mr. Raymond.

"Besides," added Diamond, "I don't quite see that she would have any better right to the crossing than the boy who has got it. Nobody gave it to her; she only took it. And now he has taken it."

"If she were to sweep a crossing—soon at least—after the illness she has had, she would be laid up again the very first wet day," said Mr. Raymond.

"And there's hardly any money to be got except on the wet days," remarked Diamond reflectively. "Is there nothing else she could do, sir?"

"Not without being taught, I'm afraid."

"Well, couldn't somebody teach her something?"

"Couldn't you teach her, Diamond?"

"I don't know anything myself, sir. I *could* teach her to dress the baby; but nobody would give her anything for doing things like that: they are so easy. There wouldn't be much good in teaching her to drive a cab, for where would she get the cab to drive? There ain't fathers and old Diamonds everywhere. At least poor Nanny can't find any of them, I doubt."

"Perhaps if she were taught to be nice and clean, and only speak gentle words—"

"Mother could teach her that," interrupted Diamond.

"And to dress babies, and feed them, and take care of them," Mr. Raymond proceeded, "she might get a place as a nurse somewhere, you know. People do give money for that."

"Then I'll ask mother," said Diamond.

"But you'll have to give her her food then; and your father, not being strong, has enough to do already without that."

"But here's me," said Diamond: "I help him out with it. When he's tired of driving, up I get. It don't make any difference to old Diamond. I don't mean he likes me as well as my father—of course he can't, you know—nobody could; but he does his duty all the same. It's got to be done, you know, sir; and Diamond's a good horse—isn't he, sir?"

"From your description I should say certainly; but I have not the pleasure of his acquaintance myself."

"Don't you think he will go to heaven, sir?"

"That I don't know anything about," said Mr. Raymond. "I confess I should be glad to think so," he added, smiling thoughtfully.

I'm sure he'll get to the back of the north wind, anyhow, said Diamond to himself; but he had learned to be very careful of saying such things aloud.

"Isn't it rather too much for him to go in the cab all day and every day?" resumed Mr. Raymond.

"So father says, when he feels his ribs of a morning. But then he says the old horse *do* eat well, and the moment he's had his supper, down he goes, and never gets up till he's called; and, for the legs of him, father says that makes no end of a differ. Some horses, sir! they won't lie down all night long, but go to sleep on their four pins, like a haystack, father says. *I* think it's very stupid of them, and so does old Diamond. But then I suppose they don't know better, and so they can't help it. We mustn't be too hard upon them, father says."

"Your father must be a good man, Diamond."

Diamond looked up in Mr. Raymond's face, wondering what he could mean.

"I said your father must be a good man, Diamond."

"Of course," said Diamond. "How could he drive a cab if he wasn't?"

"There are some men drive cabs who are not very good," objected Mr. Raymond.

Diamond remembered the drunken cabman, and saw that his friend was right.

"Ah! but," he returned. "he *must* be, you know, with such a horse as old Diamond."

"That does make a difference," said Mr. Raymond. "But it is quite enough that he *is* a good man, without our trying to account for it. Now, if you like, I will give you a proof that *I* think him a good man. I am going away on the Continent for a while—for three months, I believe—and I am going to let my house to a gentleman who does not want the use of my brougham. My horse is nearly as old, I fancy, as your Diamond, but I don't want to part with him, and I don't want him to be idle; for nobody, as you say, ought to be idle; but neither do I want him to be worked very hard. Now, it has come into my head that perhaps your father would take charge of him, and work him under certain conditions."

"My father will do what's right," said Diamond. "I'm sure of that."

"Well, so I think. Will you ask him when he comes home to call and have a little chat with me—to-day, some time?"

"He must have his dinner first," said Diamond. "No, he's got his dinner with him to-day. It must be after he's had his tea."

"Of course, of course. Any time will do. I shall be at home all day."

"Very well, sir. I will tell him. You may be sure he will come. My father thinks you a very kind gentleman, and I know he is right, for I know your very own self, sir."

Mr. Raymond smiled, and as they had now reached his

door, they parted, and Diamond went home. As soon as his father entered the house, Diamond gave him Mr. Raymond's message, and recounted the conversation that had preceded it. His father said little, but took thought-sauce to his bread and butter, and as soon as he had finished his meal, rose, saying:

"I will go to your friend directly, Diamond. It would be a grand thing to get a little more money. We do want it."

Diamond accompanied his father to Mr. Raymond's door, and there left him.

He was shown at once into Mr. Raymond's study, where he gazed with some wonder at the multitude of books on the walls, and thought what a learned man Mr. Raymond must be.

Presently Mr. Raymond entered, and after saying much the same about his old horse, made the following distinct proposal—one not over-advantageous to Diamond's father, but for which he had reasons—namely, that Joseph should have the use of Mr. Raymond's horse while he was away, on condition that he never worked him more than six hours a day, and fed him well, and that, besides, he should take Nanny home as soon as she was able to leave the hospital, and provide for her as for one of his own children, neither better nor worse—so long, that is, as he had the horse.

Diamond's father could not help thinking it a pretty close bargain. He should have both the girl and the horse to feed, and only six hours' work out of the horse.

"It will save your own horse," said Mr. Raymond.

"That is true," answered Joseph; "but all I can get by my own horse is only enough to keep us, and if I save him and feed your horse and the girl—don't you see, sir?"

"Well, you can go home and think about it, and let me know by the end of the week. I am in no hurry before then."

So Joseph went home and recounted the proposal to his

wife, adding that he did not think there was much advantage to be got out of it.

"Not much that way, husband," said Diamond's mother, "but there would be an advantage, and what matter who gets it!"

"I don't see it," answered her husband. "Mr. Raymond is a gentleman of property, and I don't discover any much good in helping him to save a little more. He won't easily get one to make such a bargain, and I don't mean he shall get me. It would be a loss rather than a gain—I do think—at least, if I took less work out of our own horse."

"One hour would make a difference to old Diamond. But that's not the main point. You must think what an advantage it would be to the poor girl that hasn't a home to go to!"

"She *is* one of Diamond's friends," thought his father.

"I could be kind to her, you know," the mother went on, "and teach her housework, and how to handle a baby; and, besides, she would help me, and I should be the stronger for it, and able to do an odd bit of charing now and then, when I got the chance."

"I won't hear of that," said her husband. "Have the girl by all means. I'm ashamed I did not think of both sides of the thing at once. I wonder if the horse is a great eater. To be sure, if I gave Diamond two hours' additional rest, it would be all the better for the old bones of him, and there would be four hours extra out of the other horse. That would give Diamond something to do every day. He could drive old Diamond after dinner, and I could take the other horse out for six hours after tea, or in the morning, as I found best. It might pay for the keep of both of them,—that is, if I had good luck. I should like to oblige Mr. Raymond, though he be rather hard, for he has been very kind to our Diamond, wife. Hasn't he now?"

"He has indeed, Joseph," said his wife, and there the conversation ended.

Diamond's father went the very next day to Mr. Raymond, and accepted his proposal; so that the week after, having got another stall in the same stable, he had two horses instead of one. Oddly enough, the name of the new horse was Ruby, for he was a very red chestnut. Diamond's name came from a white lozenge on his forehead. Young Diamond said they *were* rich now, with such a big diamond and such a big ruby.

Chapter XXX
NANNY'S DREAM

NANNY was not fit to be moved for some time yet, and Diamond went to see her as often as he could. But being more regularly engaged now, seeing he went out every day for a few hours with old Diamond, and had his baby to mind, and one of the horses to attend to, he could not go so often as he would have liked.

One evening, as he sat by her bedside, she said to him:

"I've had such a beautiful dream, Diamond! I should like to tell it you."

"Oh! do," said Diamond; "I am so fond of dreams!"

"She must have been to the back of the north wind," he said to himself.

"It was a very foolish dream, you know. But somehow it was so pleasant! What a good thing it is that you believe the dream all the time you are in it!"

My readers must not suppose that poor Nanny was able to say what she meant so well as I put it down here. She had never been to school, and had heard very little else than vulgar speech until she came to the hospital. But I have been to school, and although that could never make me able to dream so well as Nanny, it has made me able to tell her dream better than she could herself. And I am the more desirous of doing this for her that I have already done the best I could for Diamond's dream, and it would be a shame to give the boy all the advantage.

"I will tell you all I know about it," said Nanny. "The day before yesterday, a lady came to see us—a very beautiful lady, and very beautifully dressed. I heard the matron say to her that it was very kind of her to come in blue and gold; and she answered that she knew we didn't like dull colors. She had such a lovely shawl on, just like redness dipped in milk, and all worked over with flowers of the same color. It didn't shine much; it *was* silk, but it kept in the shine. When she came to my bedside, she sat down, just where you are sitting, Diamond, and laid her hand on the counterpane. I was sitting up, with my table before me, ready for my tea. Her hand looked so pretty in its blue glove, that I was tempted to stroke it. I thought she wouldn't be angry, for everybody that comes to the hospital is kind. It's only in the streets they ain't kind. But she drew her hand away, and I almost cried, for I thought I had been rude. Instead of that, however, it was only that she didn't like giving me her glove to stroke, for she drew it off, and then laid her hand where it was before. I wasn't sure, but I ventured to put out my ugly hand."

"Your hand ain't ugly, Nanny," said Diamond; but Nanny went on—

"And I stroked it again, and then she stroked mine,— think of that! And there was a ring on her finger, and I looked down to see what it was like. And she drew it off, and put it upon one of my fingers. It was a red stone, and she told me they called it a ruby."

"Oh, that is funny!" said Diamond. "Our new horse is called Ruby. We've got another horse—a red one—such a beauty!"

But Nanny went on with her story.

"I looked at the ruby all the time the lady was talking to me,—it was so beautiful! And as she talked I kept seeing deeper and deeper into the stone. At last she rose to go away, and I began to pull the ring off my finger; and what do you think she said?—'Wear it all night, if you like. Only you must take care of it. I can't give it you, for some one gave it to me; but you may keep it till to-morrow.' Wasn't it kind of her? I could hardly take my tea, I was so delighted to hear it; and I do think it was the ring that set me dreaming; for, after I had taken my tea, I leaned back, half lying and half sitting, and looked at the ring on my finger. By degrees I began to dream. The ring grew larger and larger, until at last I found that I was not looking at a red stone, but at a red sunset, which shone in at the end of a long street near where Grannie lives. I was dressed in rags as I used to be, and I had great holes in my shoes, at which the nasty mud came through to my feet. I didn't use to mind it before, but now I thought it horrid. And there was the great red sunset, with streaks of green and gold between, standing looking at me. Why couldn't I live in the sunset instead of in that dirt? Why was it so far away always? Why did it never come into our wretched street? It faded away, as the sunsets always do, and at last went out altogether. Then a cold wind began to blow, and flutter all my rags about—"

"That was North Wind herself," said Diamond.

"Eh?" said Nanny, and went on with her story.

"I turned my back to it, and wandered away. I did not know where I was going, only it was warmer to go that way. I don't think it was a north wind, for I found myself somewhere in the west end at last. But it doesn't matter in a dream which wind it was."

"I don't know that," said Diamond. "I believe North Wind can get into our dreams—yes, and blow in them. Sometimes she has blown me out of a dream altogether."

"I don't know what you mean, Diamond," said Nanny.

"Never mind," answered Diamond. "Two people can't always understand each other. They'd both be at the back of the north wind directly, and what would become of the other places without them?"

"You do talk so oddly!" said Nanny. "I sometimes think they must have been right about you."

"What did they say about me?" asked Diamond.

"They called you God's baby."

"How kind of them! But I knew that."

"Did you know what it meant, though? It meant that you were not right in the head."

"I feel all right," said Diamond, putting both hands to his head, as if it had been a globe he could take off and set on again.

"Well, as long as you are pleased I am pleased," said Nanny.

"Thank you, Nanny. Do go on with your story. I think I like dreams even better than fairy tales. But they must be nice ones, like yours, you know."

"Well, I went on, keeping my back to the wind, until I came to a fine street on the top of a hill. How it happened I don't know, but the front door of one of the houses was open, and not only the front door, but the back door as well, so that I could see right through the house—and what do you think I saw? A garden place with green grass, and the moon shining upon it! Think of that! There was no moon in the street, but through the house there was the moon. I looked and there was nobody near; I would not do any harm, and the grass was so much nicer than the mud! But I couldn't think of going on the grass with such dirty shoes: I kicked them off in the gutter, and ran in on my bare feet, up the steps, and through the house, and on to the grass; and the moment I came into the moonlight, I began to feel better."

"That's why North Wind blew you there," said Diamond.

"It came of Mr. Raymond's story about the Princess Daylight," returned Nanny. "Well, I lay down upon the grass in the moonlight without thinking how I was to get out again. Somehow the moon suited me exactly. There was not a breath of the north wind you talk about; it was quite gone."

"You didn't want her any more, just then. She never goes where she's not wanted," said Diamond. "But she blew you into the moonlight, anyhow."

"Well, we won't dispute about it," said Nanny: "you've got a tile loose, you know."

"Suppose I have," returned Diamond, "don't you see it may let in the moonlight, or the sunlight for that matter?"

"Perhaps yes, perhaps no," said Nanny.

"And you've got your dreams, too, Nanny."

"Yes, but I know they're dreams."

"So do I. But I know besides they are something more as well."

"Oh! do you?" rejoined Nanny. "I don't."

"All right," said Diamond. "Perhaps you will some day."

"Perhaps I won't," said Nanny.

Diamond held his peace, and Nanny resumed her story.

"I lay a long time, and the moonlight got in at every tear in my clothes, and made me feel so happy——"

"There, I tell you!" said Diamond.

"What do you tell me?" returned Nanny.

"North Wind——"

"It was the moonlight, I tell you," persisted Nanny, and again Diamond held his peace.

"All at once I felt that the moon was not shining so strong. I looked up, and there was a cloud, all crapey and fluffy, trying to drown the beautiful creature. But the moon was so round, just like a whole plate, that the cloud couldn't stick to her; she shook it off, and said *there*, and shone out clearer and brighter than ever. But up came a thicker cloud,—and 'You shan't' said the moon; and 'I will' said the cloud,—but it couldn't: out shone the moon, quite laughing at its impudence. I knew her ways, for I've always been used to watch her. She's the only thing worth looking at in our street at night."

"Don't call it *your* street," said Diamond. "You're not going back to it. You're coming to us, you know."

"That's too good to be true," said Nanny.

"There are very few things good enough to be true," said Diamond; "but I hope this is. Too good to be true it can't be. Isn't *true* good? and isn't *good* good? And how, then, can anything be too good to be true? That's like old Sal—to say that."

"Don't abuse Grannie, Diamond. She's a horrid old thing, she and her gin bottle; but she'll repent some day, and then you'll be glad not to have said anything against her."

"Why?" said Diamond.

"Because you'll be sorry for her."

"I am sorry for her now."

"Very well. That's right. She'll be sorry too. And there'll be an end of it."

"All right. You come to us," said Diamond.

"Where was I?" said Nanny.

"Telling me how the moon served the clouds."

"Yes. But it wouldn't do, all of it. Up came the clouds and the clouds, and they came faster and faster, until the moon was covered up. You couldn't expect her to throw off a hundred of them at once—could you?"

"Certainly not," said Diamond.

"So it grew very dark; and a dog began to yelp in the house. I looked and saw that the door to the garden was shut. Presently it was opened—not to let me out, but to let the dog in—yelping and bounding. I thought if he caught sight of me, I was in for a biting first, and the police after. So I jumped up, and ran for a little summer-house in the corner of the garden. The dog came after me, but I shut the door in his face. It was well it had a door—wasn't it?"

"You dreamed of the door because you wanted it," said Diamond.

"No, I didn't; it came of itself. It was there, in the true dream."

"There—I've caught you!" said Diamond. "I knew you believed in the dream as much as I do."

"Oh, well, if you will lay traps for a body!" said Nanny. "Anyhow, I was safe inside the summer-house. And what do you think?—There was the moon beginning to shine again—but only through one of the panes—and that one was just the color of the ruby. Wasn't it funny?"

"No, not a bit funny," said Diamond.

"If you will be contrary!" said Nanny.

"No, no," said Diamond; "I only meant that was the very pane I should have expected her to shine through."

"Oh, very well!" returned Nanny.

What Diamond meant, I do not pretend to say. He had curious notions about things.

"And now," said Nanny, "I didn't know what to do, for the dog kept barking at the door, and I couldn't get out. But the moon was so beautiful that I couldn't keep from looking at it through the red pane. And as I looked it got larger and larger till it filled the whole pane and outgrew it, so that I could see it through the other panes; and it grew till it filled them too and the whole window, so that the summer-house was nearly as bright as day.

"The dog stopped barking, and I heard a gentle tapping at the door, like the wind blowing a little branch against it."

"Just like her," said Diamond, who thought everything strange and beautiful must be done by North Wind.

"So I turned from the window and opened the door; and what do you think I saw?"

"A beautiful lady," said Diamond.

"No—the moon itself, as big as a little house, and as round as a ball, shining like yellow silver. It stood on the grass—down on the very grass: I could see nothing else for the brightness of it. And as I stared and wondered, a door opened in the side of it, near the ground, and a curious little old man, with a crooked thing over his shoulder, looked out, and said: 'Come along, Nanny; my lady wants you. We're come to fetch you.' I wasn't a bit frightened. I went up to the beautiful bright thing, and the old man held down his hand, and I took hold of it, and gave a jump, and he gave me a lift, and I was inside the moon. And what do you think it was like? It was such a pretty little house, with blue windows and white curtains! At one of the windows sat a beautiful lady, with her head leaning on her hand, looking out. She seemed rather sad, and I was sorry for her, and stood staring at her.

" 'You didn't think I had such a beautiful mistress as that!' said the queer little man. 'No, indeed!' I answered: 'who would have thought it?' 'Ah! who indeed? But you see you don't know everything.' The little man closed the door, and began to pull at a rope which hung behind it with a weight at the end. After he had pulled a while, he said—'There, that will do; we're all right now.' Then he took me by the hand and opened a little trap in the floor, and led me down two or three steps, and I saw like a great hole below me. 'Don't be frightened,' said the little man. 'It's not a hole. It's only a window. Put your face down and look through.' I did as he told me, and there was the garden and the summer-house, far away, lying at the bottom of the moonlight. 'There!' said the little man; 'we've brought you off! Do you see the little dog barking at us down there in the garden?' I told him I couldn't see anything so far. 'Can *you* see anything so small and so far off?' I said. 'Bless you, child!' said the little man; 'I could pick up a needle out of the grass if I had only a long enough arm. There's one lying by the door of the summer-house now.' I looked at his eyes. They were very small, but so bright that I think he saw by the light that went out of them. Then he took me up, and up again by a little stair in a corner of the room, and through another trap-door, and there was one great round window above us, and I saw the blue sky and the clouds, and such lots of stars, all so big, and shining as hard as ever they could!"

"The little girl-angels had been polishing them," said Diamond.

"What nonsense you do talk!" said Nanny.

"But my nonsense is just as good as yours, Nanny. When you have done, I'll tell you my dream. The stars are in it—not the moon, though. She was away somewhere. Perhaps she was gone to fetch you then. I don't think that, though, for my dream was longer ago than yours. She might have been to fetch some one else, though; for we can't fancy it's only us that get such fine things done for them. But do tell me what came next."

Perhaps one of my child-readers may remember whether the moon came down to fetch him or her the same night that Diamond had his dream. I cannot tell, of course. I know she did not come to fetch me, though I did think I could make her follow me when I was a boy—not a very tiny one either.

"The little man took me all round the house, and made me look out of every window. Oh, it was beautiful! There we were, all up in the air, in such a nice clean little house! 'Your work will be to keep the windows bright,' said the little man. 'You won't find it very difficult, for there ain't much dust up here. Only, the frost settles on them sometimes, and the drops of rain leave marks on them.' 'I can easily clean them inside,' I said; 'but how am I to get the frost and the rain off the outside of them?' 'Oh!' he said, 'it's quite easy. There are ladders all about. You've only got to go out at the door, and climb about. There are a great many windows you haven't seen yet, and some of them look into places you don't know anything about. I used to clean them myself, but I'm getting rather old, you see. Ain't I now?' 'I can't tell,' I answered. 'You see I never saw you when you were younger.' 'Never saw the man in the moon?' said he. 'Not very near.' I answered—

'not to tell how young or how old he looked. I have seen the bundle of sticks on his back.' For Jim had pointed that out to me. Jim was very fond of looking at the man in the moon. Poor Jim! I wonder he hasn't been to see me. I'm afraid he's ill too."

"I'll try to find out," said Diamond, "and let you know."

"Thank you," said Nanny. "You and Jim ought to be friends."

"But what did the man in the moon say, when you told him you had seen him with the bundle of sticks on his back?"

"He laughed. But I thought he looked offended too. His little nose turned up sharper, and he drew the corners of his mouth down from the tips of his ears into his neck. But he didn't look cross, you know."

"Didn't he say anything?"

"Oh, yes! He said: 'That's all nonsense. What you saw was my bundle of dusters. I was going to clean the windows. It takes a good many, you know. Really, what they do say of their superiors down there!' 'It's only because they don't know better,' I ventured to say. 'Of course, of course,' said the little man. 'Nobody ever does know better. Well, I forgive them, and *that* sets it all right, I hope.' 'It's very good of you,' I said. 'No!' said he, 'it's not in the least good of me. I couldn't be comfortable otherwise.' After this he said nothing for a while, and I laid myself on the floor of his garret, and stared up and around at the great blue beautifulness. I had forgotten him almost, when at last he said: 'Ain't you done yet?' 'Done what?' I asked. 'Done saying your prayers,' says he. 'I wasn't saying my prayers,' I answered. 'Oh yes, you were,' said he, 'though you didn't know it! And now I must show you something else.'

"He took my hand and led me down the stair again, and through a narrow passage, and through another, and another, and another. I don't know how there could be room for so many passages in such a little house. The heart of it must be ever so much farther from the sides than they are from each other. How could it have an inside that was so independent of its outside? There's the point. It was funny—wasn't it, Diamond?"

"No," said Diamond. He was going to say that that was very much the sort of thing at the back of the north wind; but he checked himself and only added, "All right. I don't see it. I don't see why the inside should depend on the outside. It ain't so with the crabs. They creep out of their outsides and make new ones. Mr. Raymond told me so."

"I don't see what that has got to do with it," said Nanny.

"Then go on with your story, please," said Diamond. "What did you come to, after going through all those winding passages into the heart of the moon?"

"I didn't say they were winding passages. I said they were long and narrow. They didn't wind. They went by corners."

"That's worth knowing," remarked Diamond. "For who knows how soon he may have to go there? But the main thing is, what did you come to at last?"

"We came to a small box against the wall of a tiny room. The little man told me to put my ear against it. I did so, and heard a noise something like the purring of a cat, only not so loud, and much sweeter. 'What is it?' I asked. 'Don't you know the sound?' returned the little man. 'No,' I answered. 'Don't you know the sound of bees?' he said. I had never heard bees, and could not know the sound of them. 'Those are my lady's bees,' he went on. I had heard that bees gather honey from the flowers. 'But where are the flowers for them?' I asked. 'My lady's bees gather their honey from the sun and the stars,' said the little man. 'Do let me see them,' I said. 'No. I daren't do that,' he answered. 'I have no business with them. I don't understand them. Besides, they are so bright that if one were to fly into your eye, it would blind you altogether.' 'Then you have seen them?' 'Oh, yes! Once or twice, I think. But I don't quite know: they are so very bright—like buttons of lightning. Now I've showed you all I can to-night, and we'll go back to the room.' I followed him, and he made me sit down under a lamp that hung from the roof, and gave me some bread and honey.

"The lady had never moved. She sat with her forehead leaning on her hand, gazing out of the little window, hung like the rest with white cloudy curtains. From where I was sitting I looked out of it too, but I could see nothing. Her face was very beautiful, and very white, and very still, and her hand was as white as the forehead that leaned on it. I did not see her whole face—only the side of it, for she never moved to turn it full upon me, or even to look at me.

"How long I sat after I had eaten my bread and honey, I don't know. The little man was busy about the room, pulling a string here, and a string there, but chiefly the string at the back of the door. I was thinking with some uneasiness that he would soon be wanting me to go out and clean the windows, and I didn't fancy the job. At last he came up to me with a great armful of dusters. 'It's time you set about the windows,' he said; 'for there's rain coming, and if they're quite clean before, then the rain can't spoil them.' I got up at once. 'You needn't be afraid,' he said. 'You won't tumble off. Only you must be careful. Always hold on with one hand while you rub with the other.' As he spoke, he opened the door. I started back in a terrible fright, for there was nothing but blue air to be seen under me, like a great water without a bottom at all. But what must be must, and to live up here was so much nicer than down in the mud with holes in my shoes, that I never thought of not doing as I was told. The little man showed me how and where to lay hold while I put my foot round the edge of the door on to the first round of a ladder. 'Once you're up,' he said, 'you'll see how you have to go well enough.' I did as he told me, and crept out very carefully. Then the little man handed me the bundle of dusters, saying, 'I always carry them on my reaping hook, but I don't think you could manage it properly. You shall have it if you like.' I wouldn't take it, however, for it looked dangerous.

"I did the best I could with the dusters, and crawled up to the top of the moon. But what a grand sight it was! The stars were all over my head, so bright and so near that I could almost have laid hold of them. The round ball to which I clung went bobbing and floating away through the dark blue above and below and on every side. It was so beautiful that all fear left me, and I set to work diligently. I cleaned window after window. At length I came to a very little one, in at which I peeped. There was the room with the box of bees in it! I laid my ear to the window, and heard the musical hum quite distinctly. A great longing to see them came upon me, and I opened the window and crept in. The little box had a door like a closet. I opened it—the tiniest crack—when out came the light with such a sting that I closed it again in terror—not, however, before three bees had shot out into the room, where they darted about like flashes of lightning. Terribly frightened, I tried to get out of the window again, but I could not: there was no way to the outside of the moon but through the door; and that was in the room where the lady sat. No sooner had I reached the room, than the three bees, which had followed me, flew at once to the lady, and settled upon her hair. Then first I saw her move. She started, put up her hand, and caught them; then rose and, having held them into the flame of the lamp one after the other, turned to me. Her face was not so sad now as stern. It frightened me much. 'Nanny, you have got me into trouble,' she said. 'You have been letting out my bees, which it is all I can do to manage. You have forced me to burn them. It is a great loss, and there will be a storm.' As she spoke, the clouds had gathered all about us. I could see them come crowding up white about the windows. 'I am sorry to find,' said the lady, 'that you are not to be trusted. You must go home again—you won't do for us.' Then came a great clap of thunder, and the moon rocked and swayed. All grew dark about me, and I fell on the floor, and lay half-stunned. I could hear everything but could see nothing. 'Shall I throw her out of the door, my lady?' said the little man. 'No,' she answered; 'she's not quite bad enough for that. I don't think there's much harm in her; only she'll never do for us. She would make dreadful mischief up here. She's only fit for the mud. It's a great pity. I am sorry for her. Just take that ring off her finger. I am sadly afraid she has stolen it.' The little man caught hold of my hand, and I felt him tugging at the ring. I tried to speak what was true about it, but, after a terrible effort, only gave a groan. Other things began to come into my head. Somebody else had a hold of me. The little man wasn't there. I opened my eyes at last, and saw the nurse. I had cried out in my sleep, and she had come and waked me. But, Diamond, for all it was only a dream, I cannot help being ashamed of myself yet for opening the lady's box of bees."

"You wouldn't do it again—would you—if she were to take you back?" said Diamond.

"No. I don't think anything would ever make me do it again. But where's the good? I shall never have the chance."

"I don't know that," said Diamond.

"You silly baby! It was only a dream," said Nanny.

"I know that, Nanny, dear. But how can you tell you mayn't dream it again?"

"That's not a bit likely."

"I don't know that," said Diamond.

"You're always saying that," said Nanny. "I don't like it."

"Then I won't say it again—if I don't forget," said Diamond. "But it was such a beautiful dream!—wasn't it, Nanny? What a pity you opened that door and let the bees out! You might have had such a long dream, and such nice talks with the moon-lady! Do try to go again, Nanny. I do so want to hear more."

But now the nurse came and told him it was time to go; and Diamond went, saying to himself, "I can't help thinking that North Wind had something to do with that dream. It would be tiresome to lie there all day and all night too—without dreaming. Perhaps if she hadn't done that, the moon might have carried her to the back of the north wind—who knows?"

Chapter XXXI
THE NORTH WIND DOTH BLOW

IT was a great delight to Diamond when at length Nanny was well enough to leave the hospital and go home to their house. She was not very strong yet, but Diamond's mother was very considerate of her, and took care that she should have nothing to do she was not quite fit for. If Nanny had been taken straight from the street, it is very probable she would not have been so pleasant in a decent household, or so easy to teach; but after the refining influences of her illness and the kind treatment she had had in the hospital, she moved about the house just like some rather sad pleasure haunting the mind. As she got better, and the color came back to her cheeks, her step grew lighter and quicker, her smile shone out more readily, and it became certain that she would soon be a treasure of help. It was great fun to see Diamond teaching her how to hold the baby, and wash and dress him, and often they laughed together over her awkwardness. But she had not many such lessons before she was able to perform those duties quite as well as Diamond himself.

Things however did not go well with Joseph from the very arrival of Ruby. It almost seemed as if the red beast had brought ill luck with him. The fares were fewer, and the pay less. Ruby's services did indeed make the week's income at first a little beyond what it used to be, but then there were two more to feed. After the first month he fell lame, and for the whole of the next Joseph dared not attempt to work him. I cannot say that he never grumbled, for his own health was far from what it had been; but I can say that he tried to do his best. During all that month, they lived on very short commons indeed, seldom tasting meat except on Sundays, and poor old Diamond, who worked hardest of all, not even then—so that at the end of it he was as thin as a clothes-horse, while Ruby was as plump and sleek as a bishop's cob.

Nor was it much better after Ruby was able to work again, for it was a season of great depression in business, and that is very soon felt amongst the cabmen. City men look more after their shillings, and their wives and daughters have less to spend. It was besides a wet autumn, and bread rose greatly in price. When I add to this that Diamond's mother was but poorly, for a new baby was coming, you will see that these were not very jolly times for our friends in the Mews.

Notwithstanding the depressing influences around him, however, Joseph was able to keep a little hope alive in his heart; and when he came home at night, would get Diamond to read to him, and would also make Nanny produce her book that he might see how she was getting on. For Diamond had taken her education in hand, and as she was a clever child, she was very soon able to put letters and words together.

Thus the three months passed away, but Mr. Raymond did not return. Joseph had been looking anxiously for him, chiefly with the desire of getting rid of Ruby—not that he was absolutely of no use to him, but that he was a constant weight upon his mind. Indeed, as far as provision went, he was rather worse off with Ruby and Nanny than he had been before, but on the other hand, Nanny was a great help in the house, and it was a comfort to him to think that when the new baby did come, Nanny would be with his wife.

Of God's gifts a baby is of the greatest; therefore it is no wonder that when this one came, she was as heartily welcomed by the little household as if she had brought plenty with her. Of course she made a great difference in the work to be done—far more difference than her size warranted, but Nanny was no end of help, and Diamond was as much of a sunbeam as ever, and began to sing to the new baby the first moment he got her in his arms. But he did not sing the same songs to her that he had sung to his brother; for, he said, she was a new baby and must have new songs; and besides, she was a sister-baby and not a brother-baby, and of course would not like the same kind of songs. Where the difference in his songs lay, however, I do not pretend to be able to point out. One thing I am sure of, that they not only had no small share in the education of the little girl, but helped the whole family a great deal more than they were aware.

How they managed to get through the long dreary expensive winter, I can hardly say. Sometimes things were better, sometimes worse. But at last the spring came, and the winter was over and gone, and that was much. Still Mr. Raymond did not return, and although the mother would have been able to manage without Nanny now, they could not look for a place for her so long as they had Ruby; and they were not altogether sorry for this.

One week at last was worse than they had yet had. They were almost without bread before it was over. But the sadder he saw his father and mother looking, the more Diamond set himself to sing to the two babies.

One thing which had increased their expenses was that they had been forced to hire another little room for Nanny. When the second baby came, Diamond gave up his room that Nanny might be at hand to help his mother, and went to hers, which, although a fine place to what she had been accustomed to, was not very nice in his eyes. He did not mind the change though, for was not his mother the more comfortable for it? And was not Nanny more comfortable too? And indeed was not Diamond himself more comfortable that other people were more comfortable? And if there was more comfort every way, the change was a happy one.

Chapter XXXII
DIAMOND AND RUBY

IT was Friday night, and Diamond, like the rest of the household, had had very little to eat that day. The mother would always pay the week's rent before she laid out anything even on food. His father had been very gloomy—so gloomy that he had actually been cross to his wife. It is a strange thing how the pain of seeing the suffering of those we love will sometimes make us add to their suffering by being cross with them. This comes of not having faith enough in God, and shows how necessary this faith is, for when we lose it, we lose even the kindness which alone can soothe the suffering. Diamond in consequence had gone to bed very quiet and thoughtful—a little troubled indeed.

It had been a very stormy winter; and even now that the spring had come, the north wind often blew. When Diamond went to his bed, which was in a tiny room in the roof, he heard it like the sea moaning; and when he fell asleep he still heard the moaning. All at once he said to himself, "Am I awake, or am I asleep?" But he had no time to answer the question, for there was North Wind calling him. His heart beat very fast, it was such a long time since he had heard that voice. He jumped out of bed, and looked everywhere, but could not see her. "Diamond, come here," she said again and again; but where the *here* was he could not tell. To be sure the room was all but quite dark, and she might be close beside him.

"Dear North Wind," said Diamond, "I want so much to go to you, but I can't tell where."

"Come here, Diamond," was all her answer.

Diamond opened the door, and went out of the room, and down the stair and into the yard. His little heart was in a flutter, for he had long given up all thought of seeing her again. Neither now was he to see her. When he got out, a great puff of wind came against him, and in obedience to it he turned his back, and went as it blew. It blew him right up to the stabledoor, and went on blowing.

"She wants me to go into the stable," said Diamond to himself; "but the door is locked."

He knew where the key was, in a certain hole in the wall—far too high for him to get at. He ran to the place, however: just as he reached it there came a wild blast, and down fell the key clanging on the stones at his feet. He picked it up, and ran back and opened the stable-door, and went in. And what do you think he saw?

A little light came through the dusty window from a gas-lamp, sufficient to show him Diamond and Ruby with their two heads up, looking at each other across the partition of their stalls. The light showed the white mark on Diamond's forehead, but Ruby's eye shone so bright, that he thought more light came out of it than went in. This is what he saw.

But what do you think he heard?

He heard the two horses talking to each other—in a strange language, which yet, somehow or other, he could understand, and turn over in his mind in English. The first words he heard were from Diamond, who apparently had been already quarreling with Ruby.

"Look how fat you are, Ruby!" said old Diamond. "You are so plump and your skin shines so, you ought to be ashamed of yourself."

"There's no harm in being fat," said Ruby in a deprecating tone. "No, nor in being sleek. I may as well shine as not."

"No harm?" retorted Diamond. "Is it no harm to go eating up all poor master's oats, and taking up so much of his time grooming you, when you only work six hours—no, not six hours a day, and, as I hear, get along no faster than a big dray-horse with two tons behind him?—So they tell me."

"Your master's not mine," said Ruby. "I must attend to my own master's interests, and eat all that is given me, and be as sleek and fat as I can, and go no faster than I need."

"Now really if the rest of the horses weren't all asleep, poor things—*they* work till they're tired—I do believe they would get up and kick you out of the stable. You make me ashamed of being a horse. You dare to say my master ain't your master! That's your gratitude for the way he feeds you and spares you! Pray where would your carcass be if it weren't for him?"

"He doesn't do it for my sake. If I were his own horse, he would work me as hard as he does you."

"And I'm proud to be so worked. I wouldn't be as fat as you—not for all you're worth. You're a disgrace to the stable. Look at the horse next you. *He's* something like a horse—all skin and bone. And his master ain't over kind to him either. He put a stinging lash on his whip last week. But that old horse knows he's got the wife and children to keep—as well as his drunken master—and he works *like* a horse. I dare say he grudges his master the beer he drinks, but I don't believe he grudges anything else."

"Well, I don't grudge yours what he gets by me," said Ruby.

"Gets!" retorted Diamond. "What he gets isn't worth

grudging. It comes to next to nothing—what with your fat and your shine."

"Well, at least you ought to be thankful you're the better for it. You get a two hours' rest a day out of it."

"I thank my master for that—not you, you lazy fellow! You go along like a buttock of beef upon castors—you do."

"Ain't you afraid I'll kick, if you go on like that, Diamond?"

"Kick! You couldn't kick if you tried. You might heave your rump up half a foot, but for lashing out—oho! If you did, you'd be down on your belly before you could get your legs under you again. It's my belief, once out, they'd stick out for ever. Talk of kicking! Why don't you put one foot before the other now and then when you're in the cab? The abuse master gets for your sake is quite shameful. No decent horse would bring it on him. Depend upon it, Ruby, no cabman likes to be abused any more than his fare. But *his* fares, at least when you are between the shafts, are very much to be excused. Indeed they are."

"Well, you see, Diamond, I don't want to go lame again."

"I don't believe you were so very lame after all—there!"

"Oh, but I was."

"Then I believe it was all your own fault. I'm not lame. I never was lame in all my life. You don't take care of your legs. You never lay them down at night. There you are with your huge carcass crushing down your poor legs all night long. You don't even care for your own legs—so long as you can eat, eat, and sleep, sleep. You a horse indeed!"

"But I tell you I *was* lame."

"I'm not denying there was a puffy look about your off-pastern. But my belief is, it wasn't even grease—it was fat."

"I tell you I put my foot on one of those horrid stones

they make the roads with, and it gave my ankle such a twist."

"Ankle indeed! Why should you ape your betters? Horses ain't got any ankles: they're only pasterns. And so long as you don't lift your feet better, but fall asleep between every step, you'll run a good chance of laming all your *ankles* as you call them, one after another. It's not your lively horse that comes to grief in that way. I tell you I believe it wasn't much, and if it was, it was your own fault. There! I've done. I'm going to sleep. I'll try to think as well of you as I can. If you would but step out a bit and run off a little of your fat!"

Here Diamond began to double up his knees; but Ruby spoke again, and, as young Diamond thought, in a rather different tone.

"I say, Diamond, I can't bear to have an honest old horse like you, think of me like that. I will tell you the truth: it was my own fault that I fell lame."

"I told you so," returned the other, tumbling against the partition as he rolled over on his side to give his legs every possible privilege in their narrow circumstances.

"I meant to do it, Diamond."

At the words, the old horse arose with a scramble like thunder, shot his angry head and glaring eye over into Ruby's stall, and said—

"Keep out of my way, you unworthy wretch, or I'll bite you. You a horse! Why did you do that?"

"Because I wanted to grow fat."

"You grease-tub! Oh! my teeth and tail! I thought you were a humbug! Why did you want to get fat? There's no truth to be got out of you but by cross-questioning. You ain't fit to be a horse."

"Because once I *am* fat, my nature is to keep fat for a long time; and I didn't know when master might come home and want to see me."

"You conceited, good-for-nothing brute! You're only fit for the knacker's yard. You wanted to look handsome, did you? Hold your tongue, or I'll break my halter and be at you—with your handsome fat!"

"Never mind, Diamond. You're a good horse. You can't hurt me."

"Can't hurt you! Just let me once try."

"No, you can't."

"Why then?"

"Because I'm an angel."

"What's that?"

"Of course you don't know."

"Indeed I don't."

"I know you don't. An ignorant, rude old human horse, like you, couldn't know it. But there's young Diamond listening to all we're saying; and he knows well enough there are horses in heaven for angels to ride upon, as well as other animals, lions and eagles and bulls, in more important situations. The horses the angels ride, must be angel-horses, else the angels couldn't ride upon them. Well, I'm one of them."

"You ain't."

"Did you ever know a horse tell a lie?"

"Never before. But you've confessed to shamming lame."

"Nothing of the sort. It was necessary I should grow fat, and necessary that good Joseph, your master, should grow lean. I could have pretended to be lame, but that no horse, least of all an angel-horse, would do. So I must *be* lame, and so I sprained my ankle—for the angel-horses *have* ankles—they don't talk horse-slang up there—and it hurt me very much, I assure you, Diamond, though you mayn't be good enough to be able to believe it."

Old Diamond made no reply. He had lain down again, and a sleepy snort, very like a snore, revealed that, if he was not already asleep, he was past understanding a word that Ruby was saying. When young Diamond found this, he thought he might venture to take up the dropt shuttlecock of the conversation.

"I'm good enough to believe it, Ruby," he said.

But Ruby never turned his head, or took any notice of him. I suppose he did not understand more of English than just what the coachmen and stablemen were in the habit of addressing him with. Finding, however, that his companion made no reply, he shot his head over the partition and looking down at him said—

"You just wait till to-morrow, and you'll see whether I'm speaking the truth or not.—I declare the old horse is fast asleep!—Diamond!—No I won't."

Ruby turned away, and began pulling at his hay-rack in silence.

Diamond gave a shiver, and looking round saw that the door of the stable was open. He began to feel as if he had been dreaming, and after a glance about the stable to see if North Wind was anywhere visible, he thought he had better go back to bed.

Chapter XXXIII
THE PROSPECT BRIGHTENS

THE next morning, Diamond's mother said to his father, "I'm not quite comfortable about that child again."

"Which child, Martha?" asked Joseph. "You've got a choice now."

"Well, Diamond I mean. I'm afraid he's getting into his queer ways again. He's been at his old trick of walking in his sleep. I saw him run up the stair in the middle of the night."

"Didn't you go after him, wife?"

"Of course I did—and found him fast asleep in his bed. It's because he's had so little meat for the last six weeks, I'm afraid."

"It may be that. I'm very sorry. But if it don't please God to send us enough, what *am* I to do, wife?"

"You can't help it, I know, my dear good man," returned Martha. "And after all I don't know. I don't see why he shouldn't get on as well as the rest of us. There I'm nursing baby all this time, and I get along pretty well.

I'm sure, to hear the little man singing, you wouldn't think there was much amiss with him."

For at that moment Diamond was singing like a lark in the clouds. He had the new baby in his arms, while his mother was dressing herself. Joseph was sitting at his breakfast—a little weak tea, dry bread, and very dubious butter—which Nanny had set for him, and which he was enjoying because he was hungry. He had groomed both horses, and had got old Diamond harnessed ready to put to.

"Think of a fat angel, Dulcimer!" said Diamond.

The baby had not been christened yet, but Diamond, in reading his bible, had come upon the word *dulcimer*, and thought it so pretty that ever after he called his sister Dulcimer.

"Think of a red fat angel, Dulcimer!" he repeated; "for Ruby's an angel of a horse, Dulcimer. He sprained his ankle and got fat on purpose."

"What purpose, Diamond?" asked his father.

"Ah! that I can't tell. I suppose to look handsome when his master comes," answered Diamond.—"What do *you* think, Dulcimer? It must be for some good, for Ruby's an angel."

"I wish I were rid of him, anyhow," said his father; "for he weighs heavy on my mind."

"No wonder, father: he's so fat," said Diamond. "But you needn't be afraid, for everybody says he's in better condition than when you had him."

"Yes, but he may be as thin as a tin horse before his owner comes. It was too bad to leave him on my hands this way."

"Perhaps he couldn't help it," suggested Diamond. "I dare say he has some good reason for it."

"So I should have said," returned his father, "if he had not driven such a hard bargain with me at first."

"But we don't know what may come of it yet, husband," said his wife. "Mr. Raymond may give a little to

boot, seeing you've had more of the bargain than you
wanted or reckoned upon."

"I'm afraid not: he's a hard man," said Joseph, as he
rose and went to get his cab out.

Diamond resumed his singing. For some time he car-
olled snatches of everything or anything; but at last it settled down into something like what follows. I cannot tell
where or how he got it.

> Where did you come from, baby dear?
> Out of the everywhere into here.
>
> Where did you get your eyes so blue?
> Out of the sky as I came through.
>
> What makes the light in them sparkle and spin?
> Some of the starry spikes left in.
>
> Where did you get that little tear?
> I found it waiting when I got here.
>
> What makes your forehead so smooth and high?
> A soft hand stroked it as I went by.
>
> What makes your cheek like a warm white rose?
> I saw something better than any one knows.
>
> Whence that three-cornered smile of bliss?
> Three angels gave me at once a kiss.
>
> Where did you get this pearly ear?
> God spoke, and it came out to hear.
>
> Where did you get those arms and hands?
> Love made itself into hooks and bands.
>
> Feet, whence did you come, you darling things?
> From the same box as the cherubs' wings.

How did they all just come to be you?
God thought about me, and so I grew.

But how did you come to us, you dear?
God thought about you, and so I am here.

"*You* never made that song, Diamond," said his mother.

"No, mother. I wish I had. No, I don't. That would be to take it from somebody else. But it's mine for all that."

"What makes it yours?"

"I love it so."

"Does loving a thing make it yours?"

"I think so, mother—at least more than anything else can. If I didn't love baby (which couldn't be, you know), she wouldn't be mine a bit. But I do love baby, and baby is my very own Dulcimer."

"The baby's mine, Diamond."

"That makes her the more mine, mother."

"How do you make that out?"

"Because you're mine, mother."

"Is that because you love me?"

"Yes, just because. Love makes the only myness," said Diamond.

When his father came home to have his dinner, and change Diamond for Ruby, they saw him look very sad, and he told them he had not had a fare worth mentioning the whole morning.

"We shall all have to go to the workhouse, wife," he said.

"It would be better to go to the back of the north wind," said Diamond, dreamily, not intending to say it aloud.

"So it would," answered his father. "But how are we to get there, Diamond?"

"We must wait till we're taken," returned Diamond.

Before his father could speak again, a knock came to the door and in walked Mr. Raymond with a smile on his face. Joseph got up and received him respectfully, but not very cordially. Martha set a chair for him, but he would not sit down.

"You are not very glad to see me," he said to Joseph. "You don't want to part with the old horse."

"Indeed, sir, you *are* mistaken there. What with anxiety about him, and bad luck, I've wished I were rid of him a thousand times. It was only to be for three months, and here it's eight or nine."

"I'm sorry to hear such a statement," said Mr. Raymond. "Hasn't he been of service to you?"

"Not much, not with his lameness——"

"Ah!" said Mr. Raymond, hastily—"you've been laming him—have you? That accounts for it. I see, I see."

"It wasn't my fault, and he's all right now. I don't know how it happened, but——"

"He did it on purpose," said Diamond. "He put his foot on a stone just to twist his ankle."

"How do you know that, Diamond?" said his father, turning to him. "I never said so, for I could not think how it came."

"I heard it—in the stable," answered Diamond.

"Let's have a look at him," said Mr. Raymond.

"If you'll step into the yard," said Joseph, "I'll bring him out."

They went, and Joseph, having first taken off his harness, walked Ruby into the middle of the yard.

"Why," said Mr. Raymond, "you've not been using him well."

"I don't know what you mean by that, sir. I didn't expect to hear that from you. He's sound in wind and limb—as sound as a barrel."

"And as big, you might add. Why, he's as fat as a pig! You don't call that good usage!"

Joseph was too angry to make any answer.

"You've not worked him enough, I say. That's not making a good use of him. That's not doing as you'd be done by."

"I shouldn't be sorry if I was served the same, sir."

"He's too fat, I say."

"There was a whole month I couldn't work him at all, and he did nothing but eat his head off. He's an awful eater. I've taken the best part of six hours a day out of him since, but I'm always afraid of his coming to grief again, and so I couldn't make the most even of that. I declare to you, sir, when he's between the shafts, I sit on the box as miserable as if I'd stolen him. He looks all the time as if he was a-bottling up of complaints to make of me the minute he set eyes on you again. There! look at him now, squinting round at me with one eye! I declare to you, on my word, I haven't laid the whip on him more than three times."

"I'm glad to hear it. He never did want the whip."

"I didn't say that, sir. If ever a horse wanted the whip, he do. He's brought me to beggary almost with his snail's pace. I'm very glad you've come to rid me of him."

"I don't know that," said Mr. Raymond. "Suppose I were to ask you to buy him of me—cheap."

"I wouldn't have him in a present, sir. I don't like him. And I wouldn't drive a horse that I didn't like—no, not for gold. It can't come to good where there's no love between 'em."

"Just bring out your own horse, and let me see what sort of a pair they'd make."

Joseph laughed rather bitterly as he went to fetch Diamond.

When the two were placed side by side, Mr. Raymond could hardly keep his countenance, but from a mingling of feelings. Beside the great red round barrel Ruby, all body and no legs, Diamond looked like a clothes-horse with a skin thrown over it. There was hardly a spot of him where you could not descry some sign of a bone underneath. Gaunt and grim and weary he stood, kissing his master, and heeding no one else.

"You haven't been using him well," said Mr. Raymond.

"I must say," returned Joseph, throwing an arm round his horse's neck, "that the remark had better have been spared, sir. The horse is worth three of the other now."

"I don't think so. I think they make a very nice pair. If the one's too fat, the other's too lean—so that's all right. And if you won't buy my Ruby, I must buy your Diamond."

"Thank you, sir," said Joseph, in a tone implying anything but thanks.

"You don't seem to like the proposal," said Mr. Raymond.

"I don't," returned Joseph. "I wouldn't part with my old Diamond for his skin as full of nuggets as it is of bones."

"Who said anything about parting with him?"

"You did now, sir."

"No; I didn't. I only spoke of buying him to make a pair with Ruby. We could pare Ruby and patch Diamond a bit. And for height, they are as near a match as I care about. Of course you would be the coachman—if only you would consent to be reconciled to Ruby."

Joseph stood bewildered, unable to answer.

"I've bought a small place in Kent," continued Mr. Raymond, "and I must have a pair to my carriage, for the roads are hilly thereabouts. I don't want to make a show with a pair of high-steppers. I think these will just do. Suppose for a week or two, you set yourself to take Ruby down and bring Diamond up. If we could only lay a pipe from Ruby's sides into Diamond's, it would be the work of a moment. But I fear that wouldn't answer."

A strong inclination to laugh intruded upon Joseph's inclination to cry, and made speech still harder than before.

"I beg your pardon, sir," he said at length. "I've been so miserable, and for so long, that I never thought you was only a chaffing of me when you said I hadn't used the horses well. I did grumble at you, sir, many's the time in my trouble; but whenever I said anything, my little Diamond would look at me with a smile, as much as to say: 'I know him better than you, father'; and upon my word, I always thought the boy must be right."

"Will you sell me old Diamond then?"

"I will, sir, on one condition—that if ever you want to part with him or me, you give me the option of buying him. I could *not* part with him, sir. As to who calls him his, that's nothing; for, as Diamond says, it's only loving a thing that can make it yours—and I do love old Diamond, sir, dearly."

"Well, there's a cheque for twenty pounds, which I wrote to offer you for him, in case I should find you had done the handsome thing by Ruby. Will that be enough?"

"It's too much, sir. His body ain't worth it—shoes and all. It's only his heart, sir—that's worth millions—but his heart'll be mine all the same, so it's too much, sir."

"I don't think so. It won't be at least, by the time we've got him fed up again. You take it and welcome. Just go on with your cabbing for another month, only take it out of Ruby and let Diamond rest, and by that time I shall be ready for you to go down into the country."

"Thank you, sir, thank you. Diamond set you down for a friend, sir, the moment he saw you. I do believe that child of mine knows more than other people."

"I think so too," said Mr. Raymond as he walked away.

He had meant to test Joseph when he made the bargain about Ruby, but had no intention of so greatly prolonging the trial. He had been taken ill in Switzerland, and had been quite unable to return sooner. He went away now highly gratified at finding that he had stood the test, and was a true man.

Joseph rushed in to his wife who had been standing at the window anxiously waiting the result of the long colloquy. When she heard that the horses were to go together in double harness, she burst forth into an immoderate fit of laughter. Diamond came up with the baby in his arms and made big anxious eyes at her, saying,

"What is the matter with you, mother dear? Do cry a little. It will do you good. When father takes ever so small a drop of spirits, he puts water to it."

"You silly darling!" said his mother; "how could I but laugh at the notion of that great fat Ruby going side by side with our poor old Diamond?"

"But why not, mother? With a month's oats, and nothing to do, Diamond'll be nearer Ruby's size than you will father's. I think it's very good for different sorts to go together. Now Ruby will have a chance of teaching Diamond better manners."

"How dare you say such a thing, Diamond?" said his father, angrily. "To compare the two for manners, there's no comparison possible. Our Diamond's a gentleman."

"I don't mean to say he isn't, father; for I dare say some gentlemen judge their neigbours unjustly. That's all I mean. Diamond shouldn't have thought such bad things of Ruby. He didn't try to make the best of him."

"How do you know that, pray?"

"I heard them talking about it one night."

"Who?"

"Why, Diamond and Ruby. Ruby's an angel."

Joseph stared and said no more. For all his new gladness, he was very gloomy as he re-harnessed the angel, for he thought his darling Diamond was going out of his mind.

He could not help thinking rather differently, however, when he found the change that had come over Ruby. Considering his fat, he exerted himself amazingly, and got over the ground with incredible speed. So willing, even anxious, was he to go now, that Joseph had to hold him quite tight.

Then, as he laughed at his own fancies, a new fear came upon him lest the horse should break his wind, and Mr.

Raymond have good cause to think he had not been using him well. He might even suppose that he had taken advantage of his new instructions, to let out upon the horse some of his pent-up dislike; whereas in truth, it had so utterly vanished that he felt as if Ruby too had been his friend all the time.

Chapter XXXIV
IN THE COUNTRY

B EFORE the end of the month, Ruby had got respectably thin, and Diamond respectably stout. They really
began to look fit for double harness.

Joseph and his wife had got their affairs in order, and
everything ready for migrating at the shortest notice; and
they felt so peaceful and happy that they judged all the
trouble they had gone through well worth enduring. As for
Nanny, she had been so happy ever since she left the hospital, that she expected nothing better, and saw nothing at-
tractive in the notion of the country. At the same time, she
had not the least idea of what the word *country* meant, for
she had never seen anything about her but streets and gas-
lamps. Besides, she was more attached to Jim than to Diamond: Jim was a reasonable being, Diamond in her eyes
at best only an amiable, over-grown baby, whom no
amount of expostulation would ever bring to talk sense,
not to say think it. Now that she could manage the baby
as well as he, she judged herself altogether his superior.

Towards his father and mother, she was all they could wish.

Diamond had taken a great deal of pains and trouble to find Jim, and had at last succeeded through the help of the tall policeman, who was glad to renew his acquaintance with the strange child. Jim had moved his quarters, and had not heard of Nanny's illness till some time after she was taken to the hospital, where he was too shy to go and inquire about her. But when at length she went to live with Diamond's family, Jim was willing enough to go and see her. It was after one of his visits, during which they had been talking of her new prospects, that Nanny expressed to Diamond her opinion of the country.

"There ain't nothing in it but the sun and moon, Diamond."

"There's trees and flowers," said Diamond.

"Well, they ain't no count," returned Nanny.

"Ain't they? They're so beautiful, they make you happy to look at them."

"That's because you're such a silly."

Diamond smiled with a far-away look, as if he were gazing through clouds of green leaves and the vision contented him. But he was thinking with himself what more he could do for Nanny; and that same evening he went to find Mr. Raymond, for he had heard that he had returned to town.

"Ah! how do you do, Diamond?" said Mr. Raymond; "I am glad to see you."

And he was indeed, for he had grown very fond of him. His opinion of him was very different from Nanny's.

"What do you want now, my child?" he asked.

"I'm always wanting something, sir," answered Diamond.

"Well, that's quite right, so long as what you want is right. Everybody is always wanting something; only we don't mention it in the right place often enough. What is it now?"

"There's a friend of Nanny's, a lame boy, called Jim."

"I've heard of him," said Mr. Raymond. "Well?"

"Nanny doesn't care much about going to the country, sir."

"Well, what has that to do with Jim?"

"You couldn't find a corner for Jim to work in—could you, sir?"

"I don't know that I couldn't. That is, if you can show good reason for it."

"He's a good boy, sir."

"Well, so much the better for him."

"I know he can shine boots, sir."

"So much the better for us."

"You want your boots shined in the country—don't you, sir?"

"Yes, to be sure."

"It wouldn't be nice to walk over the flowers with dirty boots—would it, sir?"

"No, indeed."

"They wouldn't like it—would they?"

"No, they wouldn't."

"Then Nanny would be better pleased to go, sir."

"If the flowers didn't like dirty boots to walk over them, Nanny wouldn't mind going to the country? Is that it? I don't quite see it."

"No, sir; I didn't mean that. I meant, if you would take Jim with you to clean your boots, and do odd jobs, you know, sir, then Nanny would like it better. She's so fond of Jim!"

"Now you come to the point, Diamond. I see what you mean, exactly. I will turn it over in my mind. Could you bring Jim to see me?"

"I'll try, sir. But they don't mind me much.—They think I'm silly," added Diamond, with one of his sweetest smiles.

What Mr. Raymond thought, I dare hardly attempt to put down here. But one part of it was, that the highest wisdom must ever appear folly to those who do not possess it.

"I think he would come though—after dark, you know," Diamond continued. "He does well at shinning boots. People's kind to lame boys, you know, sir. But after dark, there ain't so much doing."

Diamond succeeded in bringing Jim to Mr. Raymond, and the consequence was that he resolved to give the boy a chance. He provided new clothes for both him and Nanny; and upon a certain day, Joseph took his wife and three children, and Nanny and Jim, by train to a certain station in the county of Kent, where they found a cart waiting to carry them and their luggage to The Mound, which was the name of Mr. Raymond's new residence. I will not describe the varied feelings of the party as they went, or when they arrived. All I will say is, that Diamond, who is my only care, was full of quiet delight—a gladness too deep to talk about.

Joseph returned to town the same night, and the next morning drove Ruby and Diamond down, with the carriage behind them, and Mr. Raymond and a lady in the carriage. For Mr. Raymond was an old bachelor no longer: he was bringing his wife with him to live at The Mound. The moment Nanny saw her, she recognized her as the lady who had lent her the ruby-ring. That ring had been given her by Mr. Raymond.

The weather was very hot, and the woods very shadowy. There were not a great many wild flowers, for it was getting well towards autumn, and the most of the wild flowers rise early to be before the leaves, because if they did not, they would never get a glimpse of the sun for them. So they have their fun over, and are ready to go to bed again by the time the trees are dressed. But there was plenty of the loveliest grass and daisies about the house, and Diamond's chief pleasure seemed to be to lie amongst them, and breathe the pure air. But all the time, he was dreaming of the country at the back of the north wind, and trying to recall the songs the river used to sing. For this was more like being at the back of the north wind than anything he had known since he left it. Sometimes he would have his little brother, sometimes his little sister, and sometimes both of them in the grass with him, and then he felt just like a cat with her first kittens, he said, only he couldn't purr—all he could do was to sing.

These were very different times from those when he used to drive the cab, but you must not suppose that Diamond was idle. He did not do so much for his mother now, because Nanny occupied his former place; but he helped his father still, both in the stable and the harness-room, and generally went with him on the box that he might learn to drive a pair, and be ready to open the carriage-door. Mr. Raymond advised his father to give him plenty of liberty.

"A boy like that," he said, "ought not to be pushed."

Joseph assented heartily, smiling to himself at the idea of pushing Diamond. After doing everything that fell to his share, the boy had a wealth of time at his disposal. And a happy, sometimes a merry time it was. Only for two months or so, he neither saw nor heard anything of North Wind.

Chapter XXXV
I MAKE DIAMOND'S
ACQUAINTANCE

MR. RAYMOND'S house was called The Mound, be-cause it stood upon a little steep knoll, so smooth and symmetrical that it showed itself at once to be artifi-cial. It had, beyond doubt, been built for Queen Elizabeth as a hunting-tower—a place, namely, from the top of which you could see the country for miles on all sides, and so be able to follow with your eyes the flying deer and the pursuing hounds and horsemen. The mound had been cast up to give a good basement-advantage over the neighbor-ing heights and woods. There was a great quarry-hole not far off, brimful of water, from which as the current legend stated, the materials forming the heart of the mound—a kind of stone unfit for building—had been dug. The house itself was of brick, and they said the foundations were first laid in the natural level, and then the stones and earth of the mound were heaped about and between them, so that its great height should be well buttressed.

Joseph and his wife lived in a little cottage a short way from the house. It was a real cottage, with a roof of thick thatch, which, in June and July, the wind sprinkled with the red and white petals it shook from the loose topmost sprays of the rose-trees climbing the walls. At first Diamond had a nest under this thatch—a pretty little room with white muslin curtains, but afterwards Mr. and Mrs. Raymond wanted to have him for a page in the house, and his father and mother were quite pleased to have him employed without his leaving them. So he was dressed in a suit of blue, from which his pale face and fair hair came out like the loveliest blossom, and took up his abode in the house.

"Would you be afraid to sleep alone, Diamond?" asked his mistress.

"I don't know what you mean, ma'am," said Diamond. "I never was afraid of anything that I can recollect—not much, at least."

"There's a little room at the top of the house—all alone," she returned: "perhaps you would not mind sleeping there?"

"I can sleep anywhere, and I like best to be high up. Should I be able to see out?"

"I will show you the place," she answered; and taking him by the hand, she led him up and up the oval-winding stair in one of the two towers.

Near the top they entered a tiny little room, with two windows from which you could see over the whole country. Diamond clapped his hands with delight.

"You would like this room, then, Diamond?" said his mistress.

"It's the grandest room in the house," he answered. "I shall be near the stars, and yet not far from the tops of the trees. That's just what I like."

I daresay he thought also, that it would be a nice place for North Wind to call at in passing; but he said nothing of that sort. Below him spread a lake of green leaves, with glimpses of grass here and there at the bottom of it. As he looked down, he saw a squirrel appear suddenly, and as suddenly vanish amongst the topmost branches.

"Aha! little squirrel," he cried, "my nest is built higher than yours."

"You can be up here with your books as much as you like," said his mistress. "I will have a little bell hung at the door, which I can ring when I want you. Half-way down the stair is the drawing-room."

So Diamond was installed as page, and his new room got ready for him.

It was very soon after this that I came to know Diamond. I was then a tutor in a family whose estate adjoined the little property belonging to The Mound. I had made the acquaintance of Mr. Raymond in London some time before, and was walking up the drive towards the house to call upon him one fine warm evening, when I saw Diamond for the first time. He was sitting at the foot of a great beech-tree, a few yards from the road, with a book on his knees. He did not see me. I walked up behind the tree, and peeping over his shoulder, saw that he was reading a fairy-book.

"What are you reading?" I said, and spoke suddenly, with the hope of seeing a startled little face look round at me. Diamond turned his head as quietly as if he were only obeying his mother's voice, and the calmness of his face rebuked my unkind desire and made me ashamed of it.

"I am reading the story of the Little Lady and the Goblin Prince," said Diamond.

"I am sorry I don't know the story," I returned. "Who is it by?"

"Mr. Raymond made it."

"Is he your uncle?" I asked at a guess.

"No. He's my master."

"What do you do for him?" I asked respectfully.

"Anything he wished me to do," he answered. "I am busy for him now. He gave me this story to read. He wants my opinion upon it."

"Don't you find it rather hard to make up your mind?"

"Oh dear no! Any story always tells me itself what I'm to think about it. Mr. Raymond doesn't want me to say whether it is a clever story or not, but whether I like it, and why I like it. I never can tell what they call clever from what they call silly, but I always know whether I like a story or not."

"And can you always tell why you like it or not?"

"No. Very often I can't at all. Sometimes I can. I always know, but I can't always tell why. Mr. Raymond writes the stories, and then tries them on me. Mother does the same when she makes jam. She's made such a lot of jam since we came here! And she always makes me taste it to see if it'll do. Mother knows by the face I make whether it will or not."

At this moment I caught sight of two more children approaching. One was a handsome girl, the other a pale-faced, awkward-looking boy, who limped much on one leg. I withdrew a little, to see what would follow, for they seemed in some consternation. After a few hurried words, they went off together, and I pursued my way to the house, where I was as kindly received by Mr. and Mrs. Raymond as I could have desired. From them I learned something of Diamond, and was in consequence the more glad to find him, when I returned, seated in the same place as before.

"What did the boy and girl want with you, Diamond?" I asked.

"They had seen a creature that frightened them."

"And they came to tell you about it?"

"They couldn't get water out of the well for it. So they wanted me to go with them."

"They're both bigger than you."

"Yes, but they were frightened at it."

"And weren't you frightened at it?"

"No."

"Why?"

"Because I'm silly. I'm never frightened at things."

I could not help thinking of the old meaning of the word *silly*.

"And what was it?" I asked.

"I think it was a kind of an angel—a very little one. It

had a long body and great wings, which it drove about it
so fast that they grew a thin cloud all round it. It flew
backwards and forwards over the well, or hung right in the
middle, making a mist of its wings, as if its business was
to take care of the water."

"And what did you do to drive it away?"

"I didn't drive it away. I knew, whatever the creature
was, the well was to get water out of. So I took the jug,
dipped it in, and drew the water."

"And what did the creature do?"

"Flew about."

"And it didn't hurt you?"

"No. Why should it? I wasn't doing anything wrong."

"What did your companions say then?"

"They said—'Thank you, Diamond. What a dear silly
your are.'"

"And weren't you angry with them?"

"No! Why should I? I should like if they would play
with me a little; but they always like better to go away together when their work is over. They never heed me. I
don't mind it much, though. The other creatures are
friendly. They don't run away from me. Only they're all so
busy with their own work, they don't mind me much."

"Do you feel lonely, then?"

"Oh, no! When nobody minds me, I get into my nest,
and look up. And then the sky does mind me, and thinks
about me."

"Where is your nest?"

He rose, saying, "I will show you," and led me to the
other side of the tree.

There hung a little rope-ladder from one of the lower
boughs. The boy climbed up the ladder and got upon the
bough. Then he climbed further into the leafy branches,
and went out of sight.

After a little while, I heard his voice coming down out
of the tree.

"I am in my nest now," said the voice.

"I can't see you," I returned.

"I can't see you either, but I can see the first star peeping out of the sky. I should like to get up into the sky. Don't you think I shall, some day?"

"Yes, I do. Tell me what more you see up there."

"I don't see anything more, except a few leaves, and the big sky over me. It goes swinging about. The earth is all behind my back. There comes another star! The wind is like kisses from a big lady. When I get up here I feel as if I were in North Wind's arms."

This was the first I heard of North Wind.

The whole ways and look of the child, so full of quiet wisdom, yet so ready to accept the judgment of others in his own dispraise, took hold of my heart, and I felt myself wonderfully drawn towards him. It seemed to me, somehow, as if little Diamond possessed the secret of life, and was himself what he was so ready to think the lowest living thing—an angel of God with something special to say or do. A gush of reverence came over me, and with a single *good night*, I turned and left him in his nest.

I saw him often after this, and gained so much of his confidence that he told me all I have told you. I cannot pretend to account for it. I leave that for each philosophical reader to do after his own fashion. The easiest way is that of Nanny and Jim, who said often to each other that Diamond had a tile loose. But Mr. Raymond was much of my opinion concerning the boy; while Mrs. Raymond confessed that she often rang her bell just to have once more the pleasure of seeing the lovely stillness of the boy's face, with those blue eyes which seemed rather made for other people to look into than for himself to look out of.

It was plainer to others than to himself that he felt the desertion of Nanny and Jim. They appeared to regard him as a mere toy, except when they found he could minister to the increase of their privileges or indulgences, when they made no scruple of using him—generally with success. They were however well-behaved to a wonderful degree; while I have little doubt that much of their good behavior was owing to the unconscious influence of the boy they called God's baby.

One very strange thing is, that I could never find out where he got some of his many songs. At times they would be but bubbles blown out of a nursery-rhyme, as was the following, which I heard him sing one evening to his little Dulcimer. There were about a score of sheep feeding in a paddock near him, their white wool dyed a pale rose in the light of the setting sun. Those in the long shadows from the trees were dead white; those in the sunlight were half glorified with pale rose.

Little Bo Peep, she lost her sheep,
   And didn't know where to find them;
They were over the height and out of sight,
   Trailing their tails behind them.

Little Bo Peep woke out of her sleep,
   Jump'd up and set out to find them:
"The silly things, they've got no wings,
   And they've left their trails behind them.

"They've taken their tails, but they've left their trails,
   "And so I shall follow and find them";
For wherever a tail had dragged a trail,
   The long grass grew behind them.

And day's eyes and butter-cups, cow's lips and crow's feet
   Were glittering in the sun.
She threw down her book, and caught up her crook,
   And after her sheep did run.

She ran, and she ran, and ever as she ran,
   The grass grew higher and higher;
Till over the hill the sun began
   To set in a flame of fire.

She ran on still—up the grassy hill,
  And the grass grew higher and higher;
When she reached its crown, the sun was down
  And had left a trail of fire.

The sheep and their tails were gone, all gone—
  And no more trail behind them!
Yes, yes! they were there—long-tailed and fair,
  But, alas! she could not find them.

Purple and gold, and rosy and blue,
  With their tails all white behind them,
Her sheep they did run in the trail of the sun,
  She saw them, but could not find them.

After the sun, like clouds they did run,
  But she knew they were her sheep:
She sat down to cry, and look up at the sky,
  But she cried herself asleep.

And as she slept the dew fell fast
  And the wind blew from the sky;
And strange things took place that shun the day's face,
  Because they are sweet and shy.

Nibble, nibble, crop! she heard as she woke:
  A hundred little lambs
Did pluck and eat the grass so sweet
  That grew in the trails of their dams.

Little Bo Peep caught up her crook,
  And wiped the tears that did blind her;
And nibble nibble crop! without a stop,
  The lambs came eating behind her.

Home, home she came, both tired and lame,
  With three times as many sheep.
In a month or more, they'll be as big as before,

And then she'll laugh in her sleep.

But what would you say, if one fine day,
    When they've got their bushiest tails,
Their grown up game should be just the same,
    And she have to follow their trails?

Never weep, Bo Peep, though you lose your sheep,
    And do not know where to find them;
'Tis after the sun the mothers have run,
    And there are their lambs behind them.

I confess again to having touched up a little, but it loses far more in Diamond's sweet voice singing it than it gains by a rhyme here and there.

Some of them were out of books Mr. Raymond had given him. These he always knew, but about the others he could seldom tell. Sometimes he would say, "I made that one"; but generally he would say, "I don't know; I found it somewhere"; or "I got it at the back of the north wind."

One evening I found him sitting on the grassy slope under the house, with his Dulcimer in his arms and his little brother rolling on the grass beside them. He was chanting in his usual way, more like the sound of a brook than anything else I can think of. When I went up to them he ceased his chant.

"Do go on, Diamond. Don't mind me," I said.

He began again at once. While he sang, Nanny and Jim sat a little way off, one hemming a pocket-handkerchief, and the other reading a story to her, but they never heeded Diamond. This is as near what he sang as I can recollect, or reproduce rather.

What would you see if I took you up
    To my little nest in the air?
You would see the sky like a clear blue cup
    Turned upside downwards there.

What would you do if I took you there
 To my little nest in the tree?
My child with cries would trouble the air,
 To get what she could but see.

What would you get in the top of the tree
 For all your crying and grief?
Not a star would you clutch of all you see—
 You could only gather a leaf.

But when you had lost your greedy grief,
 Content to see from afar,
You would find in your hand a withering leaf,
 In your heart a shining star.

As Diamond went on singing, it grew very dark, and just as he ceased there came a great flash of lightning, that blinded us all for a moment. Dulcimer crowed with pleasure; but when the roar of thunder came after it, the little brother gave a loud cry of terror. Nanny and Jim came running up to us, pale with fear. Diamond's face too was paler than usual, but with delight. Some of the glory seemed to have clung to it, and remained shining.

"You're not frightened—are you, Diamond?" I said.

"No. Why should I be?" he answered with his usual question, looking up in my face with calm shining eyes.

"He ain't got sense to be frightened," said Nanny, going up to him and giving him a pitying hug.

"Perhaps there's more sense in not being frightened, Nanny," I returned. "Do you think the lightning can do as it likes?"

"It might kill you," said Jim.

"Oh no, it mightn't!" said Diamond.

As he spoke there came another great flash, and a tearing crack.

"There's a tree struck!" I said; and when we looked round, after the blinding of the flash had left our eyes, we saw a hugh bough of the beech-tree in which was Diamond's nest, hanging to the ground like the broken wing of a bird.

"There!" cried Nanny; "I told you so. If you had been up there you see what would have happened, you little silly!"

"No, I don't," said Diamond, and began to sing to Dulcimer. All I could hear of the song, for the other children were going on with their chatter, was—

> The clock struck one,
> And the mouse came down.
> Dickery, dickery, dock!

Then there came a blast of wind, and the rain followed in straight-pouring lines, as if out of a watering-pot. Diamond jumped up with his little Dulcimer in his arms, and Nanny caught up the little boy, and they ran for the cottage. Jim vanished with a double shuffle, and I went into the house.

When I came out again to return home, the clouds were gone, and the evening sky glimmered through the trees, blue, and pale-green towards the west, I turned my steps a little aside to look at the stricken beech. I saw the bough torn from the stem, and that was all the twilight would allow me to see. While I stood gazing, down from the sky came a sound of singing, but the voice was neither of lark nor of nightingale: it was sweeter than either: it was the voice of Diamond, up in his airy nest:—

> The lightning and thunder,
>   They go and they come;
> But the stars and the stillness
>   Are always at home.

And then the voice ceased.

"Good night, Diamond," I said.

"Good night, sir," answered Diamond.

As I walked away pondering, I saw the great black top of the beech swaying about against the sky in an upper wind, and heard the murmur as of many dim half-articulate voices filling the solitude around Diamond's nest.

Chapter XXXVI
DIAMOND QUESTIONS
NORTH WIND

MY readers will not wonder that, after this, I did my very best to gain the friendship of Diamond. Nor did I find this at all difficult, the child was so ready to trust. Upon one subject alone was he reticent—the story of his relations with North Wind. I fancy he could not quite make up his mind what to think of them. At all events it was some little time before he trusted me with this, only then he told me everything. If I could not regard it all in exactly the same light as he did, I was, while guiltless of the least pretence, fully sympathetic, and he was satisfied without demanding of me any theory of difficult points involved. I let him see plainly enough, that whatever might be the explanation of the marvellous experience, I would have given much for a similar one myself.

On an evening soon after the thunderstorm, in a late twilight, with a half-moon high in the heavens, I came upon Diamond in the act of climbing by his little ladder into the beech-tree.

"What are you always going up there for, Diamond?" I heard Nanny ask, rather rudely, I thought.

"Sometimes for one thing, sometimes for another, Nanny," answered Diamond, looking skywards as he climbed.

"You'll break your neck some day," she said.

"I'm going up to look at the moon to-night," he added, without heeding her remark.

"You'll see the moon just as well down here," she returned.

"I don't think so."

"You'll be no nearer to her up there."

"Oh, yes! I shall. I must be nearer her, you know. I wish I could dream as pretty dreams about her as you can, Nanny."

"You silly! you never have done about that dream. I never dreamed but that one, and it was nonsense enough, I'm sure."

"It wasn't nonsense. It was a beautiful dream—and a funny one too, both in one."

"But what's the good of talking about it that way, when you know it was only a dream? Dreams ain't true."

"That one was true, Nanny. You know it was. Didn't you come to grief for doing what you were told not to do? And isn't that true?"

"I can't get any sense into him," exclaimed Nanny, with an expression of mild despair. "Do you really believe, Diamond, that there's a house in the moon, with a beautiful lady, and a crooked old man and dusters in it?"

"If there isn't, there's something better," he answered, and vanished in the leaves over our heads.

I went into the house, where I visited often in the evenings. When I came out, there was a little wind blowing, very pleasant after the heat of the day, for although it was late summer now it was still hot. The tree-tops were swinging about in it. I took my way past the beech, and called up to see if Diamond were still in his nest in its rocking head.

"Are you there, Diamond?" I said.

"Yes, sir," came his clear voice in reply.

"Isn't it growing too dark for you to get down safely?"

"Oh, no, sir—if I take time to it. I know my way so well, and never let go with one hand till I've a good hold with the other."

"Do be careful," I insisted—foolishly, seeing the boy was as careful as he could be already.

"I'm coming," he returned. "I've got all the moon I want to-night."

I heard a rustling and a rustling drawing nearer and nearer. Three or four minutes elapsed, and he appeared at length creeping down his little ladder. I took him in my arms, and set him on the ground.

"Thank you sir," he said. "That's the north wind blowing, isn't it, sir?"

"I can't tell," I answered. "It feels cool and kind, and I think it may be. But I couldn't be sure except it were stronger; for a gentle wind might turn any way amongst the trunks of the trees."

"I shall know when I get up to my own room," said Diamond. "I think I hear my mistress's bell. Good night, sir."

He ran to the house, and I went home.

His mistress had rung for him only to send him to bed, for she was very careful over him, and I daresay thought he was not looking well. When he reached his own room, he opened both his windows, one of which looked to the north and the other to the east, to find how the wind blew. It blew right in at the northern window. Diamond was very glad for he thought perhaps North Wind herself would come now: a real north wind had never blown all the time since he left London. But, as she always came of herself, and never when he was looking for her, and indeed almost never when he was thinking of her, he shut the east window, and went to bed. Perhaps some of my readers may wonder that he could go to sleep with such an expectation; and, indeed, if I had not known him, I should have wondered at it myself; but it was one of his peculiarities, and seemed nothing strange in him. He was so full of quietness that he could go to sleep almost any time, if he only composed himself and let the sleep come. This time he went fast asleep as usual.

But he woke in the dim blue night. The moon had vanished. He thought he heard a knocking at his door.

"Somebody wants me," he said to himself, and jumping out of bed, ran to open it.

But there was no one there. He closed it again, and, the noise still continuing, found that another door in the room was rattling. It belonged to a closet, he thought, but he had never been able to open it. The wind blowing in at the window must be shaking it. He would go see if it was so.

The door now opened quite easily, but to his surprise, instead of a closet he found a long narrow room. The moon, which was sinking in the west, shone in at an open window at the further end. The room was low with a coved ceiling, and occupied the whole top of the house, immediately under the roof. It was quite empty. The yellow light of the half-moon streamed over the dark floor. He was so delighted at the discovery of the strange desolate moonlit place close to his own snug little room, that he began to dance and skip about the floor. The wind came in through the door he had left open, and blew about him as he danced, and he kept turning towards it that it might blow in his face. He kept picturing to himself the many places, lovely and desolate, the hill-sides and farm-yards and tree-tops and meadows, over which it had blown on its way to The Mound. And as he danced, he grew more and more delighted with the motion and the wind; his feet grew stronger, and his body lighter, until at length it seemed as if he were borne up on the air, and could almost fly. So strong did his feeling become, that at last he began to doubt whether he was not in one of those precious dreams he had so often had, in which he floated about on the air at will. But something made him look up, and to his unspeakable delight, he found his uplifted hands lying in those of North Wind, who was dancing with him, round and round the long bare room, her hair now falling to the floor, now filling the arched ceiling, her eyes shining on him like twinkling stars, and the sweetest of grand smiles playing breezily about her beautiful mouth. She was, as so often before, of the height of a rather tall lady. She did not stoop in order to dance with him, but held his hands high in hers. When he saw her, he gave one spring, and his arms were about he neck, and her arms holding him to her bosom. The same moment she swept with him through the open window in at which the moon was shining, made a circuit like a bird about to alight, and settled with him in his nest on the top of the great beech-tree. There she placed him on her lap and began to hush him as if he were her own baby, and Diamond was so entirely happy that he did not care to speak a word. At length, however, he found that he was going to sleep, and that would be to lose so much, that, pleasant as it was, he could not consent.

"Please, dear North Wind," he said, "I am so happy that I'm afraid it's a dream. How am I to know that it's not a dream?"

"What does it matter?" returned North Wind.

"I should cry," said Diamond.

"But why should you cry? The dream, if it is a dream, is a pleasant one—is it not?"

"That's just why I want it to be true."

"Have you forgotten what you said to Nanny about her dream?"

"It's not for the dream itself—I mean, it's not for the pleasure of it," answered Diamond, "for I have that, whether it be a dream or not; it's for you, North Wind: I can't bear to find it a dream, because then I should lose you. You would be nobody then, and I could not bear that. You ain't a dream, are you, North Wind? Do say *No*, else I shall cry, and come awake, and you'll be gone for ever. I daren't dream about you once again if you ain't anybody."

"I'm either not a dream, or there's something better

that's not a dream, Diamond," said North Wind, in a rather sorrowful tone, he thought.

"But it's not something better—it's you I want, North Wind," he persisted, already beginning to cry a little.

She made no answer, bu rose with him in her arms and sailed away over the tree-tops till they came to a meadow, where a flock of sheep was feeding.

"Do you remember what the song you were singing a week ago says about Bo-Peep—how she lost her sheep, but got twice as many lambs?" asked North Wind, sitting down on the grass and placing him in her lap as before.

"Oh yes, I do, well enough," answered Diamond; "but I never just quite liked that rhyme."

"Why not, child?"

"Because it seems to say one's as good as another, or two new ones are better than one that's lost. I've been thinking about it a great deal, and it seems to me that although any one sixpence is as good as any other sixpence, not twenty lambs would do instead of one sheep whose face you knew. Somehow, when once you've looked into anybody's eyes, right deep down into them, I mean, nobody will do for that one any more. Nobody, ever so beautiful or so good, will make up for that one going out of sight. So you see, North Wind, I can't help being frightened to think that perhaps I am only dreaming, and you are nowhere at all. Do tell me that you are my own real beautiful North Wind."

Again she rose, and shot herself into the air, as if uneasy because she could not answer him; and Diamond lay quiet in her arms, waiting for what she would say. He tried to see up into her face, for he was dreadfully afraid she was not answering him because she could not say that she was not a dream; but she had let her hair fall all over her face so that he could not see it. This frightened him still more.

"Do speak, North Wind," he said at last.

"I never speak when I have nothing to say," she replied.

"Then I do think you must be a real North Wind, and no dream," said Diamond.

"But I'm looking for something to say all the time."

"But I don't want to you to say what's hard to find. If you were to say one word to comfort me that wasn't true, then I should know you must be a dream, for a great beautiful lady like you could never tell a lie."

"But she mightn't know how to say what she had to say, so that a little boy like you would understand it," said North Wind. "Here, let us get down again, and I will try to tell you what I think. You mustn't suppose I am able to answer all your questions, though. There are a great many things I don't understand more than you do."

She descended on a grassy hillock, in the midst of a wild furzy common. There was a rabbit-warren underneath, and some of the rabbits came out of their holes, in the moonlight, looking very sober and wise, just like patriarchs standing in their tent-doors, and looking about them before going to bed. When they saw North Wind, instead of turning round and vanishing again with a thump of their heels, they cantered slowly up to her and snuffed all about her with their long upper lips, which moved every way at once. That was their way of kissing her; and, as she talked to Diamond, she would every now and then stroke down their furry backs, or lift and play with their long ears. They would, Diamond thought, have leaped upon her lap, but he was there already.

"I think," said she, after they had been sitting silent for a while, "that if I were only a dream, you would not have been able to love me so. You love me when you are not with me, don't you?"

"Indeed I do," answered Diamond, stroking her hand. "I see! I see! How could I be able to love you as I do if you weren't there at all, you know? Besides, I couldn't be able to dream anything half so beautiful all out of my own head; or if I did, I couldn't love a fancy of my own like that, could I?"

"I think not. You might have loved me in a dream,

dreamily, and forgotten me when you woke, I daresay, but
not loved me like a real being as you love me. Even then,
I don't think you could dream anything that hadn't something real like it somewhere. But you've seen me in many
shapes, Diamond: you remember I was a wolf once—don't
you?"

"Oh yes—a good wolf that frightened a naughty
drunken nurse."

"Well, suppose I were to turn ugly, would you rather I
weren't a dream then?"

"Yes; for I should know that you were beautiful inside all the same. You would love me, and I should love
you all the same. I shouldn't like you to look ugly, you
know. But I shouldn't believe it a bit."

"Not if you saw it?"

"No, not if I saw it ever so plain."

"There's my Diamond! I will tell you all I know about
it then. I don't think I am just what you fancy me to be.
I have to shape myself various ways to various people. But
the heart of me is true. People call me by dreadful names,
and think they know all about me. But they don't. Sometimes they call me Bad Fortune, sometimes Evil Chance,
sometimes Ruin; and they have another name for me
which they think the most dreadful of all."

"What is that?" asked Diamond, smiling up in her face.

"I won't tell you that name. Do you remember having
to go through me to get into the country at my back?"

"Oh yes, I do. How cold you were, North Wind! and so
white, all but your lovely eyes! My heart grew like a lump
of ice, and then I forgot for a while."

"You were very near knowing what they call me then.
Would you be afraid of me if you had to go through me
again?"

"No. Why should I? Indeed I should be glad enough, if
it was only to get another peep of the country at your
back."

"You've never see it yet."

"Haven't I, North Wind? Oh! I'm so sorry! I thought I had. What did I see then?"

"Only a picture of it. The real country at my real back is ever so much more beautiful than that. You shall see it one day—perhaps before very long."

"Do they sing songs there?"

"Don't you remember the dream you had about the little boys that dug for the stars?"

"Yes, that I do. I thought you must have had something to do with that dream, it was so beautiful."

"Yes; I gave you that dream."

"Oh! thank you. Did you give Nanny her dream too—about the moon and the bees?"

"Yes. I was the lady that sat at the window of the moon."

"Oh, thank you. I was almost sure you had something to do with that too. And did you tell Mr. Raymond the story about the Princess Daylight?"

"I believe I had something to do with it. At all events he thought about it one night when he couldn't sleep. But I want to ask you whether you remember the song the boy-angels sang in that dream of yours."

"No. I couldn't keep it, do what I would, and I did try."

"That was my fault."

"How could that be, North Wind?"

"Because I didn't know it properly myself, and so I couldn't teach it to you. I could only make a rough guess at something like what it would be, and so I wasn't able to make you dream it hard enough to remember it. Nor would I have done so if I could, for it was not correct. I made you dream pictures of it, though. But you will hear the very song itself when you do get to the back of——"

"My own dear North Wind," said Diamond, finishing the sentence for her, and kissing the arm that held him leaning against her.

"And now we've settled all this—for the time, at least," said North Wind.

"But I can't feel quite sure yet," said Diamond.

"You must wait a while for that. Meantime you may be hopeful, and content not to be quite sure. Come now, I will take you home again, for it won't do to tire you too much."

"Oh! no, no. I'm not the least tired," pleaded Diamond.

"It is better, though."

"Very well; if you wish it," yielded Diamond with a sigh.

"You are a dear good boy," said North Wind. "I will come for you again to-morrow night and take you out for a longer time. We shall make a little journey together, in fact. We shall start earlier; and as the moon will be later, we shall have a little moonlight all the way."

She rose, and swept over the meadow and the trees. In a few moments the Mound appeared below them. She sank a little, and floated in at the window of Diamond's room. There she laid him on his bed, covered him over, and in a moment he was lapt in a dreamless sleep.

Chapter XXXVII
ONCE MORE

THE next night Diamond was seated by his open window, with his head on his hand, rather tired, but so eagerly waiting for the promised visit that he was afraid he
could not sleep. But he started suddenly, and found that
he had been already asleep. He rose, and looking out of
the window saw something white against his beech-tree. It
was North Wind. She was holding by one hand to a top
branch. Her hair and her garments went floating away behind her over the tree, whose top was swaying about while
the others were still.

"Are you ready, Diamond?" she asked.

"Yes," answered Diamond, "quite ready."

In a moment she was at the window, and her arms came
in and took him. She sailed away so swiftly that he could
at first mark nothing but the speed with which the clouds
above and the dim earth below went rushing past. But
soon he began to see that the sky was very lovely, with
mottled clouds all about the moon, on which she threw
faint colors like those of mother-of-pearl, or an opal. The

night was warm, and in the lady's arms he did not feel the wind which down below was making waves in the ripe corn, and ripples on the rivers and lakes. At length they descended on the side of an open earthy hill, just where, from beneath a stone, a spring came bubbling out.

"I am going to take you along this little brook," said North Wind. "I am not wanted for anything else to-night, so I can give you a treat."

She stooped over the stream, and holding Diamond down close to the surface of it, glided along level with its flow as it ran down the hill. And the song of the brook came up into Diamond's ears, and grew and grew and changed with every turn. It seemed to Diamond to be singing the story of its life to him. And so it was. It began with a musical tinkle which changed to a babble and then to a gentle rushing. Sometimes its song would almost cease, and then break out again, tinkle, babble, and rush, all at once. At the bottom of the hill they came to a small river, into which the brook flowed with a muffled but merry sound. Along the surface of the river, darkly clear below them in the moonlight, they floated; now, where it widened out into a little lake, they would hover for a moment over a bed of water-lilies, and watch them swing about, folded in sleep, as the water on which they leaned swayed in the presence of North Wind; and now they would watch the fishes asleep among their roots below. Sometimes she would hold Diamond over a deep hollow curving into the bank, that he might look far into the cool stillness. Sometimes she would leave the river and sweep across a clover-field. The bees were all at home, and the clover was asleep. Then she would return and follow the river. It grew wider and wider as it went. Now the armies of wheat and of oats would hang over its rush from the opposite banks; now the willows would dip low branches in its still waters; and now it would lead them through stately trees and grassy banks into a lovely garden, where the roses and lilies were asleep, the tender flowers quite folded up, and only a few wide-awake and sending out their life in sweet strong odors. Wider and wider grew the stream, until they came upon boats lying along its banks, which rocked a little in the flutter of North Wind's garments. Then came houses on the banks, each standing in a lovely lawn, with grand trees; and in parts the river was so high that some of the grass and the roots of some of the trees were under water, and Diamond, as they glided through between the stems, could see the grass at the bottom of the water. Then they would leave the river and float about and over the houses, one after another—beautiful rich houses, which, like fine trees, had taken centuries to grow. There was scarcely a light to be seen, and not a movement to be heard: all the people in them lay fast asleep.

"What a lot of dreams they must be dreaming!" said Diamond.

"Yes," returned North Wind. "They can't surely be all lies—can they?"

"I should think it depends a little on who dreams them," suggested Diamond.

"Yes," said North Wind. "The people who think lies, and do lies, are very likely to dream lies. But the people who love what is true will surely now and then dream true things. But then something depends on whether the dreams are home-grown, or whether the seed of them is blown over somebody else's garden-wall. Ah! there's some one awake in this house!"

They were floating past a window in which a light was burning. Diamond heard a moan, and looked up anxiously in North Wind's face.

"It's a lady," said North Wind. "She can't sleep for pain."

"Couldn't you do something for her?" said Diamond.

"No, I can't. But you could."

"What could I do?"

"Sing a little song to her."

"She wouldn't hear me."

"I will take you in, and then she will hear you."

"But that would be rude, wouldn't it? You can go where you please, of course, but I should have no business in her room."

"You may trust me, Diamond. I shall take as good care of the lady as of you. The window is open. Come."

By a shaded lamp, a lady was seated in a white wrapper, trying to read, but moaning every minute. North Wind floated behind her chair, set Diamond down, and told him to sing something. He was a little frightened, but he thought a while, and then sang:—

> The sun is gone down,
>   And the moon's in the sky;
> But the sun will come up,
>   And the moon be laid by.
>
> The flower is asleep,
>   But it is not dead;
> When the morning shines,
>   It will lift its head.
>
> When winter comes,
>   It will die—no, no;
> It will only hide
>   From the frost and the snow.
>
> Sure is the summer,
>   Sure is the sun;
> The night and the winter
>   Are shadows that run.

The lady never lifted her eyes from her book, or her head from her hand.

As soon as Diamond had finished, North Wind lifted him and carried him away.

"Didn't the lady hear me?" asked Diamond, when they were once more floating down with the river.

"Oh, yes, she heard you," answered North Wind.

"Was she frightened then?"

"Oh, no."

"Why didn't she look to see who it was?"

"She didn't know you were there."

"How could she hear me then?"

"She didn't hear you with her ears."

"What did she hear me with?"

"With her heart."

"Where did she think the words came from?"

"She thought they came out of the book she was reading. She will search all through it to-morrow to find them, and won't be able to understand it at all."

"Oh, what fun!" said Diamond. "What *will* she do?"

"I can tell you what she won't do: she'll never forget the meaning of them; and she'll never be able to remember the words of them."

"If she sees them in Mr. Raymond's book, it will puzzle her, won't it?"

"Yes, that it will. She will never be able to understand it."

"Until she gets to the back of the north wind," suggested Diamond.

"Until she gets to the back of the north wind," assented the lady.

"Oh!" cried Diamond, "I know now where we are. Oh! do let me go into the old garden, and into mother's room, and Diamond's stall. I wonder if the hole is at the back of my bed still. I should like to stay there all the rest of the night. It won't take you long to get home from here, will it, North Wind?"

"No," she answered; "you shall stay as long as you like."

"Oh, how jolly!" cried Diamond, as North Wind sailed over the house with him, and set him down on the lawn at the back.

Diamond ran about the lawn for a little while in the moonlight. He found part of it cut up into flower-beds, and the little summer-house with the coloured glass and the great elm-tree gone. He did not like this, and ran into the stable. There were no horses there at all. He ran upstairs. The rooms were empty. The only thing left that he cared about was the hole in the wall where his little bed had stood; and that was not enough to make him wish to stop. He ran down the stair again, and out upon the lawn. There he threw himself down and began to cry. It was all so dreary and lost!

"I thought I liked the place so much," said Diamond to himself, "but I find I don't care about it. I suppose it's only the people in it that make you like a place, and when they're gone, it's dead, and you don't care a bit about it. North Wind told me I might stop as long as I liked, and I've stopped longer already.—North Wind!" he cried aloud, turning his face towards the sky.

The moon was under a cloud, and all was looking dull and dismal. A star shot from the sky, and fell in the grass beside him. The moment it lighted, there stood North Wind.

"Oh!" cried Diamond, joyfully, "were you the shooting star?"

"Yes, my child."

"Did you hear me call you then?"

"Yes."

"So high up as that?"

"Yes; I heard you quite well."

"Do take me home."

"Have you had enough of your old home already?"

"Yes, more than enough. It isn't a home at all now."

"I thought that would be it," said North Wind. "Everything, dreaming and all, has got a soul in it, or else it's worth nothing, and we don't care a bit about it. Some of our thoughts are worth nothing, because they've got no soul in them. The brain puts them into the mind, not the mind into the brain."

"But how can you know about that, North Wind? You haven't got a body."

"If I hadn't, you wouldn't know anything about me. No creature can know another without the help of a body. But I don't care to talk about that. It's time for you to go home."

So saying, North Wind lifted Diamond and bore him away.

Chapter XXXVIII
AT THE BACK OF THE NORTH WIND

I DID not see Diamond for a week or so after this, and then he told me what I have now told you. I should have been astonished at his being able even to report such conversations as he said he had had with North Wind, had I not known already that some children are profound in metaphysics. But a fear crosses me, lest, by telling so much about my friend it should lead people to mistake him for one of those consequential, priggish little monsters, who are always trying to say clever things, and looking to see whether people appreciate them. When a child like that dies, instead of having a silly book written about him, he should be stuffed like one of those awful big-headed fishes you see in museums. But Diamond never troubled his head about what people thought of him. He never set up for knowing better than others. The wisest things he said came out when he wanted one to help him with some difficulty he was in. He was not even offended with Nanny and Jim for calling him a silly. He supposed there was something in it, though he could not quite understand what. I suspect however that the other name they gave him, *God's Baby*, had some share in reconciling him to it.

Happily for me, I was as much interested in metaphysics as Diamond himself, and therefore, while he recounted his conversations with North Wind, I did not find myself at all in a strange sea, although certainly I could not always feel the bottom, being indeed convinced that the bottom was miles away.

"*Could* it be all dreaming, do you think, sir?" he asked anxiously.

"I daren't say, Diamond," I answered. "But at least there is one thing you may be sure of, that there is a still better love than that of the wonderful being you call North Wind. Even if she be a dream, the dream of such a beautiful creature could not come to you by chance."

"Yes, I know," returned Diamond; "I know."

Then he was silent, but, I confess, appeared more thoughtful than satisfied.

The next time I saw him, he looked paler than usual.

"Have you seen your friend again?" I asked him.

"Yes," he answered, solemnly.

"Did she take you out with her?"

"No. She did not speak to me. I woke all at once, as I generally do when I am going to see her, and there she was against the door into the big room, sitting just as I saw her sit on her own door-step, as white as snow, and her eyes as blue as the heart of an iceberg. She looked at me, but never moved or spoke."

"Weren't you afraid?" I asked.

"No. Why should I?" he answered. "I only felt a little cold."

"Did she stay long?"

"I don't know. I fell asleep again. I think I have been rather cold ever since though," he added with a smile.

I did not quite like this, but I said nothing.

Four days after, I called again at the Mound. The maid who opened the door looked grave, but I suspected nothing. When I reached the drawing-room, I saw Mrs. Raymond had been crying.

"Haven't you heard?" she said, seeing my questioning looks.

"I've heard nothing," I answered.

"This morning we found our dear little Diamond lying on the floor of the big attic-room, just outside his own door—fast asleep, as we thought. But when we took him up, we did not think he was asleep. We saw that——"

Here the kind-hearted lady broke out crying afresh.

"May I go and see him?" I asked.

"Yes," she sobbed. "You know your way to the top of the tower."

I walked up the winding stair, and entered his room. A lovely figure, as white and almost as clear as alabaster, was lying on the bed. I saw at once how it was. They thought he was dead. I knew he had gone to the back of the north wind.

Afterword

"People call me by dreadful names," says North Wind late in the book, after we have had some experience of her, "and think they know all about me. But they don't. Sometimes they call me Bad Fortune, sometimes Evil Chance, sometimes Ruin; and they have another name for me which they think the most dreadful of all."

That name, which she will not tell Diamond, is Death.

At the Back of the North Wind is a book about death.

George MacDonald spent most of his life mulling over the problem of death. Or, to state the problem another way: Why do terrible things happen to innocent people? How does one reconcile the doctrine of a loving deity with the random cruelty of the human condition? What loving purpose, for instance, was served by the death of Mac-Donald's mother when he was eight years old?

All his life, MacDonald kept a single letter of his mother's, written to a relative when he was a toddler, in which she expressed her affection for him and her grief for his suffering when she was forced to wean him. MacDonald remembered his mother. Although he must have missed her terribly when she died, he did not want to forget her; he filled his novels with loving mothers—Diamond's mother in *At the Back of the North Wind*, for instance. But also, look at North Wind herself. Loving, lovely, as big as the world, fearsomely strong, sometimes angry, sometimes smiling, frightening and adored—is she not MacDonald's mother? Not a sentimentalized Victorian mother, but isn't she his real mother, his pick-you-up-and-toss-you-around mother, his all-powerful capital-M Mother, remembered as he experienced her when he was just a tyke?

And she is Death.

I need to take a deep breath just thinking about it.

And she is North Wind. Not the god Boreas, and not just a character named (last name first) Wind, North—but she is really the north wind, the physical manifestation that sometimes wafts through the garden as a gentle breeze and other times flattens trees, breaks windows, wrecks ships, takes lives. In an imaginative leap, making the sort of intuitive connection that has earned him his reputation for creative genius, MacDonald has taken the myth of Hyperborea and the existence of the north wind, given the latter a human face, turned her loose, provided her with Diamond to talk with, and watched her grow into a powerful metaphor for the nature of good and evil. Moreover, North Wind became the personification of the problem George MacDonald resolved with a paradox: Death is kind, he said. The North Wind is kind, and she is death.

MacDonald does not tell you this, of course. No one is going to want to read a book if you tell them it is about death; MacDonald has enough sense to know that. Also, he is being careful not to preach. The country at the back of the north wind, for instance, is never represented as a doctrinaire Christian heaven. Rather, Hyperborea has a wonderfully mythic feel to it, reminding me of the land beyond Lethe, or the Elysian Fields, or the Celtic paradise beyond the western sea, the Islands of the Mighty.

Death happens, MacDonald seems to be saying, and it is

nothing to fear. By staying away from the traditional Heaven, he neatly sidesteps questions of salvation and what one must do to achieve it. It is true that Diamond must be brave, that Diamond must go through an ordeal to get to the back of the North Wind—but Diamond's trust of the North Wind is such that the ordeal is a gentle one and he barely suffers at all. You or I might not have done so well, but MacDonald shows us that when the wind blows, it touches everyone. The North Wind gives Nanny a dream and Mr. Raymond a story. Dreams and stories are the ways that North Wind speaks to us, MacDonald is saying; the North Wind is for all of us.

Dreams and stories. Faced with a grim life, George MacDonald found peace in his own mythic dreams, and in his stories he attempts to pass that peace on to us. In a sense North Wind is a face of his God, much as the lion Aslan in C.S. Lewis's Narnia stories is a face of the Christian God. But unlike Lewis, MacDonald never chides. MacDonald lets the North Wind speak for herself.

When I was a child reading about Diamond riding at the back of the North Wind, nesting in her amazing black hair, I understood nothing of the meaning behind the story, nothing whatsoever—yet I sensed the profound serenity of MacDonald's vision. He gave a gift of peace to me. I hope that he has also given such a gift to you.

About the Author

From a very early age, George MacDonald lived his life expecting to die. His beloved mother died of tuberculosis when he was eight years old, and his father lost a leg to the same disease. Two of his brothers died in childhood. George himself suffered from pleurisy (an inflamation of the chest cavity) while he was still in his teens, when he underwent bleeding in an attempt at a cure. By the time he was in his twenties, he himself had tuberculosis. His wedding in 1850 was postponed by a severe hemorrhage. Three years later, his half-sister and one of his surviving brothers died of tuberculosis. Under the circumstances, MacDonald's expectation that he might die at any time was not an unreasonable one.

Nor was it necessarily an unpleasant one. Born in northern Scotland in 1824, MacDonald inherited a strong strain of Celtic mysticism to balance his strict Calvinist upbringing. Christian doctrine combined with poetic genius in MacDonald to help him think of death as life's ultimate good, as birth into another sort of life.

At the same time, MacDonald wished to lead a good, useful life in this world. He wanted to be a doctor, but his poor health stood in the way. He became a Congregationalist minister, but his unconventional and liberal views (for instance, favoring the education of women) caused so many complaints from his parishioners that he gave it up. He must have been a bit of a character. Despite all the usual protests from family members, he grew a perfectly enormous beard.

Recurrent bouts with tuberculosis kept him from supporting himself with any sort of manual labor, so after he left the ministry, he lived in poverty—but poverty did not embitter him. He and his beloved wife Louisa had eleven children, and counted every one a blessing, even though there were times when they were literally down to their last few shillings. The family lived hand to mouth, often helped by MacDonald's father (who had told him that he could grow his beard until he had to tuck it in his pants for all he cared) and MacDonald became a lay pastor, preaching in any pulpit that would have him, often for little or no pay.

His literary career began almost by accident. He liked to write; he wrote poems and recited them or gave them to his friends. He published a play. Then Lady Byron, Lord Byron's wife, whom he had never met, became the first of his patrons, offering to pay for him to spend a winter in Algiers to nurse his tuberculosis and write. After that, one thing followed another; in his lifetime, MacDonald published over fifty books.

At the height of his fame, in the 1860s and 1870s, MacDonald moved in the highest cultural and literary circles. A friend named Charles Dodgson gave MacDonald and family the manuscript of something called Alice In Wonderland, asking whether he ought to get it published. Alfred Lord Tennyson used to come over and borrow from MacDonald's library. Matthew Arnold was a friend. MacDonald dined with Ruskin, Charles Kingsley, Leslie Stephen, Leigh Hunt, Thackeray, Dickens, Trollope, Wilkie Collins. Mark Twain came to visit. On a lecture tour to America in 1872, MacDonald was welcomed by Emerson, Longfellow, and Whittier.

All this, and the MacDonald family was still just getting by. (Try supporting eleven children on a writer's intermittent pay!) But I hope and imagine that MacDonald had a wonderful time.

He was a big, handsome man with the biggest beard of all the male Victorian writers, and he was known to appear on the streets of London or New York in full Highland regalia, dirk and all, with his Tartan plaid fastened at the left shoulder by a topaz brooch. Other times he wore a scarlet cloak, waistcoats with gilt buttons, black velvet jackets or a complete suit of white flannel. He wore diamond pins and jeweled shirt-studs. MacDonald loved precious stones and colorful clothes; anything beautiful spoke of God to him. He is said to have been a kindly, almost a saintly, man. Men and women of all classes came to him with their troubles, and he would listen and try to help.

Most of MacDonald's books were standard Victorian novels for adults, mawkish and largely forgotten. But his fairy stories are likely to be remembered for a long time. C.S. Lewis said of MacDonald: "What he does best is fantasy—fantasy that hovers between the allegorical and the mythopoeic. And this, in my opinion, he does better than any man ... MacDonald is the greatest genius of this kind whom I know." MacDonald's great fantasy books are *The Princess and the Goblin*, *The Princess and Curdie*, *At the Back of the North Wind*, *Phantastes*, and *Lilith*.

George MacDonald finally died after a far longer, more eventful life than he expected, in 1905, at the age of eighty-one.

Nancy Springer